The Adventures of CLARISSA HARDY

CHLOE GILLIS

OMNIFIC PUBLISHING
LOS ANGELES

Omnific Publishing
1901 Avenue of the Stars, 2nd floor
Los Angeles, CA 90067
www.omnificpublishing.com

First Omnific eBook edition, April 2015
First Omnific trade paperback edition, April 2015

The characters and events in this book are fictitious.
Any similarity to real persons, living or dead,
is coincidental and not intended by the author.

Library of Congress Cataloguing-in-Publication Data

Gillis, Chloe.
The Adventures of Clarissa Hardy / Chloe Gillis – 1st ed.
ISBN: 978-1-623422-00-4
1. Erotica — Fiction. 2. Romance — Fiction.
3. Flapper Era — Fiction. 4. 1920s — Fiction. I. Title

10 9 8 7 6 5 4 3 2 1

Cover Design by Micha Stone and Amy Brokaw
Interior Book Design by Coreen Montagna

Printed in the United States of America

*This book is dedicated to my husband,
for all the reasons you might suspect.*

PROLOGUE
The Discovery

This morning I made a truly extraordinary discovery when I had taken a break from writing. Sitting at the computer for hours on end can get you "all stove up," as my grandmother used to say. The kids were in school, my husband was at work. It was just the dogs and me. Ordinarily, when I get to a difficult place in the manuscript, I shut the computer top and go outside to work in the garden or mow the lawn or do errands in town. I glanced out the window. No outside work today. It was pouring down rain, one of those soaking rains of early spring that sets the seeds to germinating, the flowers to blooming, and turns the grass the lushest green.

The struggle with the manuscript had left me feeling worn out and lethargic. Yet I had to move around. I decided to go up into the attic and look for a couple of paintings that I knew had been sitting up there for ages, waiting to be brought down and hung. Now, finally, because of some recent renovations to the house, I had just the place to put them.

I went upstairs, the dogs trailing behind me. The attic door was in the hall on the second floor and had a tendency to stick, so I gave a mighty pull. It opened reluctantly, and I carefully climbed the steep, narrow stairway. At the top, I pulled a long string and the single light bulb flicked on, illuminating several generations of boxes, books, bureaus, and worn out sporting paraphernalia of all kinds. It was junk or treasure, depending on your outlook of the day. I scanned the topography and saw the paintings across the room. One was laid across a low rafter that braced a gable roof. The other was propped up against the wall just below it.

"Wouldn't you know it!" I groused to myself as I began the trek to retrieve them. I know that in some households, things are put away for posterity in a particular manner. They are neatly wrapped, tenderly tucked into boxes, and carefully labeled to assure positive and swift identification should they ever be needed in the future. Not so in our house. Unwanted things were stuffed. If we were feeling so inclined, they were stuffed into boxes, like old clothes, and then the boxes themselves were stuffed into the maw of the attic. There was no system. There were no walkways left to leave easier access to the stuff at the back. It was just one big pile of crap. Who knew how many generations had stuffed. The house had been in my family for at least two hundred years. And it did seem that the Stuffing Gene had been dominant through each generation.

It was a large, old attic. I crept over the rubble slowly so as not to fall through the piles of boxes. I'd never be found if that happened. The dogs wisely stood at the top of the stairs, watching. At last, I reached the objects of my expedition. I tucked the larger picture under my arm and extended my free hand to fetch the smaller one from the rafter. At that moment, the box upon which I teetered collapsed on one side and I was thrown forward into the gable. I stopped my head from cracking into the eave by dropping the painting and rolling over on my side. I ended up in a heap against the outer wall with a loud, "Oooff!"

The dogs must have thought it was hilarious because they began to wag their tails and the little one barked hysterically. Slowly I sought to regain my feet and my booty. When I reached up and grabbed the outer eave to pull myself up, my fingers touched something. It felt like a block of wood, but there was something else. Curiosity made me forget any injury I might have sustained. Keeping my head low, I scrambled to a half-standing position and peered under the eave. There was something there. I reached in with both hands and gently lifted it out.

"Oh, my!" I said aloud. It was a wooden box, a very beautiful box. In the dim light, I could make out some carving.

Slowly I made my way back over the moonscape of boxes, bags, and detritus and stood under the light. The box was of a smooth, dark wood, like walnut or a darkly stained oak. It was hinged with tiny iron hinges and an ornately wrought iron clasp. On the lid was carved the figure of a reclining nude woman, another nude behind her brushing her hair, and a nude male seated on the floor, leaning back against the reclining woman. They were rendered in a very Aubrey Beardsley manner, surrounded by intricately scrolled patterns. I have never been able to quite separate Art Nouveau, Art Deco, and Arts and Crafts, but the carving, if original, put the piece somewhere in that period.

Carefully, I undid the clasp and raised the lid. Inside were papers. Perhaps they were letters. What a treasure! I made my way to the stairs, turned off the light, and went back down to my desk.

Breathless with anticipation, I lifted the papers out. They were in remarkably good condition, and written in a clean, clear hand. I leafed quickly through the pile. Some of the pages were handwritten, but some were typed on obviously very early manual typewriters. Some of the paper was writing paper, but some of the pages were mismatched, as though the writer used whatever was available to get the story told. I shook them gently into a loose pile and picked up the first page. I read, "Clarissa Hardy Saves The Day."

"Oh, my!" I exclaimed aloud to the dogs. "It's an old manuscript!" How wonderful, I thought. Who could have written it? There was no name that I could see anywhere. *Well,* I thought to myself, *I'll read and maybe the writer will give up his or her name. Maybe I found a real masterpiece!* My imagination began to run a little wild. What if I had discovered an old F. Scott Fitzgerald or early Ernest Hemingway!

Whether the author had been male or female, I couldn't tell, but the hand was clear and precise. I began to read.

Clarissa Hardy Saves The Day

Clarissa Hardy was a girl of her time. She was what they called, a true flapper. She was lithe and trim and wore her blond hair in a chic bob. The fashions of the times looked good on her. She was built like a reed. She smoked (when her mother wasn't watching) and she had been known to swear here and there (when her father wasn't around). She was also a girl of means, albeit nouveau, enjoying life from the comfort and security provided by her father's successful paper mill. She lived with him, her nervous, society-conscious mother, and her younger brother in a huge house built in the rather gaudy Victorian style situated high on a hill overlooking the river, the canal that harnessed the power of the river, and the paper mill that used the power to make the Hardys rich.

Clarissa had just graduated from a fine finishing school for girls. "A fine institution for the complete education of your young woman," the brochure had read when her father had set the material in front of her one morning and announced that this would be where she was to spend the next two years.

Clarissa had thrown a tizzy, having just fallen in love with Eddie O'Malley, the son of her father's banker. She had had her first kiss and she wanted more kisses. She wailed and cried and refused to go, but in the end, go she did. Eddie wrote her long, passionate letters declaring he would love her always and shower her with kisses, if that was what she wanted.

It was indeed what Clarissa wanted, and, on her last holiday home from school, she and Eddie sneaked into the back drawing room one evening when they had returned from a dance before everybody else. He pinned her up against the wall, and his hand stole up under her dress. She felt his fingers prying between her legs. There was nothing to do but open them...

Wait! What was this? What kind of manuscript did I discover? Was it some sort of vintage erotica? Some private stash of porn? Those Victorians had a reputation for such things. Fingers prying? This discovery had my attention. I moved myself, the box, and the manuscript to the couch. Curling up in a comfortable position, I pulled the throw over me and continued to read in earnest.

PART ONE
Clarissa Saves the Day

ddie poked and prodded, driving Clarissa to distraction as she wriggled around, trying to guide him to the spot between her thighs that felt on fire. It was one of the most wonderful feelings Clarissa had ever experienced, and yet, she knew it would be this way, just from that first kiss. She loved those intimate touches. She had experimented with herself, but this was much more intense, much more exciting. There was a feeling building inside her right now that nearly made her swoon to unconsciousness. She must have Eddie's finger now!

Impatiently, she reached down and took his hand, drawing it between her legs. She was becoming wetter and slipperier by the second. At last he seemed to find the place and tentatively pushed his middle finger in.

"It's all hot. Hot and wet!" he gasped.

Clarissa ignored him, squirming to be closer to his hand. "Farther," she whispered. "Push it in farther."

He had his face buried in her neck. Lifting his head, he said, "What?"

"I said push it in farther!" Clarissa was becoming agitated. Clarissa arched her back. She had never had even her own finger inside of her, but suddenly, it was all she could focus on.

"My cock is getting hard," he gasped into her ear. "Feel it!" He withdrew his hand and put it on the bulge in his slacks.

Clarissa had an idea. Why not? "Stop!" she hissed. He looked at her like a beaten dog. "Just for a minute. Here, come over here!" She led him to the big sofa, sat down and leaned back against the arm, hoisting her dress as she did so. She was naked underneath, with only her garter belt and stockings on.

"Hurry," she said. "Hurry. Touch me there. Put your finger inside me." She opened her legs. Eddie looked at her dumbly. The aching burn between her legs was nearly unbearable. "Now, Eddie, before they all come home!"

Suddenly, Eddie sprang into action. Tentatively, he ran his fingertips shyly over her cunt. His fingers slipped between the lips. Clarissa gasped. "Feel me," she whispered hoarsely. "Inside."

Eddie did as he was commanded and pushed around with his finger until Clarissa felt it slip inside her. She gave a little squeal. Eddie pushed it in deeper. Clarissa began to writhe.

"Yes! That's it!" she cried out, but suddenly Eddie pulled his finger out of her. Her eyes, which had been squeezed shut, popped open. Eddie had dropped his slacks to the floor.

"Open your legs," he gasped.

Clarissa needed no such encouragement. The throbbing between her legs was nearly unbearable. She spread her knees and Eddie knelt between Clarissa's milky thighs. She watched him as he took his turgid cock in both hands, and guided it into her.

"Open it for me," he said desperately. She spread the lips of her cunt for him, exposing the orifice. He groaned as he pushed into her, and she gave a little yelp when he began his shaky thrusting. She heaved her hips up to meet him. It was beginning to feel so wonderful! Then his face contorted, his eyes rolled back in his head. He made an awful noise, and his whole body shuddered and jerked.

"Eddie!" Clarissa whispered hoarsely. "Keep going! What's wrong?"

Eddie withdrew. Clarissa felt the now limp cock slip from her still throbbing, still begging cunt. "Nothing's wrong," he said matter-of-factly. "I'm done."

"Done?"

"Yes. That's what happens."

"I'm not done," said Clarissa peevishly. "I'm not done in the least!" In fact, she was mightily disappointed.

"You must be done if I am."

Well, this was not what Clarissa had envisioned at all. There went her virginity, not that it had ever meant that much to her, but she had thought it would be more fun to lose it. She had always thought of it as a sort of send-off, like breaking a bottle of champagne on the bow of a newly christened ship. Something like that. Not just a few gyrations, and then nothing but a mess between your legs. She would have to see what to do about it. Maybe Eddie was not up to the job. She was fond of him, though.

Clarissa's was a buoyant character. She managed a smile, sighed, and said, "Oh well, we shall just have to practice, Eddie. Get yourself together and wait in the hallway like we've just walked in. I have to go freshen up. You've managed to wrinkle my beading!"

That was four months ago. Clarissa mulled the incident over in her mind and wondered whether Eddie could have improved. She had also done some research. At school, she had snuck into the nurse's office and studied the anatomy books. Some of it had been quite shocking, but it fascinated her.

However, the biggest victory of her education had come when it was her turn to clean the headmistress's office. All the girls had to perform one menial task each week, just to build character and to understand the social order of the classes. On a bright Saturday morning two weeks before graduation, Clarissa reported to Miss White's office. Miss White was a tall woman, ramrod straight, and stern. She would not accept a half-baked job.

"Miss Hardy," she said in her faintly English accent, "you are to dust and sweep thoroughly. And by dusting, I mean take the library ladder and make sure the bookshelves are done properly. The spines of the books should all be shining! Sweep the floor and wash the windows."

There was a knock on the door. "That would be Miss Harris," said Miss White. "We are going to my apartments for our Saturday lunch. I will be back at three o'clock sharp to check your work."

Clarissa could always set her mind to a job. She wasted no time thinking about how much she would rather be playing tennis, but instead accepted the task as a means to an end and began her work.

Her discovery came as she carefully stood on the library ladder and struggled to reach the top shelf with her feather duster. Clarissa could see a stubborn cobweb hanging from a large volume just out of her reach. As she was not a tall girl, she had to stretch to reach the cobweb. In doing so, she nearly fell off the ladder. She made a mad grab for the shelf, and the large volume tumbled to the floor. When Clarissa looked down at it, her eyes grew wide with surprise. The book had sprung open. It was not a book at all, but a box. Its contents were strewn on the floor.

Clarissa descended the ladder and stooped to examine the items. The book-shaped box contained two smaller books, what looked to be postcards, and two objects she could not identify. One of the objects was a smooth, cylindrical thing about six inches long. It was made of soft rubber and possessed what appeared to be a handle. The other object was a strand of what looked like big pearls, but they were set and knotted about two inches apart on a fine, smooth chain of gold. She replaced them carefully in the box.

Clarissa picked up the small volumes and the postcards. She read the titles on the book covers. One was *Memoirs of a Woman of Pleasure,* and the other was a small volume with the intriguing title of *The Romance of Lust.*

Curious, Clarissa sat down on the carpet and began to scan one of the books. Her eyes opened wide with wonder and delight as she read. Here was a wealth of the information she had been looking for! And told in such a delightful manner.

Clarissa felt a tingle between her legs. She picked up the postcards. They depicted half-nude women in comprising positions with nude men. She reached up under her skirt as she examined the pictures, rubbing herself, enjoying her own wetness. Finally, she was so excited, she had to set her book aside and give herself over to her climax, which she accomplished quite satisfactorily.

After that, Clarissa frequented Miss White's office as often as possible when she knew there would be nobody around. By the time she left school, she considered her education complete.

Now she found herself back home. Eddie was returning from Harvard next week and Clarissa dearly hoped for an improvement in his lovemaking. In the meantime, there was nothing to do but go over her wardrobe, weed it out, and wait for her best friend Bonnie Lovell, a teacher at the public school, to be out for the summer.

Clarissa was sorting out her summer dresses and deep in thought about the effectiveness of Eddie's cock when there was a knock on her bedroom door.

"Come in," she said pleasantly. It was Nan, the upstairs maid.

"Visitor for you, Miss Clarissa," she said.

"Why, who is it, Nan?"

"It's your friend, Bonnie," answered the maid in an urgent whisper. "And she is some upset! She's crying, she is!"

Clarissa let the dress she was holding fall to the floor. "Crying! Oh, dear! Send her up immediately, Nan!"

The maid nodded vigorously and left the room. Two minutes later, Bonnie came in, a lacy handkerchief held to her nose. She was a pretty girl, with dark hair worn in stylish waves, longer in the front and jauntily cut short up the back. Clarissa envied Bonnie her chest. Her beautiful bosom swelled against the dark blue middy blouse in a most provocative manner.

Clarissa wrapped the poor girl in a warm embrace. "Why, darling! Whatever can have made you cry?" She guided her friend to the bed and sat her down. "Tell me all about it!"

Bonnie snuffled pitifully. "I-I-I'm not sure I can, Clarissa. I'm really not."

"What do you mean?" scoffed Clarissa. "Of course you can tell me! We tell each other everything." Which was not exactly true. Clarissa had never told Bonnie of her tryst with Eddie, not the details.

Bonnie looked at her with the saddest eyes. "Harry and I are to be engaged. Next month."

Clarissa broke into laughter. "This is the best news! Are you crying for happiness?"

"I am not."

"I thought you were in love with him. I thought you wanted to marry him. You certainly have whined about it for ages on end!" It was an undeniable fact that when Clarissa was puzzled, she became irritable.

"Oh, Clarissa, don't be short with me, please. Not now. I-I shall tell you. You know Roger Downs?"

"Why yes," replied Clarissa. "He's the principal of the high school."

"Yes. And he is my superior in my career. And-and yesterday he called me into his office. Of course I went directly and immediately there. It was strange, though. His secretary was not there, and when I knocked at the door, he said, 'Come in and lock the door behind you.' I, of course, did as I was told. Then-then, oh, Clarissa! He took me in his arms and kissed me on the mouth! Only Harry has ever kissed me on the mouth!"

Clarissa's mouth gaped opened in shock. "Good heavens, Bonnie! What on earth! Wait, wait. Hold your story. We must light up."

Clarissa dropped to her knees and, reaching under the bed, brought out two long cigarette holders, an engraved silver cigarette case, and a crystal ashtray. Deftly, she inserted the cigarettes into the holders and handed one to Bonnie, who gratefully accepted. Clarissa lit Bonnie's and then her own. "Go on," she said, blowing the smoke to the ceiling.

"Clarissa, Roger Downs told me he lusted for me. *Lusted.* That was the word he used. He told me he must have me. In every way you imagine he meant."

Clarissa could barely speak for shock. Finally, she collected her emotions. "He's married! Why, he and his wife have been here in this house for dinner. He has business dealings with my father and my father holds part of the mortgage on his house! Whatever did you do?"

"I told him I was to marry Harry. He said, go ahead and marry Harry. It was no concern of his. He said he didn't care. He told me to meet him this Saturday noon in his office at the school or-or—"

"Or what?"

"Or he would see that I was fired from my job! He said he would help me financially. He would give me things. He would see that Harry and I could afford a small place of our own, but if I didn't agree to-to be with him, he would fire me and force me to leave town."

"The cad!" Clarissa's head was spinning. She could not believe her ears. She rose from the bed and began to pace back and forth, like a cat. "I shan't let this happen! I shall go straight to Father!"

"Oh, no! Please, no!"

"We must stop this man! He cannot use you like this."

"Then we must think of something else to do. I won't risk Harry hearing a breath of it."

"Okay, then. This is a challenge, but I shall think of something. Leave it to me. Do not go to the school tomorrow."

"Oh, what shall I do?"

"Wait at home until I call for you. Tell everybody you have a sick headache, and stay in bed."

That night, Clarissa tossed and turned in her bed. She was never at a loss for courage. Hadn't she made short work of Livinia Small when she bullied Missy Talbot to tears in front of the whole student body at dinner? However, the sensitivity of the matter at hand was paramount. The plan would take cunning, and the plan she was formulating under her neat blond bob would take all the courage she could muster. Roger Downs was bigger than Livinia Small.

The next morning, Clarissa awoke, a woman with her mind made up. She rose, slipped into her blue silk dressing gown, because it gave her confidence, and went down to breakfast. She sat at the table alone. "Where is everybody?" she asked when Rose, the housekeeper, came in to pour her coffee.

"Mr. Hardy went to the baseball game at the park with Michael Junior. He pitches today, you see, Michael Junior does. Against Winslet Paper."

"Oh, that's right. The whole town will be there. Where's Mommy?"

"Mrs. Hardy went to the hospital auxiliary board meeting, then Mrs. Roger Downs will drop her off to watch Michael Junior pitch in the big game. I'm going myself soon's I get the dishes done." She went back through the swinging kitchen door.

Clarissa sipped her coffee. So this was his plan, she thought. Of course. He would pick a day when most of the town was occupied. It was a cagey thing to do. No children or teachers at school. No people free to stop in. His wife on the auxiliary board with Mommy. Harry played on Michael Junior's team, as well, so he would also be duly occupied.

Rose came in with a plate of scrambled eggs and two sausage links. Clarissa promptly dismissed them. It would not do to have one's stomach bloated with sausage or to smell of scrambled egg. Rose looked irritated, but said nothing, and disappeared again through the swinging doors. Clarissa went upstairs to dress.

Dress was paramount. It had to be exactly right. Would she appear at Roger's office a demure ingénue, cloaked modestly in her white middy blouse and skirt, evoking in him the desire to deflower the winsome virgin? Or would she go for the siren look? Show a little cleavage in the middle of the day? Perhaps a short skirt, exposing her plump knees. No, she decided, she would not force him to compare her physical attributes with Bonnie's amazing bosom and inherent sexiness. She would hit him on a different level, somehow goading him into having the guts to deflower (for he would never know the difference) his friend and business partner's daughter.

Clarissa dressed carefully in a demure white, drop-waisted frock with a wide powder blue collar. She wore dark blue stockings, like a girl would wear, but underneath it all, she took extra care. On a soiree to the city one day, she had visited a lingerie shop in a part of town known to be not quite proper. She'd purchased a bustier in a shop there, made of white lace and trimmed with red ribbon. It laced down the front in the same ribbon. The edges didn't quite meet, so her skin was visible all the way down to her navel in a soft, white strip.

Once dressed, she set out, walking to the school, which was only half a mile away. On the way she perfected her plan and reflected on Roger Downs. He was not as old as her father, but she suspected he was nearly forty. Still, he had a certain youthfulness about him, being quite good-looking, even at his age. His hair was thick and dark brown. He wore glasses, but she had seen him playing tennis last summer with Michael Junior, and his physique, she had to admit, was impressive.

Clarissa walked up the wide stone steps to the front door of the high school. She pulled on the heavy door, and it opened. The building was completely silent. The floorboards creaked softly as she made her way around the corner to the principal's office. She could see there was a light on in the back office, but the anteroom, where the secretary sat, was empty and unlit.

She tapped at the door quietly. She heard movement and through the frosted glass saw the figure of a man approach. The door opened, and there stood Roger Downs, fully dressed in his suit, waistcoat, white shirt, and tie.

Roger could not hide his surprise. Perhaps to gather his thoughts, he looked at the clock. Clarissa followed his gaze. It was just noon.

"Why, Clarissa," he said smoothly, "whatever are you doing here?"

"I am on an errand for a friend," said Clarissa. Her heart was beating so hard she hoped he could not see it beneath her dress. "May I come in?" Without waiting for a reply, she slipped past him into the office. "May we sit down privately?" she asked. She was afraid to break her stream of conversation. She passed quickly across the outer room and through the open door of his private office.

She sat in a large wooden chair facing his desk. She could tell he was agitated as he followed her, confused, into the room. He closed the door behind him. "What is this all about?"

Clarissa cut to the chase. It was the best strategy, after all. Take him between wind and water and don't allow him to rally his forces.

"My friend, my *best* friend, Miss Bonnie Lovell, with whom I am sure you are acquainted," Clarissa paused for just the slightest tick of the clock before she continued, "asked me to come here today. She is down with a sick headache and did not want you to think that under any circumstances she had forgotten your meeting, nor the ramifications of it."

"Well, thank you, Clarissa," said Roger amiably, standing in front of her. Clarissa demurely tucked her legs closer to her chair. "Miss Lovell and I have some very important discussions involving future curriculum."

"And that is what I would like to discuss with you, Mr. Downs. This curriculum and the importance of it." He was silent, which is just what Clarissa wanted. "I know the nature of this curriculum, you see. A sort of natural science, as it were, which is perfectly acceptable, except that it is unacceptable to my friend, and I must ask that you drop your outrageous demands, apologize to her, and leave her alone now and in the future. Such behavior is dangerous to your family life, and the threats you have leveled are indeed unsportsmanlike!"

A terrible cloud passed over Roger's face, darkening it to nearly uncontrolled anger. For a brief moment, Clarissa was frightened, but she held her own and remained outwardly collected. Roger began to pace.

"This is atrocious!" he cried. "What lies has the girl been telling? What is her plan now? She never leaves me alone! What is a man to do?"

Now Clarissa laughed outright. "Oh, do not try to throw me off the trail, Mr. Downs! I am indeed a bloodhound when it comes to these things. I have known Bonnie intimately all our growing years. She is mad for Harry and will marry him before fall. You tried to seduce her and failed, and so you are angry and blackmail is your choice of revenge!"

"There is nobody to believe you! The girl must do as I say, and lest you tarnish your own reputation, you had better stay out of my business."

It was going just the way Clarissa had hoped. He was beginning to talk to her man-to-man, even if she was a girl. That meant he was frightened. Now Clarissa delivered the blow that would cast the agreement in stone.

"I have a proposition for you, Mr. Downs," she said. He didn't answer, but stood, glowering at her. "I propose a fulfillment of your offer to Bonnie Lovell. A fulfillment by proxy, you might say."

"What are you talking about?" he growled, shoving his hands deep in his pockets.

"I propose this: I will fulfill Bonnie's end of the bargain, and you will agree to apologize to her, wish her a wonderful marriage, and leave her alone now and in the future."

"What?" he shouted.

Clarissa smiled. She loved when a plan came to fruition, when the pieces began to fit and form the picture.

"Don't be stupid," Roger sputtered. "Why, why, you're nothing but a girl!"

"I am exactly Bonnie's age. I am as good as my word and prepared to cut the deal now."

Roger took his hands slowly out of his pockets. He walked slowly around to the back of Clarissa's chair and put his hands on her shoulders. "You are a virgin. Are you prepared for what will happen?"

Neither affirming or denying his statement, she said winsomely, "Mr. Downs, I know you will respect my…innocence." She nearly choked on the word. "I know you will be a gentle and kind teacher just as I will be a perfectly pliable student and let you do whatever you must." She tucked her head meekly.

He bent down and whispered in her ear. "I agree," he said.

Clarissa's thighs clenched automatically, and she felt a little thrill in her stomach.

Roger moved his hands down over her shoulders and cupped her breasts. "Don't move," he said. He squeezed lightly. Clarissa sat still. Then he moved around in front of her. He took off his glasses and laid them on the desk. His eyes locked on hers as he removed his suit coat and hung it carefully over the back of his chair. Then he stripped off his tie, undid his collar stays and cuff links, and unbuttoned his shirt. Clarissa watched his face flush as he let the shirt fall to the floor and pulled his undershirt over his head. He stood before her naked from the waist up.

Clarissa could not help but smile. He was wonderfully built, with taut stomach muscles, strong biceps, and a muscled loin that descended into his slacks. Well, thought Clarissa, this may be a business deal with a scalawag, but there was no reason it couldn't be fun.

"Oh, Mr. Downs," she whispered, feigning timidity, "what will you do?"

"Stand up," he said. Clarissa did his bidding. He approached her and, without touching her anywhere else, he kissed her on the mouth. His lips were full and sensuous, soft, and yet there was an aggression to his kiss that Clarissa found extremely titillating. She kissed him back.

"So you do know how to kiss," he said. "And what else do you know?"

"I will do whatever you teach me," she said with all the guileless-ness of an innocent.

He went down on his knees in front of her and lifted her skirt and petticoat. "Hold your skirts up so I can look at you," he said. "You may find this entirely pleasant."

Clarissa did as she was bidden. Pulling down her drawers, he ran his finger around the tops of her stockings. Eddie had never done anything like this. Clarissa was thrilled. It was all she could do to remember to play the ingénue. Her mons was bared to him now. He reached up and spread the lips, running his finger along the in-side edges. Clarissa was nearly driven to distraction. Then he leaned forward and kissed the lips of her cunt. It was something she had never before experienced. She groaned outright, in spite of herself. His tongue reached into her, igniting a fire in her inner most self.

"I-I can't stand," she gasped, grabbing his thick hair in her fingers.

Mr. Downs chuckled. "A fantastic first response," he said. "You are a courageous and lusty girl."

Gently, he pulled her down to the carpet on the floor and laid her on her back. He rolled up her dress, slipping it over her head. He smiled with approval at the bustier. "Ah, we have a little wild one here in disguise!" He bent his head again and licked and lapped until, moaning with ecstasy, she spread her legs as wide as she could. Roger knelt between them and spread the lips of her wet cunt as well, then inserted his finger in that place, pumping it in and out, all the while stroking her with his other hand.

Clarissa was wild with desire. She ached for her climax. She felt she could not survive unless the fever was satiated immediately. She moaned and twisted her body this way and that. Who could have thought something could feel so supremely wonderful?

"I will make you come as you should," he said. "And I will show you how." She tried to calm her breathing enough to pay attention. He spread the outer lips of her cunt. "Here is the place," he said, and he grabbed hold of something, something she was unaware belonged to her. "This is called your clit, and it is the seat of all these gyrations and desires." So saying, he twirled it between his fingers, pulling at it, rubbing it. Then he bent down and sucked it.

Clarissa cried out as her climax crashed around her and continued to crash in the most elegant and intoxicating manner. In the midst of her passion, she hadn't seen that he had freed his cock until he said, "Now, I must have my part of the bargain."

Clarissa opened her eyes and beheld a grown man's cock, large and thick. She grew frightened, wondering if she could take the massive thing inside her. She was not that big, after all.

His next remark surprised her greatly. "You must take it in your mouth," he said.

"What!" Clarissa gasped.

"The bargain was for you to adhere to my wishes. Take my cock in your mouth. Suck it. Suck it as you would a piece of candy, for that is what it is!" He laughed and held the erect monster up to her face. "Take a lick," he prodded.

Clarissa was not prepared for this, but he had, after all, given her much pleasure with his own tongue. "Well," she said, eying the piston of love admiringly, "why not?"

She licked it gingerly with her tongue. There was a dampness about it, around the tip. She wrapped her lips around it and sucked gently. Mr. Downs groaned a bit. "Take it in your own hands. Rub and pull on it. Suck hard. Put as much of it into your mouth as you can. Relax your throat and more of it will fit."

Always a good student, Clarissa did as she was bade. It seemed to give him immense pleasure. He began to move back and forth, in a slow fucking motion, moaning softly all the while. Clarissa doubled her efforts, nearly swallowing the whole, hard shaft. It was quite lovely to feel that thing hard in her mouth. She rolled her tongue around it and cupped his ball sack with her hands. He began to thrust harder and she could hear him breathing heavily.

"That is enough," he breathed at last, withdrawing from her. "I do not want to come into your mouth this time." It was then she realized there was another way of making a man climax. Before she could reflect more on the details, he spoke again.

"Keep your legs spread," he ordered. "I am going to sink my cock into you. It may hurt at first, in a virgin such as yourself, but you will soon forget the pain." Expertly, Mr. Downs drove his cock home to the prize. He gasped as his balls smacked against her, and he began his thrusts. They were so vigorous, Clarissa moved along the carpet on her back until he grabbed her hips and hoisted her up to a sitting position on his lap. He moved her up and down, impaling her, all the while sucking on her nipples which had long ago burst forth from their garment. The heat between her legs grew until she felt another wash of ecstasy flowing over her. Breathless, she let him lay her back upon the carpet. Then his thrusts were harder and faster still.

"I will fuck you!" he grunted, laboring gloriously. "Tell me you want me to fuck you!"

Clarissa took up the cause eagerly. "Oh, Mr. Downs! Roger!" she nearly screamed. "Fuck me! I say, fuck me hard. Don't stop. Please! Your cock! Your cock!"

At that, he suddenly let out a huge breath, shuddered all over, and collapsed upon her, his face between her breasts. They lay still for a time, until their breathing had returned to a more normal level.

At last, Roger raised himself up. He gave her twat a playful squeeze and stood up. "You have indeed stuck to your word," he said. "However, I will need you to make another visit. You see, my wife no longer sleeps in my bed, and being a man who loves cunt, I will need to fuck you again."

Clarissa straightened her bustier and stockings. She stood and watched as he dressed. As he slipped his undershirt over his head, Clarissa made a swift motion and snatched up his collar stays and one cufflink from the desk. Discretely, she tucked them into her décolletage. He was none the wiser.

Before she put her drawers and dress back on, she looked at him with narrowed eyes and said, "Mr. Downs, I understood the agreement was for today only." She stood before him, purposely twirling the curly hair of her mons.

Roger Downs gave a hearty laugh. "Ah, that is the way it may have started, but I think I like your little twat. It accommodates my cock quite nicely. And you taste good, too!" He approached her and slipped a finger between her legs up into her still hot cunt.

Clarissa tried, but she could not suppress the thrill that surged through her.

"We shall see, Mr. Downs," she said, with forced determination. "Now let me dress."

He chuckled again and withdrew his finger.

On her walk back home, Clarissa wrestled with some issues she had not foreseen, the most disturbing of which was the fact that she had thoroughly enjoyed herself. Another meeting with Mr. Downs would not bother her in the least. In fact, she wished for it already. And yet, there was such a thing as loyalty, and she had gone into this with her best friend's welfare at stake. There was nothing, not even a cock of such impressive size and wielded so expertly, as Mr. Down's had been, that would sway Clarissa from her duty to her friend. The man was a cad and must be controlled.

However, Clarissa Hardy was nothing if not resourceful. By the time she arrived home, she had worked out a further course of action that might benefit all parties concerned, not the least of which was herself. She skipped happily up the stairs and sat down at her writing desk. Taking pen in hand, she wrote the following:

Dear Mr. Downs,

Thank you for a wonderful time today. You do yourself proud as a teacher and as a man. I am an adventurous girl, that is true, but this was an adventure to be remembered always! Now, I must remind you of something. You spoke to me of modifying the original terms of our agreement. This was not to my liking—at first. However, on my walk home, I realized I had enjoyed myself so much that I would be jolly for another session at the time you propose. You may expect me at the appointed time and place.

Your humble student,
Clarissa Hardy

P.S. In the event that you may be tempted to withdraw in any way from our agreement and from the overtures you promised to make to my dearest friend Miss Bonnie Lovell, I have taken your collar stays and a cufflink as a kind of insurance. In the event that something ugly occurs, I would not stop from returning said items. To Mrs. Downs.

~CH

Clarissa glanced at the clock. It was nearly time for the big baseball game between the rival paper companies! She carefully folded the note, addressed it as private correspondence to the principal of the high school, and stamped the envelope. Quickly, she changed her clothing, skipped down the stairs, and set out for the ball park. She would post the letter on the way.

Clarissa hummed to herself as she walked briskly along. Somehow, she couldn't help but think, though she knew the thought was scandalous, that perhaps Bonnie Lovell had missed out!

PART TWO
Clarissa Aboard Ship

Clarissa learned of her next adventure in a suspiciously similar manner as she had learned of her going off to finishing school. It was on a Saturday morning, again. At breakfast. Again. Her brother was absent from the table as he had been when the previous news had been leveled upon her. Her mother and father were both sitting in their more formal positions, one at each end of the table.

Well, you can fool Clarissa Hardy once, but never a second time. She walked into the room, dressed in her tennis attire and quite hungry. She was meeting Bonnie Lovell for a set that morning. As soon as she surveyed the scene, she could smell trouble.

"What's going on?" she demanded, halting her approach at the door.

"What do you mean, darling?" said her mother, in a tone far too innocent to be taken seriously.

"Sit down, Clarissa," said her father in his big baritone voice that he used for important occasions. "We've something to discuss with you."

"Oh, no!" sighed Clarissa crossly. "What's happening to me now?"

"Don't be difficult, girl," ordered her father. "Sit here by me."

Reluctantly, Clarissa crossed the room and plunked herself dejectedly into the chair at her father's elbow.

"Now, Clarissa," piped up her mother from the far end of the table, "don't be recalcitrant until you hear what your father is proposing."

"I'm proposing nothing!" said the senior Hardy firmly. "I'm telling the girl what she's about this summer!"

Clarissa rolled her eyes and prepared for the worst.

"Clarissa, as you know, your mother has a dear first cousin who is married to Sir Terrance Handcock, in England. Now, Mama has recently received an invitation to Lady Handcock's only daughter Annabelle's wedding. Annabelle is to be married to William Barnes-Putnam on August tenth at the Handcock country estate outside London."

"How nice," said Clarissa with a hint of sarcasm.

Her father chose to ignore her as he continued. "Due to your mother's delicate constitution, your brother's internship at Harvard Law, and my current business dealings, we are not able to attend. You, however, my dear, seem to have very little going this season, so we've decided to send you as our family representative. Your ship sails on the tenth of July. I've telegraphed Sir Terrence to put forth our regrets, but explained you will represent our family eagerly."

Clarissa thought she had not heard correctly. A trip abroad? To England? It was a dream come true. She leaped up from her chair.

"Now, don't get hysterical on us," said her father, holding up his hands, but Clarissa squealed and wrapped her arms around her father's neck and showered him with kisses.

"Oh, Daddy! Thank you! Thank you! A trip on my own! Abroad! Why, it's a dream!" She turned and ran to her mother. "Oh, Mommy! I love you so much for this! I will indeed represent our family. You will be proud of me!" She gave her mother a big hug and kiss. "I am going to find Bonnie right now and tell her! Oh! Oh! So exciting!"

July tenth came about much more quickly than Clarissa had anticipated. It was all she could do, with the help of Nan, to pack her new wardrobe and prepare for her trip. She sat on her bed the morning before the trip and waited for Nan to bring her some freshly starched blouses.

It was a good time for a trip. Her father had spoken truthfully. She faced a fairly vapid summer. Nothing too exciting on the docket. Most of the loose ends were tied up. She had spoken to Eddie as soon as he had returned from school and graciously backed out of their association, pointing out there was much more for him outside the small town from whence they hailed and she had no right to hold him back from his future. He had taken it rather badly, at first, but Clarissa had no intention of resuming the relationship simply to provide Eddie with a learning outlet for his newly discovered sexual appetite. Bonnie Lovell was making happy plans with Harry for their wedding in the fall. After receiving Clarissa's letter, Roger Downs had lived up to his word. He visited Bonnie, apologized, wished her happiness, and promised to behave in a strictly professional manner toward her in the future.

And there was the only rub in Clarissa's plan. It would be a little difficult to leave Roger Downs. Not so much because she valued his company or admired him. They rarely saw each other, except for the weekly meeting. However, Clarissa would dearly miss those weekly meetings. Having little in common except for their passion for sex, they had concentrated on perfecting their mutual interests. Roger had really taught her quite a lot, and she had succeeded in bringing him around to satisfying her own desires.

He had taken the news with some disappointment and made her promise to resume their activities upon her return. Of course, Clarissa had promised. She did not look forward to a summer without some outlet for her physical needs. However, she reasoned, she would probably be so busy partaking of the new and interesting adventures upon which she was embarking, that she would be able to manage somehow.

Most of the next day was a complete blur to Clarissa. Somehow, she and her parents had arrived at the boarding point. Somehow, she was at the railing, waving good-bye. Somehow, she found herself settling, with the help of a steward, into her first class cabin aboard the huge ship that would take her three thousand miles in less than a week! Exhausted, she lay back on the bed and fell asleep, only to awaken nearly three hours later to a knock at the door.

Clarissa struggled against the grogginess that stupefied her and opened the door. A uniformed maid stood there with a silver tray. On the tray was an envelope with her name on it.

"Message for you, miss," said the maid.

"Why, thank you," replied Clarissa. Curious, she took the envelope and closed the door. The envelope bore the seal of the ship line and the name of the ship. It said "Captain Robert Windham" on the flap. Clarissa opened it. It was an invitation to her to join the captain and his party at their table for dinner on their first night at sea. Clarissa was thrilled.

Hurriedly, she looked at herself in the mirror, hoping her eyes were not puffy from that impromptu nap. And she would have to decide what to wear. Oh, what a letter this would make to send Bonnie Lovell!

The seven o'clock cocktail hour found Clarissa dressed in a lovely fringed peach number with adorable matching heels tied with satin ribbon. She wore long white gloves and carried a crystal beaded clutch, which held her lipstick and cigarettes. Around her high forehead, she wore a smashing headdress, sparkling with rhinestones. When her name was announced, she gave herself a covert glance as she passed the large mirror at the entry way to the dining room. She was pleased to see that she looked quite stunning. She would play the coquette tonight! There was no telling who one might meet at the captain's table.

Imagine Clarissa's disappointment when, after two cocktails, and a pleasant mingling with some of the other travelers, she was escorted to the captain's table and found it occupied by only the captain, a man of about fifty, his wife, his widowed younger sister, and two other couples older than her own mother and father! Why, there was nobody there with whom Clarissa could look forward to chumming about with during the voyage! However, she managed to hide her disappointment under a brilliant smile as she prepared to take her assigned seat beside the captain's widowed sister, a handsome woman almost twenty years Clarissa's senior. Still, Clarissa thought, these people might be some interesting boy's parents or know some young people with whom she might enjoy her crossing.

The men stood as the steward pulled out her chair and the captain introduced her all round. "Mr. and Mrs. Reginald Clarkson, Sir Anderson and Lady Ann Tallman, Mrs. Gertrude Windham, and my sister, Mrs. Eleanora Harriman, please welcome our most pleasant, and certainly youngest," there was a titter round the table at that, "member of our party tonight, Miss Clarissa Hardy." The gentlemen sat back down and conversation began.

"Haha!" laughed Sir Anderson. "You are much too pleasing to the eye to be sitting at this table!" More good spirited laughter followed.

"Oh, my," smiled Clarissa demurely, "thank you for the compliment!"

Mrs. Harriman patted Clarissa on the thigh reassuringly. "They are only being truthful, my dear. You are quite pretty, you know!" Here, she offered her hand to Clarissa, who took it politely.

Clarissa was surprised at the strength of the woman's handshake. "I am pleased to make your acquaintance," continued Mrs. Harriman in a strong, firm voice. "I like the cut of your jib! I say, do you play tennis?"

The first course had been placed before them and Clarissa chewed daintily on an oyster. "Why, yes," she said, truly surprised. "How on earth did you make that out?"

"Why, my dear, you have an athletic figure and the tone of your skin shows that you are outside and upright a good deal of the time. Like myself!"

"I am so pleased to see your love of life returning, my dear," said Mrs. Captain Windham, poking at her oysters with her fork. She looked at Clarissa and said, "Mrs. Harriman lost Mr. Harriman five years ago."

"Oh, I am so sorry to hear of it," said Clarissa.

"Well," remarked Mrs. Harriman, cheerily enough, "five years is five years, and one must get on with it!" She turned to Clarissa and said, "I have just returned from a trip to Africa to sail upon the Nile. I found it quite uplifting. The pyramids defy description! Now I plan to travel through Europe and make my way to Greece where I will explore the ancient world that lingers there."

"How fascinating!" exclaimed Clarissa, trying to scan the crowd of diners around her in search of people more like herself. Propriety prevented Clarissa from asking outright about the other passengers, or more than very discreet gawking about for them herself. The dinner passed, boringly enough, until, after coffee, Captain Windham stood up and called for the room's attention.

"Everybody, you are all invited to the ballroom. A new jazz band is playing the most red hot dance numbers there, and we should make the most of it!" He was met with great applause. Captain Windham took his wife's arm and led the way to the next room.

Clarissa walked with Mrs. Harriman. When they entered the room, Clarissa was truly impressed.

"Oh, my!" she exclaimed. "Look, Mrs. Harriman, it's so glittery and glorious!"

"Eleanora, please," answered the woman, taking up Clarissa's hand and giving it a warm squeeze. "Now, I am sure your dance card will be filled before you can draw breath." She looked Clarissa up and down.

"And by the look of you, I am sure you are a fabulous dancer. Have fun, my girl. Perhaps we shall see each other at breakfast tomorrow!"

"Oh, yes, indeed, Mis—I mean Eleanora," replied Clarissa, and without a glance backward, she walked forward to conquer the room.

The next morning, Clarissa awoke to see That the sun was shining in through the porthole near her bed. She yawned and stretched luxuriously as she glanced at the clock. It was seven thirty. Breakfast started at eight thirty, but Clarissa planned on nine. She had slept quite well and enjoyed lying in bed a bit longer, reflecting on the evening.

Of course, it had been as Mrs. Harriman had said. Her dance card had filled immediately. There were a number of young men she met, but none really struck her as particularly interesting. However, it was only the first night, and when she got to know people better, she would perhaps discover some very interesting things about them. With this thought, Clarissa climbed out of bed, dressed in a smart ensemble, and wandered out on the promenade to the first class dining room.

The wonderful aroma of elegant coffee greeted Clarissa as she came through the door. A handsome steward approached, saying, "Breakfasting alone this morning, miss? Let me show you to a wonderful table by the big window." He gestured to a lovely window that looked out across the ocean.

She followed him across the room and that was when she heard, "Yoo hoo! Miss Hardy! I say, Miss Hardy! Over here!" Clarissa focused on a female figure waving vigorously to her from near the window. Yes. It was Mrs. Harriman. Clarissa suppressed a sigh. She had been quite looking forward to being seated alone, hoping to perhaps attract an interesting young man.

The steward looked at her. "Oh, why not," said Clarissa.

He nodded and led her to Mrs. Harriman's table. He pulled out her chair, and she seated herself opposite her new friend.

"Good morning, my dear!" The older woman smiled radiantly at Clarissa. "Did the dance end well for you? I saw you several times, swirling past me with yet another man in your arms!" She laughed gaily. Clarissa smiled back at her. Mrs. Harriman wasn't a bad sort at all, really. Her energy was infectious.

"Good morning, Mrs. Harriman."

"Eleanora. Please."

"Why not?" said Clarissa. "Eleanora it is, then. And yes, the dance was lovely."

"Did you meet any young men? Did you meet anybody of interest?"

"Well, I'm not sure. I danced with several young men who might show possibilities yet."

"Now that's what I like to hear! A positive, adventurous spirit!"

The steward was at Clarissa's elbow, filling her coffee cup. "Your order for breakfast, miss?"

Clarissa ordered a soft-boiled egg, toast and jam, with a large glass of orange juice.

Eleanora went on. "I must say, it is important to meet a man who is adventurous! My dear departed husband was as fine a man as you could imagine, but, to be perfectly frank, a trifle dull. He did not share my sense of adventure!" She bent her head to her fruit cup, then looked up at Clarissa with a sly little smile. "You seem to have a well-developed sense of adventure, setting out all by yourself for a place you've never been!"

"Well, I would like to think your assessment of me is correct! I love new experiences." She felt a sudden pang as she recalled her most recent tryst with Roger Downs. She would certainly miss those adventures! "I am very eager to see England and to see my cousin, whom I have never met. I hope they are nice people!"

"I am sure you will find them lovely. A wedding in the English countryside. At the family estate, no less! Why, it will be fabulous!"

Their breakfast passed jovially. Eleanora was very entertaining, telling Clarissa stories of her trips to Egypt and the Orient and the fascinating things she had seen.

After breakfast, as they were exiting the dining room, Eleanora said, "I must meet my brother and sister-in-law now. It was wonderful having breakfast with you. Enjoy your day, my dear." She leaned forward and gave Clarissa a soft peck on the cheek. Then she turned to leave. Clarissa decided to explore in the other direction and set out to stroll the decks. Suddenly, she heard Eleanora calling.

"I say, Clarissa, would you like to meet me in my cabin for this afternoon's tea? My friends will be otherwise occupied and so I have the afternoon alone. I don't enjoy being alone. What do you say?"

"Why not?" Clarissa called back.

"Wonderful! I will send my steward to fetch you at four o'clock!"

After an invigorating walk around the massive vessel, Clarissa returned to her room to catch up on her correspondence. Of course, she wrote to her mother and father first, then a rather long one to Bonnie. She followed her letter writing with a lengthy entry into her diary, trying to leave no detail unrecorded. She would want to look back on this voyage throughout the years.

Clarissa was so engrossed in her activity, she started when there was a knock at her door. A male voice called, "Mr. Simon, miss, here to escort you to Mrs. Harriman's cabin."

Clarissa jumped up. The time had flown by! Quickly, she looked in the mirror, smoothed her hair, and reapplied her lipstick. She checked her little clutch to make sure her cigarettes and holder were there and went to follow the steward to Eleanora's stateroom.

When they arrived, the steward opened the door and motioned Clarissa inside. Then he closed the door behind her. She stood, expecting to see Eleanora. She looked around the room. It was a beautiful sitting room with lovely white upholstered furniture and plush carpeting. A low, gilt table had been set for tea, with two cups and a three-tiered stand overflowing with tiny sandwiches and other sweet mouthfuls.

Clarissa, having skipped lunch, was delighted. She called out, "Eleanora?"

There were two doors off this main sitting room. Clarissa felt a little envious. Even though her own cabin was first class, it was not this large or elaborate. It must pay to be the captain's sister, thought Clarissa.

Suddenly, one of the doors opened and Eleanora came into the room. She was dressed in flowing white silk slacks and a long, silk jacket of Oriental design.

"Oh, my dear Clarissa! Come in! Come in!" She sat on the sofa and patted the cushions beside her. "Sit here and we will have our tea! I have just come from my bath, so you must excuse my dishabille!"

Clarissa sat as she was invited. Eleanora poured her a cup of tea and set a tiny plate of goodies on the table in front of her.

"Well, this is indeed relaxing. I must say, it always takes a period of time to adjust to travel, no matter how eager one is to get somewhere."

"Are you stopping in England for a stay or will you sail straight on to Greece?"

"Oh, I will change my vessel and go straight on to the Mediterranean islands off Greece. I am so very eager to explore that region."

"What do you hope to see there?" asked Clarissa, sipping her tea.

"Oh, there is so, so much to see! The ancient Greeks, as you know, were a particularly civilized culture. I am especially interested in their social and familial lives. They were a very tolerant bunch, really, eating, drinking, playing games — in the nude, no less — and loving whomever they chose! I thought I might visit some of the places these people frequented, like the Island of Lesbos. Are you familiar with the poet Sappho, dear?"

"No, no, I don't think so."

"Well, I shall tell you about her. At least what I have been told about her. She was a wonderful poet, very admired in her day as well as now. The special thing about Sappho was that she loved both men and women."

"Don't we all?"

Eleanora tipped back her head and laughed. "Oh, no, dear. I mean, Sappho loved both men and women physically." Clarissa stared at her, quite blankly. Eleanora's face became serious. "I must ask you a question, dear. A personal question."

"Of course."

"Fine. Have you ever had relations with a man? Physical relations?"

Clarissa colored deeply. "Well, um, yes. Yes, I have." Suddenly, it felt very liberating to tell somebody. "Yes, I have," she repeated. "On more than one occasion. Although, to be perfectly frank, you are the first person to know!" She found herself giggling softly. As it turned out, Eleanora was very interesting. Perhaps she would tell Clarissa of her own adventures. She, after all, had been married.

"Did you enjoy it?"

"Oh, yes! It was jolly fun!"

"Thank goodness! I am glad to hear it. I knew you were one for a good time! Now, as I was telling you, the Greeks often had relations with people of their own sex. Men with men, women with women. Whomever took their fancy. They enjoyed each other without reservation, loving whomever they would."

Clarissa turned this over in her mind. It had never occurred to her. "How curious! I cannot quite picture it! I mean, if I may speak openly, where does one man...how do two men...how do they join?"

Eleanora laughed again. "That is something I can tell you, if you would like to know. Right now, I want to tell you about a technique that was practiced by the Greeks, as it has been in all great cultures. The art of massage!"

"Oh, I know massage."

"Have you had an Oriental massage?"

"Oh, no. Our athletic trainer at school would simply rub our backs and shoulders after a vigorous game of tennis or softball."

"Well, then I have a proposition for you. I have recently learned Oriental massage from a wonderful woman I met on my trip to the Orient. I wonder if I might practice on you. It imparts the most amazing relaxation on the body, making it stronger and fitter than ever, removing every stress! Will you agree to it?"

Clarissa had always enjoyed the back rubs from the athletic trainer at school. "Why not! I'm always game for something new."

"Wonderful girl!" Eleanora exclaimed as she rose from the couch. "Now, I shall fetch you a silk robe. Go into the bathroom, undress, and put on the robe. I shall unroll my massage mat on the floor. It is a silken mat stuffed with cotton. Most comfortable and expressly designed to impart relaxation. It is infused with the essential oils of lavender to help in the process."

Clarissa took the beautiful robe that Eleanora held out to her and went into the bath. She was not a particularly modest girl and had never been uncomfortable dressing and undressing in front of the rest of the team, as some of the other girls had been. They were all girls, after all.

When she re-entered the sitting room, the drapes had been drawn, dimming the light. Eleanora knelt on the white silk mat and bade Clarissa to lie down. "On your front," she said. "I shall work on your back first, then come round to the front."

At the first touch of Eleanora's hands, Clarissa could feel the tension leaving her body. The older woman's fingers were strong and sure, and the soft kneading and pulling on her shoulders and back felt amazingly good. Clarissa had always loved to be touched.

"Ah. I feel you giving in," said Eleanora softly. "Very good. Just go with it."

Slowly, she worked her way down Clarissa's back to just above her buttocks. Here she concentrated her efforts. Something about the pressure there made Clarissa's legs relax and they parted slightly. Now, Eleanora's hands were skimming lightly over her buttocks in a circular motion. She began to squeeze them softly. Clarissa had never felt quite so peaceful. The feeling was unexpected and very pleasurable. Eleanora's hands proceeded down each leg, right to the foot.

"Such lovely little feet," she said, rubbing each one gently. "Now, my dear, I don't want to alarm you, but I will roll up your robe. I need skin to skin contact on your buttocks to rub you with warm oils."

Clarissa did not object. Eleanora effortlessly raised the robe, and Clarissa's bare behind was exposed. The next thing she felt was the warm oil, then the gentle massaging continued.

"There is much tension residing in the buttocks," explained Eleanora patiently. She spread Clarissa's bottom, her fingertips tracing the valley between them, stopping short of the tight little sphincter. Clarissa let out a deep sigh and opened her legs ever so slightly.

"Ah, that's a good girl," whispered Eleanora. "Are you surprised by the feeling?"

Clarissa was surprised, but enjoying herself too much to give it serious thought. "Well, it certainly is relaxing," she answered.

"I think you are ready to turn over. Here, I will assist you."

Eleanor rolled her over and opened the silk robe, exposing Clarissa completely. "A lovely body, a lovely body," said Eleanora, pouring more oil upon Clarissa. Her hands began again the deep rubbing and kneading motion across Clarissa's breasts, circling her nipples, down her belly. "I will do your thighs next," said Eleanora. "Please bring up your knees and spread your legs slightly, feet on the mat."

Clarissa hesitated for an instant, but Eleanora reached out and drew up her knees, prying them gently apart. She rubbed and massaged them until Clarissa thought her legs had turned to rubber. Then, before she knew it, Eleanora's fingers were massaging the insides of her thighs on both sides of her most private places.

"What do you call it?" asked Eleanora.

"Call what?"

"This." Eleanora touched her cunt with a lightest touch of a fingertip.

"I call it my cunt."

"Fair enough," said Eleanora. "I call it a similar thing. A cunny. Or a twat."

While she was talking, she continued to stroke Clarissa on both sides, squeezing harder and harder. Clarissa found herself aching to be touched on her cunt. In her cunt. She could feel the wetness growing within her. As if in answer to her desires, Eleanora gently parted the outer lips of her cunt and dripped some of the fantastic warm oil between them. Clarissa felt it ooze down within her.

"I am going to rub your cunt. Do you like it?" She rubbed Clarissa with a gentle pressure.

Clarissa indeed liked it and said so.

"I will insert my finger into you." Slowly, she entered Clarissa, who moaned in ecstasy. "You like that feeling. You see, a woman knows what another woman wants. There is no hurry, no roughness, as with a man. It is a different, most enjoyable experience." She began to move her finger in and out of Clarissa, then squeezed her now rigid clit between her thumb and forefinger. Clarissa groaned again. Eleanora's hand moved farther down, caressing Clarissa's anus.

"Oh, you have a tight little bung hole, too," laughed the older woman. "All the parts of your body are connected. Relaxation in every part is paramount to total rest." She placed her fingertip directly on Clarissa's nether hole and pushed gently. It felt divine.

Suddenly, Clarissa felt Eleanora draw back. She raised her head and looked up. "Are-are we done?" Clarissa did not feel that they were done.

Eleanor laughed. "Oh, no! Not in the least, my girl. Here, I have something to show you." The older woman rose and disappeared into the bedroom. When she returned, she held something in her hand.

"What is it?" asked Clarissa, her curiosity getting the better of her.

Eleanor settled on her knees beside Clarissa and held the object out in her hands. It was a long, smooth cylinder with a handle attached.

"Oh, oh," cried Clarissa, sitting up. "I have seen one before! Yes, when I was a student. When I was cleaning the headmistress's office! What is it?"

"Well, we find that the headmistress was more of a woman than we assumed!" chuckled Eleanora. "This, my dear, is a cock, of sorts. Yes. It is rather like having the pleasure of a man without the bother of the attached man! Now lie back and let me demonstrate."

Clarissa lay back on the massage mat. "Open your lovely thighs for me," whispered Eleanora.

Clarissa spread her legs. Eleanora opened the outer lips of Clarissa's cunt and dripped the warm oil between them. She massaged Clarissa's clit until Clarissa began to gyrate with heightened desire.

"Now, here I introduce you to a new folly!" said Eleanora. With that, she deftly slipped the cylinder into Clarissa and began to pump it slowly in and out, all the while fondling Clarissa's taut clit between her thumb and forefinger. Clarissa groaned. Her gyrations grew more frantic as she lusted after her desire to climax. Eleanor did not stop fucking her with the cylinder. Instead, she let go Clarissa's clit and bent her lips to it, sucking and pulling at it. At the same time, she slipped her well-oiled finger into Clarissa's "bung hole," as she had referred to it. Clarissa's body jerked with the new found sensation. There was nothing she could do. Giving herself over to her physical passion, Clarissa was swept away by her climax, as it washed over her in relentless waves and left her panting in warm fulfillment.

Clarissa's liaison with Eleanora certainly gave a new spin to her transatlantic crossing. Instead of wasting her time looking for attractive young men to squire her to and from dinners and dances, or sitting in a deck chair reading an abysmally boring book, or worse yet, the newspapers, she had stumbled upon a lively and intelligent friend, from whom she was learning much about many things. She found herself every night at Captain Windham's table, which was always exciting, because there were new guests each night. Sometimes there were handsome men, and Clarissa did take a couple of walks around the deck with one or two, but she found her relationship with Eleanora fascinating and quite enlightening.

In Eleanora, Clarissa had a friend who willingly taught her about all manner of things, from the location of all her erogenous zones, to how to make a man or a woman, wild with desire for her, to the very practical matter of how to avoid an unwanted pregnancy. Eleanor fearlessly answered any question Clarissa had, told her amazing stories, and listened to Clarissa with interest when she herself had something to say.

Three days into their voyage, with only two to go until they reached England, Eleanora and Clarissa were walking on the deck after dinner, having elected not to go to the dance. The night was quite balmy and they stood for a while, leaning on the rail, to watch the sun set.

"I say," began Eleanora, "we don't have too much longer together. Of course, a friend made is a friend forever, and we will always write."

"Indeed," murmured Clarissa, "I shall miss you, Eleanora, but we will keep a correspondence. You must go on where your fancies lead you. Explore Greece. Revisit your Oriental friend. You never know, she may have more playthings!"

Eleanora laughed at this. "You are so jolly, Clarissa! And you are right. Our paths must go their separate ways, but there is one more facet of our physicality in which I would like to tutor you."

Clarissa chuckled. "What could that possibly be? I reckon you have tutored me in nearly every aspect of man and woman!"

"Let us retire to my cabin and I will show you."

When they had reached the cabin, Eleanora poured them each a snifter of fine sherry. They lit their cigarettes and sat on the white couch.

"Let me begin with a little explanation," said Eleanora. "I do not limit myself to men or women. I do not prefer one over another. I truly believe we love whom we love. At least that is the way it is for me. I was married to a man I adored, but since his passing, I have experienced other avenues of physical pleasure, with both men and women, sometimes both at the same time."

Clarissa's hand flew to her mouth. There was always a surprise to Eleanora! "No! Really! You are making fun!"

"I am telling you the truth," went on Eleanora. "When the opportunity for pleasure arises, I feel one should take every advantage of it, as far as one is comfortable. Which is why we find ourselves together here. I am pleased with your obvious passion for such activities, but thus far, I have been the one who has been, well, the dominant actor, the initiator, if you will. Oh, you have pleased me very well, at my direction, but I would like to see you take charge. Men, as well as women, find titillation in this." She leaned in toward Clarissa. "Besides, there is a small surprise, or it might be taken as an example, that I have prepared for you."

"I am intrigued," said Clarissa, catching on to the game. "You always intrigue me, Eleanora. I hope I may find a man who is such a good friend to me as you are! I should love to fall in love."

"It is a wonderful experience. You shall find a man and marry, I am sure. Just be sure he is a good man and your friend. Love is so personal, my young friend. Women love men. Men love women. Women love women. Men love men. The important thing is being true to that love and not bringing other people any pain. Love in its physical and psychological manifestations is the most wonderful thing we have in this world. Seek it, pursue it, enjoy it. Value it, my dear."

Clarissa put her cigarette out in the crystal ashtray on the low table. She leaned forward and embraced her friend. "You are so wise!" She felt the woman's breast heave against her own, their nipples brushing against one another through their dresses. Clarissa whispered in Eleanora's ear. "Now go stand in the middle of the room and strip. Stark naked. And stand there."

Clarissa saw Eleanora suppress a smile as she went to do her bidding.

Slowly, the dark-haired beauty shed her clothes. When she had stripped only to her lacy slip, she turned away from Clarissa. The slip dropped to the floor. Eleanora turned back to face Clarissa, entirely naked. Clarissa saw immediately that she had shaved most of the curly dark hair from her mons. Clarissa laughed appreciatively.

"Oh, my dear! You do surprise me! Why look how tailored and ship-shape you look! I quite like it, I do! I can see you more clearly! Come here."

Eleanora approached Clarissa and stood before her.

"What a lovely cunt," breathed Clarissa. She kissed it gently, slipping her tongue between the lips. With her fingers, she spread those lips and looked closely at Eleanora's clit. Then she stood up to face her friend. Passionately, she kissed the other woman, tasting the sherry on her lips. She ran her hands down Eleanora's chest and played with her generous breasts. Eleanora sighed contentedly. Clarissa lowered her mouth and sucked each nipple in turn, teasing them with little bites. Clarissa took Eleanora's hand and led her to the couch.

"Lie down, dear," she said. The older woman obeyed. Clarissa sat down, taking one of Eleanora's long legs and draping it over her own lap. With both hands, she caressed her thighs, edging closer to the fragrant cunt between them. Clarissa licked her finger and probed between the hot lips. Eleanora was wet and that fired the desire in Clarissa. She spread Eleanora's cunt and began to lick. Eleanora groaned in ecstasy. Clarissa licked vigorously, sucking and pulling at Eleanora's clit, reaching into the deep recesses with her tongue.

She drew back to admire the sight. Eleanora was indeed beautiful and the trim which she had given her womanly parts had set off her private beauty exactly. Clarissa reached for the bottle of almond oil on the low table and dripped it generously between Eleanora's legs. Then she entered her with one finger, rolling it around inside the woman, pushing and reaching deep within. Once lubricated, Clarissa put three fingers into Eleanora and pumped vigorously.

"Do you like this, my dear? Do you feel the heat of it?"

"Yes! Oh, it is lovely!" gasped Eleanora.

"Turn over and lie with your beautiful bottom across my lap," whispered Clarissa, depositing another kiss on Eleanora's mouth. Her friend smiled and complied.

The plump, blushing orbs were exposed on Clarissa's lap. "You have a most adorable bottom!" exclaimed Clarissa.

She felt them all over, squeezing and pinching, kneading and spreading them, until she herself felt a sudden surge of passion. Slowly, slowly, she ran her index finger down between those sweet mounds until she could feel the wet place and the pulsing clit. Sinking three fingers into Eleanora once again, she fucked her with her fingers until the older woman squirmed and gasped. Clarissa suddenly ceased and withdrew her fingers. Reaching for a small wooden box on the table, she took out the dildo, poured oil on it and inserted it deep into Eleanora.

"Be still, Eleanora," said Clarissa. "I am going to leave it in you while I examine you. I want to see everything about you."

Eleanora did not reply, but endeavored to remain still, although Clarissa could feel her trembling. Gently, Clarissa spread Eleanora's buttocks until she revealed the puckered opening above the turgid clit. She ran her finger gently around that nether door, shaking the dildo a little at the same time. She had such a desire to explore. Tentatively, she pushed her finger onto the sphincter. To her surprise, she found the opening to be quite relaxed. She pushed with more determination and her finger entered. She pushed up to the first knuckle, feeling, turning, exploring within her friend.

Eleanora whispered, "Yes. How wonderful! Fuck my arse with the dildo, dear. Fuck my nether hole."

Clarissa withdrew her finger. She could not resist fucking Eleanora's twat quite aggressively for a minute or two before she withdrew the dildo. It was dripping with wet and oil. Clarissa slipped it into Eleanora's eagerly awaiting arse. The dark-haired woman moaned aloud as Clarissa sank it to the hilt and began to move it around and in and out. Reaching with her other hand, she filled Eleanora's cunt with her fingers. Eleanora seemed entirely swept away by the action. She gave a squeal. Clarissa felt her body jerk and twitch with the intense feelings that overcame her. At last she lay quietly breathing across Clarissa's lap. Clarissa kissed each plump cheek and withdrew the dildo.

Eleanora rose and wrapped herself in a silk robe. She lit a cigarette and resumed her seat on the couch. "Oh, Clarissa. You have a loving and generous heart, and I know you will be successful in anything you attempt. You will make many friends. This has been a lovely crossing, when it could have been the opposite. Thank you for joining me."

Clarissa lit a cigarette for herself and leaned back against the soft arm of the sofa, blowing the smoke to the ceiling. "It has been such an education! And for that I thank you and am grateful. I know you will have a marvelous journey through Greece."

The two embraced warmly and spent the evening in spirited discussion.

Two days later, the magnificent liner docked in London. Clarissa, clutching her overnight bag, looked out on the cheering crowds, her heart beating excitedly in anticipation of the adventure that awaited her. The gangplanks were lowered and secured.

Clarissa and Eleanora gave each other a final embrace and walked down the gangplank together. At the bottom, they each set out in separate directions. Once, Clarissa looked back over her shoulder, but Eleanora had disappeared in the teeming crowd.

Clarissa gave a little smile. She would always fondly remember the beautiful woman who had taught her so much.

PART THREE
Clarissa Helps Out

The early morning sun shone softly through the bedroom window. Clarissa stirred in her sleep and opened her eyes. It took her a moment to get her bearings. She was snuggled in a huge four-poster bed, hung with a delft blue canopy and curtains. She was covered in the softest and puffiest down-filled duvet she could imagine.

Still pleasantly half-asleep, she looked around the room. It was a big room, furnished with antiques. There was a large clothespress against one wall, a vanity table with a gilt mirror, and a chaise lounge. The walls were papered in a subtle beige and cream swan and scroll pattern, and hung with various works of art, large and small. Where was she? Then she remembered.

Clarissa was in the English countryside, at the country estate of her second cousin, Lady Edith Handcock. She had been sent as an emissary of sorts to represent her family at the wedding of Lady Edith's only daughter, Annabelle. She had arrived last night after dark and, being tired after her transatlantic crossing, she had gone to bed shortly after greeting Lord and Lady Handcock and her cousin.

Now she was waking in this beautiful bedroom. There was a light tapping at her door. "Who is it?" called Clarissa.

"It's Lizzie, miss, with your morning tea."

"Oh! Well, how nice. Please come in."

The door opened and a small, uniformed maid carrying a tray entered the room. Clarissa sat up. The maid set the tray down on the table beside the bed and poured steaming tea into a dainty, flowered teacup. There was a matching plate laden with assorted toast points, pots of jam, and gooey breakfast breads. Clarissa was enchanted.

"How lovely!" she exclaimed.

"It's eight o'clock, miss," said Lizzie. "This is just to get you going. Breakfast begins in the dining room at nine."

"Oh, my! Well, I shall dress and be in the dining room at nine. Thank you, Lizzie."

The maid smiled. "I will be helping you during your visit here, miss. You may call on me for anything."

She departed, and Clarissa was left to her own devices. She reached over and brought the teacup to her lips, sipping the fragrant, hot liquid. After half a cup, she felt much more awake. She climbed out of bed and stood in front of the long window in her silk pajamas, gazing out on the green meadows, dotted here and there with horses, cattle, and sheep. It was most spectacular. Clarissa felt invigorated.

Nine o'clock found her in the massive dining room. Clarissa looked around the room and estimated there were about twenty people collected at the huge sideboard, looking over the array of breakfast foods.

Clarissa paused, not entirely sure how to proceed, but Annabelle called to her, waving from across the room. "Clarissa! Clarissa, dear! Come here."

Clarissa smiled in reply and made her way across the room.

Annabelle clasped both Clarissa's hands in her own. "Oh, how wonderful you have come to be a part of our celebration! There are only a few people from America here, and we find them quite droll! The Americans surely keep things interesting!"

"Do they?" said a young man, coming up beside Annabelle. "Whom do I have the pleasure of meeting?" He was quite good-looking, tall, with brown hair and brown eyes. He was dressed in white flannel slacks and a pale blue shirt with a regimental tie.

"Oh, darling!" exclaimed Annabelle. "Do meet my cousin from America. Miss Clarissa Hardy. We have only just met ourselves upon her arrival, but I know we shall become fast friends. Clarissa, this is my betrothed, Mr. William Barnes-Putnam."

"So pleased to make your acquaintance, Mr. Barnes-Putnam," said Clarissa politely, extending her hand. Clarissa's manners were impeccable. She had been to finishing school, after all.

Mr. Barnes-Putnam gave her a friendly smile as he took her hand. "William, please. I am sure I am equally pleased to meet our American cousin," he said. "Welcome, welcome!" He looked Clarissa up and down. "I say, Annabelle! I think she might quite enjoy meeting Andrew." He winked at Clarissa in a good natured way.

Annabelle giggled. "Oh, you are incorrigible!"

Clarissa said, "I should enjoy meeting any friend of yours, I'm sure."

A bell tinkled, breaking through the steady drone of low conversation that filled the room.

Annabelle's father said in a loud voice, "My dear guests, please be seated. You will find your name at your place. My wife is an expert seater, and I am sure you will thoroughly enjoy those seated at each of your elbows!" He laughed heartily.

Lady Handcock tittered behind her lace handkerchief as she took her seat at the opposite end of the table from her husband.

Annabelle bent in to whisper in Clarissa's ear. "We have put you between William and William's school chum, Andrew Milton. I think you will enjoy Andrew."

Breakfast turned out to be a charming affair. Coddled eggs were served in adorable porcelain ramekins, along with slices of ham, breast of pheasant, tiny sausages, boiled potatoes, and the ever-present toast points. Clarissa found Andrew Milton very interesting. He was only a little older than herself, and planning a trip to Egypt by ship, returning to England via the Continent. He had a quick smile and was quite handsome. At one point during the meal, his knee brushed ever so slightly against her thigh. Clarissa was beginning to feel quite at home amongst her new friends.

"I say, Clarissa," said Andrew, setting down his knife and fork and leaning back in his chair, "do you fancy a set? Say, after breakfast settles, just before lunch?"

Before she could answer, Annabelle positively yelped with excitement. "Oh, yes! Andrew, what a lovely idea! You will love our court, Clarissa! We can play doubles. Boys against girls! Boy and girl against boy and girl. What fun!"

Clarissa replied, "Yes, yes. That sounds capital! Absolutely capital!" Secretly, she would rather have played one-on-one with Andrew.

"Then it's on!" Annabelle clapped her hands together. "Oh, I know I am anxious about our big day, William, and this physical activity will surely help settle our nerves!"

The tennis game did turn out to be invigorating. Clarissa held back a little and did not play with her usual competitive tenacity and accuracy, feeling it might not be proper to show up one's hosts. Andrew was indeed a good player, and she would have loved to meet him head-to-head. Perhaps another day. There was still a week to go to the wedding.

They stopped playing as the morning began to reach midday. It was getting rather warm, and the boys were sweating up a storm. Clarissa and Annabelle played less and less vigorously, trying to keep their perspiration to a fine mist.

At last, William said, "I say, it's getting quite humid! Annabelle, if you have a fainting fit, we will have to postpone the wedding, and that will be too much to bear! Let's all quit while we're ahead!"

Clarissa was more than ready to hang up her racquet. "What a grand time!" she said, smiling at Andrew, who winked back at her.

"Walk me to the house, please, William," said Annabelle. "I think I shall take a short nap before lunch."

Andrew trotted to catch up to Clarissa, who walked beside Annabelle and William. "I say, Clarissa, old sport," he said, taking her hand, "you don't feel ready for a nap, do you? Let's cool down with a walk in the gardens instead!"

"Why not!" said Clarissa eagerly. Her heart gave a little leap.

Annabelle called over her shoulder to them, "Have a look at the horses at the stable while you're walking around. Clarissa, you ride, don't you? Good! Well, tomorrow we will go for a hack before breakfast. There is a fine bay mare there, who I am sure you will find a lovely ride. Her name is Pimpernel."

Before she could reply, Andrew had pulled her, not too gently, onto the path through the rhododendrons that led to the stables. As soon as they disappeared into the foliage, he drew her to him and planted the most delightful kiss right on her lips.

"Oh, Andrew!" she gasped when he released her. She could feel her blood rising.

"I say! I wanted to do that all through the stupid game! Hope you don't mind, old girl!"

"I must say, it's a bit of surprise," replied Clarissa coyly. "However, I can't say I didn't imagine the same thing myself! I thought that game would never end!"

"This wedding may prove to be fun after all! Let's go find a place to play some other kinds of games, shall we?"

Andrew led her through the thicket of rhododendrons to the stable. They went in. The place had the sweet smell of hay and the comforting scent of horses and leather.

"Follow me," whispered Andrew, taking her by the hand. A steep stair led up through a trap door in the ceiling. Clarissa followed closely behind him as he climbed the stairs. She found herself in the dim light of the haymow.

Andrew lay back against a fragrant pile of loose hay. Reaching up, he took Clarissa's hand and pulled her gently down to him. Clarissa lay back in the soft hay, exhaling softly as Andrew rolled over onto her body and kissed her deeply. She could feel all her senses coming alive as the handsome young man's kisses blazed a trail down her throat and between her breasts. Instinctively, she opened her thighs. Andrew looked up from his kissing and smiled at her. He slipped his hand under her cute, white cotton tennis dress, and the gauzy slip underneath it, gasping a little when he suddenly realized she was wearing no other underwear.

"I say, Clarissa!" he whispered hoarsely.

Clarissa gave a little laugh. "It was hot today," she explained. "I thought the slip would be enough."

"You are a capital girl!" Andrew raised himself up, kneeling between her legs. Deftly, he undid his belt and dropped his white flannels, freeing his erect and ready cock.

Clarissa sized up the shiny head on the generous shaft and smiled up at him. "Why, Andrew, you are fairly capital yourself!"

"Open your legs. Let me in, please!"

"Not so fast!" Clarissa sat up.

"Be a sport, Clarissa! You can't shut a bloke down at this stage of the game!"

"Oh, I'm not shutting anybody down!" Clarissa laughed and took the rigid member in both hands, stroking and squeezing it softly. Carefully she placed a kiss right on the glossy head and then took it between her lips. She was gratified to hear an audible, ecstatic moan escape Andrew. She began to suck his cock, gently at first, then harder and harder, running it deeper into her mouth. Andrew's head rolled on his shoulders in euphoric delirium. She took his balls in one hand, squeezing and massaging them. He began to thrust himself into her mouth. Finally, she stopped. It would be no good for her to finish him off here. Lying back in the hay, she lifted her skirts, spreading her legs wide.

"Is this where you want to be?" she whispered, slipping one of her fingers into her wet cunt. She spread her lips for him. Andrew made no reply, but taking his cock in his hand, he guided it into the waiting warmth and wetness. Clarissa felt the relief of it as it filled her cunt.

"Fuck my twat," she commanded. "Fuck me hard!"

Andrew needed no encouragement. With renewed vigor, he began to hammer her relentlessly, driving his hard cock, which only seemed to grow harder, in and out of her. He gripped her hips and lifted her bottom onto his lap, all the while ramming into her with delectable force. The pure power with which he pounded her fired a wantonness in Clarissa. She felt a dizzying swirl engulf her. Her wet cunt spasmed, and suddenly, her climax crashed around her. She cried aloud with the overwhelming frenzy of it, twisting and humping her hips to meet his. Suddenly, he gripped her, doubling over, with a grunting groan. He pulled out quickly and collapsed upon her, his juice running over her heaving belly.

The two of them lay there for a while. At last Andrew raised his head. He kissed her on the cheek and said, "I say, old girl! You are jolly good fun!"

"Why thank you, Andrew," replied Clarissa. "I do enjoy a good romp once in a while. You have made my stay here much more enjoyable than I could have predicted!"

After that, the rest of the week went quite quickly. Clarissa woke each morning looking forward to that day's adventures. She came to truly like Annabelle, and the two of them spent a good deal of the daytime together until two days before the wedding when Annabelle's bridesmaids began to arrive and the wedding preparations began to take precedence over all other activities in the home.

Clarissa was grateful, therefore, for Andrew's friendship and attentions. He slipped into her room nearly every night after everybody was abed—and then slipped into her.

They had much fun. Clarissa was especially impressed with Andrew's staying power. The piston-like repetitions of his vigorous thrusts had the power to bring her to multiple climaxes, something she had heretofore not considered. It was delightful!

The week passed quickly. Finally, the wedding was only a day away. The ceremony was scheduled for late afternoon, with the party to follow in the garden through the long English twilight. Clarissa did not see much of Andrew that day. He was best man for William and had much to attend to. Clarissa was not a bridesmaid, being only introduced to Annabelle two weeks before, so she kept mostly to her room. She and Lizzie went over her clothing for the next day. Lizzie was quite sure Clarissa would be the most beautiful girl there.

"It is certainly fortunate you are not a bridesmaid, miss," said the maid, "or you would outshine the bride!"

"Why, thank you, Lizzie! You are a beautiful girl yourself, and I wager there are many young men vying for your attentions!"

Lizzie blushed deeply in a way that stirred a desire within Clarissa. She was reminded of her lovely time aboard ship with Eleanora. It would be fun to explore Lizzie beneath that uniform, but, no, Clarissa decided not to press the matter. Andrew was more than enough entertainment for now, and no matter how much fun girls could have together, there was nothing quite a like cock for fulfilling one's needs.

Dinner that night was spectacular. The groom's family was the guest of the bride's family. The dining room was set for seventy-two people, who all appeared dressed in glitter and glitz. Candlelight sparkled off the silver and the crystal on the table, and the tiaras and diamonds worn by the guests. The food was elegant, and both champagne and the finest wines flowed ceaselessly. Andrew was very attentive and after dinner swirled her around the dance floor almost exclusively, which irritated Clarissa ever so slightly because, being an American, and therefore a bit of a curiosity, she was in high demand. Young men lined up to sign her dance card, and often cut in during dances. Clarissa found herself slightly breathless at one point, after a very athletic jazz number.

"Good show! Good show, Miss Hardy!" complimented her dance partner.

Clarissa could not remember his name. She thanked him demurely, and slipped away. Once lost in the crowd, she cast a furtive eye around the room, and thankfully not seeing Andrew, she tiptoed out onto the veranda for a breath of fresh air and a cigarette. She had been dying for a smoke all evening. Reaching into her evening clutch, she brought out her holder and a cigarette. She put the cigarette in the holder and took it daintily between her full lips. It was then she realized she had forgotten her lighter. It was too much! She was tired and just a bit homesick. "Damn it!" she swore.

"May I be of assistance?" said a male voice behind her.

Clarissa yelped. There was just no other word for it.

"I'm terribly sorry," said the voice. "I didn't mean to startle you."

Clarissa spun around and found herself face to face with one of the most handsome men she had ever seen. About six feet tall, he was broad shouldered with a trim waist and exquisitely fitting clothing. His hair was dark and cut in such a way that even though it was evident he meant to sweep it back from his face, it dipped in the most tantalizing way over his forehead. His skin was ever so slightly swarthy, as though he spent time in the sun, and his eyes were large and dark blue. He was standing very close to her.

"You didn't startle me," lied Clarissa, regaining her composure. "It is I who owe you an apology. I am really very much better than my language just now."

He laughed heartily and held out a lighter. "I think you are charming," he said. His accent betrayed him. He was an American. Clarissa dipped her cigarette to the lighter and inhaled. The flame caught. She blew the smoke delicately skyward.

"Thank you, sir," she said, meeting his eyes.

"I say! There you are! Clarissa, old sport, where have you been hiding!" She turned. It was Andrew. She found herself immediately annoyed. She turned to introduce herself and Andrew to the stranger, but he had departed silently. She could just see him as he melted into the crowd.

"What is it, Andrew?" she asked shortly.

"Where have you been?"

Clarissa was feeling nastily unsettled. "You know, Andrew, I'm feeling rather woozy, and I do not want to be compromised tomorrow. I think I shall slip away now and go up to bed." She had been feeling so lively, so good. What was wrong? Perhaps she had had too much champagne. Under the circumstances, it was easy to lose track. She squeezed Andrew's hand and ducked through a side door to the stairwell that led to her room.

Once in the privacy of her boudoir, Clarissa stripped off her clothing and stood naked in front of the mirror. She tried to look at herself objectively. She was indeed pretty, with her pale blond hair cut in a flawless bob. Her neck was long and graceful. She wished her breasts were larger, but nobody had ever complained, so she was grateful for what she had. Her waist was small and trim, and her belly was flat and muscular. Her bottom was full and round. Everybody seemed to love her bottom. Her legs could be longer, but they were well shaped and athletic, like a dancer's.

She played her fingers in the triangle of curls that grew between her legs. Suddenly, she was feeling quite amorous. She lay down on the bed and worked her finger between the lips of her cunt, feeling the wetness there. She fell asleep, naked on the bed, with her fingers in her cunt.

It must have been some hours later when she was wakened by the turning of the key in the lock. The door to her bedroom opened, and Andrew stole in.

"Clarissa! Clarissa!" he whispered. "I say, let's have a romp! You know, a celebratory thing!"

Clarissa sat up abruptly and pulled the sheet around her. "Andrew! You can't burst into my room uninvited!"

Andrew was busy taking off his shirt. He crossed the room and turned on a small light on her vanity table.

"Andrew! Did you hear me?"

"Come on, Clarissa! I'm dying for you. Let's do it now."

Andrew's demeanor was different, and somewhat alarming. Clarissa tucked her legs under her. He had dropped his pants to the floor and was standing, naked, before her. "Please, be a sport, Clarissa. Don't keep a bloke waiting!"

"You stay right where you are, Andrew! Don't take a step near me until you explain what's going on!"

Suddenly, there was a bumping and a thumping from inside the large clothespress.

Clarissa gave a little yip. "Oh! Oh! What is it? There is something in my clothespress!"

Andrew's shoulders slumped. Clarissa threw him a questioning look, but he was staring at the floor. "It's no use," he called out to the clothespress. "She's on to us. You may as well come out."

Clarissa watched incredulously as the clothespress doors opened. Crouched inside was William, dressed in silk pajamas.

"What! What madness is this? Explain yourself, Andrew! William, get out of there right now! You are crumpling my wardrobe! Out! Out, I say!" Clarissa was very angry.

William stepped sheepishly out of the clothespress and closed the doors behind him. Clarissa looked at the two young men, one in dark blue silk pajamas, the other stark naked. She was quite curious, so she overcame her anger and said quietly and calmly, "Now, one of you please tell me what is going on."

William took a tentative step toward the bed. "You see, Clarissa, it's like this. I…well, I…oh, you tell, Andrew, old chap. I'm too ashamed."

"Ashamed?" echoed Clarissa, switching her attention to Andrew.

Andrew lifted his eyes from the floor. He looked over at William, and then met Clarissa's gaze. "You see, old girl, it's like this. William is due to marry Annabelle tomorrow afternoon. Tomorrow at this time, they are supposed to be rolling around under the blankets having a grand old time."

"I don't understand," said Clarissa dryly.

"William's never done it," said Andrew bluntly.

"Well, of course he's never been married!"

"Not that," said Andrew, squirming slightly. "He's never…done… it, you know. *It*. He's never been with a girl!"

Clarissa leaned forward. "You mean you've never had sex, William?"

William shook his head.

"What about school? You've been to school."

"I went to an all-boys school."

"Oh, well, didn't you at least—you know—experiment?"

Both young men were silent. Clarissa cleared her throat and did not press the matter. "Well, what does that have to do with me?"

Andrew and William exchanged glances. Andrew said, "Well, the truth is, Clarissa, dear, the truth is we were hoping you'd give old William here some pointers. The plan was that you and I would get down to business, and William could see how it's done and then join in and get some practice."

Clarissa's eyes grew wide. "You astound me!" she ejaculated. "Andrew, you positively astound me! And you, too, William! Get out of my room this minute!"

Now Andrew took a truly pleading tone. "Oh, be a sport, Clarissa! Come on! We can't send old William into battle without training! What if the bride turns out to have more experience than he does? Think about it, Clarissa! Be a sport! I say, let's give it a go!"

Clarissa did think about it. She remembered her disappointment with Eddie. She really did like Annabelle, and it was not fair for Clarissa to know the lay of the land and not do what she could to spare her new friend a similar distasteful experience. She heaved a sigh.

"Oh, why not!" she said. After all, it could turn in to quite the adventure.

William gave a broad smile, and Andrew fairly yelled with delight. "Oh, Clarissa! You're the cat's meow! Thanks so much, old girl! You'll have fun, too." He rubbed his hands together and took a step toward the bed, his cock already at attention.

"Stay right where you are, Andrew," ordered Clarissa. "William, strip off those silly pajamas and approach the bed." With the sheet still held tightly around her, Clarissa knelt on the edge of the big four-poster. William shyly shed his pajamas and stood in front of Clarissa.

"Why, William, you are quite luscious to look at!" she said. Reaching out, she ran her hand across his abdomen and down his groin, lifting his flaccid cock in her hand. She bent her head and placed a tender kiss upon its tip, squeezing the shaft as she did so. She felt it stir and grow in her hand. Smiling up at William, she said, "Ah, I think you are going to be a very astute student!" She pointed to Andrew. "Look, you have just as lovely equipment as Andrew. He is all ready to go. Andrew, you may approach."

Andrew flashed Clarissa a big smile, and without further ado, climbed onto the bed. He went around and knelt behind Clarissa, pulling down the sheet and baring her breasts. He reached around and squeezed her nipples. Clarissa could feel his hard cock pressing against her back. This could turn out to be quite fun, she decided.

"A lady likes her breasts played with," explained Andrew. "Give them a kiss on each nipple, old boy." Andrew cupped Clarissa's breasts in his hands and hoisted them up. William leaned in and timidly pecked at each nipple. "Not like that! Give them a good suck!" commanded Andrew, squeezing them provocatively. William obeyed, sucking quite successfully. Clarissa leaned back again Andrew's chest and groaned with pleasure.

"Let me work on him a bit, Andrew," she said, at last. William stood up and leaned in over the bed. Clarissa took his now erect cock in her hands. "Well, I am glad to see you are paying attention!" she laughed. She took the tip into her lips and ran the shaft into her mouth, sucking and licking as she went.

William's breathing grew faster. He began to thrust. Clarissa sucked harder, feeling the cock grow stiffer as well, with her efforts. William groaned.

Andrew said, somewhat alarmed, "Stop, Clarissa. William, hang on to it, old boy. We've more to do! Don't blow it here!" William stepped back reluctantly.

"That felt capital!" he said, gasping. "Do you think Annabelle will do that?"

"If you treat her right," said Clarissa. Andrew was gently pushing her back onto the bed. She lay there, waiting to see what he would do.

"Now for a look at the prize," he said, beckoning to William. "Come up onto the bed, Will." Andrew spread Clarissa's legs wide. "Open up for us, Clarissa. There. Look there, William." Andrew parted the lips of Clarissa's cunt. "You need to stroke and tickle her twat, to get it all wet. A lady likes to have her cunt licked and kissed, too."

Andrew bent his head and began to lick Clarissa's cunt. He pushed his tongue in and out of her, sucking at her clit, rolling his tongue around it. Clarissa heaved her hips to meet his mouth. What a heavenly feeling!

Andrew straightened up. "You see," he continued instructing William. "You see how the lady reacts. She finds it quite pleasurable, and it makes her positively ache for your cock." Andrew slipped a finger into Clarissa and began to pump it in and out of her. "See how wet she is," Andrew pointed out. "That's what you want to see. It feels excellent on the cock. Clarissa knows the ropes. She's already wet. It takes some girls a little longer. Sometimes you just need to be patient."

"Give me a go, Andrew," asserted William, pushing his friend aside. Clarissa reached down and spread the lips of her cunt for him.

"Finger me, William," she instructed. "My cunt is wet and juicy, and my clit is hard."

William gave a little giggle. He settled on his knees between her legs. Clarissa closed her eyes as he inserted his finger and slid it in and out. In the meantime, Andrew was sucking at her nipples. Clarissa was enjoying herself, and William was catching on fast. He used both hands, fingering her, pulling and pinching her clit, reaching as far into her as he could.

She whispered, "Put your cock in me, William. Put it right in there!"

William straightened up. Andrew looked up to watch. William's cock was certainly worthy of the job. Andrew reached down and spread the lips of Clarissa's wet cunt. William took his cock in both hands and guided it into the opening. Clarissa let out a moan as he sank it to the hilt into her throbbing orifice. She wiggled her hips, and he began to thrust. At first, they were short, soft thrusts, but the passion hit him and he began to bang her in earnest.

"Hoho!" exclaimed Andrew. "Ride her, my friend." Andrew bent around and gave William a smart whack on the buttocks. "Faster!" He reached underneath and between William's legs and squeezed his ball sack. "Good job!" he grunted in encouragement, whacking William again.

William's head rolled back just then. Clarissa felt his big cock swell within her. She felt William shudder and convulse as he groaned aloud and collapsed on top of her at the height of his climax. He lay there panting until Andrew rolled him off.

"My turn," he gasped, turning Clarissa over onto her stomach. Her cunt was still throbbing, sticky and hot from the pounding it had just received. She had not yet reached her climax. Andrew grabbed her hips and set her on her knees, her bottom hoisted into the air.

"There are a number of positions," Andrew grunted to William. "Watch carefully." Andrew proceeded to ram into Clarissa with his eager, hard shaft and began to fuck her from behind, squeezing her buttocks all the while. A white hot heat infused Clarissa's whole body as he pounded away. He reached under her, taking her whole mons in his hand and massaging and pinching it. She gasped and moaned and groaned.

"Fuck me! Fuck me!" she cried, but at that, he pulled out. "Oh! Oh! Don't stop, please," she begged. He sat up and dragged her on her tummy across his lap.

"A lady likes to be titillated, old chum," Andrew explained, breathing hard. "Sometimes, it's fun to tease them until they come. You have to make sure they come, too. It makes them want more the next time and that is only good for you. Sit here and take part."

William lifted Clarissa's legs. He sat beside Andrew on the edge of the bed, Clarissa face down across their laps. She felt deliciously exposed and vulnerable. Andrew's hands were stroking her buttocks.

"Put your finger into her and fuck her twat," said Andrew. "I'll show you something."

Clarissa felt a thrill as Andrew spread her buttocks, exposing her tight arsehole. He began to tickle and tease it. Clarissa wriggled in ecstasy.

"See the bung hole, here?" said Andrew. "It's really quite sensitive. Girls love it when you tickle it. You can even put a finger in there. Just make sure you have her permission. How about it, Clarissa? You like a finger in the bum, don't you?"

"Oh, yes, yes!" breathed Clarissa, wild with anticipation.

Andrew pushed his finger into her twat beside William's, to get it wet. Then he began to tickle and tease her arsehole, pushing against it, stroking it with his finger. "Keep fucking and playing with her twat. We want to drive her wild!"

Indeed, Clarissa was wild. She writhed and heaved on their laps. William had three fingers in her, pumping them in and out. Andrew traced her arse with his finger and then slipped it into her, knuckle-deep. She gave out a little yelp of pleasure. Slowly, he began to finger fuck her, turning it this way and that inside her. The sensation of being full in every orifice overcame Clarissa. She reached the pinnacle of pleasure, and her climax crashed over her in a series of exquisite waves.

"Why, I feel her twitching inside!" exclaimed William.

"Yes," replied Andrew, withdrawing his finger. "She's come and come hard! Bravo, Clarissa!"

Clarissa giggled and crawled over them to collapse on the bed in a satiated heap.

"I say," William said, "not so fast, Clarissa. Look what's happened!"

Clarissa opened her eyes and saw, with amusement, that William's cock had resurrected itself quite gloriously.

Andrew looked at him with admiration. "I say, old chap, good show!"

Clarissa watched while Andrew took his own cock in his hands and rubbed it up and down. Clarissa reached over and took it lazily in her mouth, sucking the shaft to attention.

William looked mischievously at Andrew. "What say we try to both go in at once? How's that, Clarissa? Do you think you could take it? Two cocks in a bush?"

The young men laughed. Clarissa laughed and spread her legs. "Why not!" she said gamely. "Have a try!"

Both on their knees, each man hoisted one of Clarissa's legs. Clarissa felt herself being stretched as the two cocks were pushed together into her cunt.

At last Andrew collapsed in laughter. "Stand back, old chap," he said to William. "I've not had my turn yet. Clarissa, prepare to be fucked once again!"

Clarissa smiled up at him. Andrew took both her legs and bent them up over her shoulders, ramming his cock home as he did so. He fucked her with a passion that brought the heat of another climax washing over her again, pumping in and out until he fell over her with a groan.

When they opened their eyes a minute later, William was smiling down at them, already dressed in his pajamas.

"Damned fine lesson!" he said. "I can't thank you enough! I am a new man. I am! Damn good sports, the two of you! Capital friends! Capital friends! Well, see you tomorrow!" He gave them a wink and left the room.

The wedding was a lovely affair. The bride was exquisite in white lace that clung to her lithesome figure, and flared out into a delicate train behind her. The groom smiled ear-to-ear throughout the entire ceremony and garden party afterward. Clarissa's heart swelled with happiness for them, and not a little pride in herself, knowing that, all things considered, she had given them the best gift of all.

PART FOUR
Clarissa Sees Things Clearly

Clarissa stood at the window of her bedroom in Lord and Lady Handcock's vast, well-appointed English country house. The wedding had been a jolly affair, but that had been over two weeks ago. Annabelle and William had departed for their month-long honeymoon touring the continent, no doubt enjoying themselves (and each other) immensely. Worse yet, Clarissa's special friend, Andrew Milton, had abandoned her, catching his scheduled steamer to pursue archeological studies in Egypt. Clarissa was alone in a cavernous home with two old people and a stream of elderly visitors. And to top it all off, the weather had been rainy for nearly a week!

To fight the boredom, Clarissa wrote. She wrote bawdy, funny letters to Bonnie and Eleanora. She wrote long, descriptive letters to her mother and father. She also kept a journal and recorded her daily activities and observations for later scrutiny.

Clarissa turned away from the window to dress. Why were the visitors always so old and dull? One would think the Handcocks, with all their connections, would know some young people. Clarissa hugged her long cashmere cardigan around herself and went down to breakfast.

"Clarissa, dear! Good morning!" Lady Handcock greeted her warmly.

"Good morning, my dear," said Lord Handcock. "Please be seated." He stood and, as there was no other man in the room, pulled the chair out for her himself. Clarissa sat and at that moment, Tina, the kitchen maid, came out with teapot in one hand and coffee pot in the other.

"Coffee or tea, miss?"

"Oh, coffee, please," answered Clarissa. Tina duly filled her cup with the steaming black liquid. Clarissa helped herself to the cream from the dainty little pitcher on the table at her place.

"My!" exclaimed Lady Edith. "Aren't we the lonely little family this morning!"

Clarissa raised her cup to her lips in order to avoid making a reply. Lord Terrence chuckled through his mustache, as if he knew a secret.

Lady Edith went on. "Clarissa, dear, I have a confession to make." Clarissa looked at her quizzically. Lady Edith continued, "Clarissa, dear, I was in the library and there were some papers on the library table. I thought perhaps Lord Terrance had left them, so I gathered them up. As I was doing so, I noticed it was not his hand. I stopped and read some of what was on the pages."

Clarissa gave a little gasp. "Oh, Lady Edith! I am so sorry! It must have been the letter that I was writing to my mother! I am so sorry to have abandoned it. Something caught my attention, and I left the room and forgot to come back for my papers!"

Lady Edith gave a little laugh. "No, my dear. No apology is necessary! The fact is, I was so caught up in your letter, I read through it. It was a description of Annabelle's wedding, and it was wonderful! Why, I felt as though I was reliving it! It was so captivating! You are truly talented. I am very impressed. And I do apologize to you for reading a personal epistle."

"Certainly, it was I who was amiss by being so careless in your home," replied Clarissa. "However, I am so glad you liked my description of the wedding. I enjoyed writing it."

Lord Terrence set down his fork and dabbed at his mustache with his napkin. "My dear, Lady Edith and I would like to ask your permission to send this report of Annabelle's wedding to the *Times* and the *Tribune*. We would keep it anonymous, of course, to protect your identity amongst your peers, but your writing is superior. Truly superior."

Clarissa blinked. "Lord Terrence, I am, of course, flattered that you both think so much of my little report, but wasn't there a detailed description of the affair already published in the *Times?*"

"There was indeed," spoke up Lady Edith. "It was a dry, dull, positively common report. It made no mention of the bride's attendants, no mention of the groom's heritage. There was no description of our wonderful home. It was a special event. An important event. Important people were here. The Duke and Duchess of Cornwall were here! I was terribly disappointed. And they were supposed to forward the article on to the *Tribune* so that our American friends and peers here and abroad might read of it, also. No mention, no mention at all, in the *Tribune*!"

"My dear, do not upset yourself. If Clarissa will agree to it, I have a plan," said Lord Terrence, patting his wife's hand soothingly. "Follow me, ladies, into the library."

When they had settled themselves in the library, Lord Terrence explained. "Today we are expecting the arrival of our dear friends, Sir Anderson and Lady Anne Tallman. They are also bringing with them their younger son Bruce, and Bruce's old school chum Chauncey Chelmsford. They are about your age, Clarissa, and both very eligible! However, before you get excited, there is more. Chauncey Chelmsford is the social editor of the *Tribune*! Yes! I think with a little diplomatic maneuvering, we will get our just desserts in the *Tribune* and a repeat mention of worth in the *Times*!"

Lady Edith clapped her hands together.

Clarissa exclaimed, "I certainly would agree to that, Lord Terrence." It seemed so important to him and to Lady Edith that Clarissa spoke with added enthusiasm. However, it was not the actual publication of her report that made Clarissa's heart leap. It was the fact that not one, but two young men were coming to visit. At last, some fun!

At two-thirty that afternoon, Lord Terrence sent the car to the train to collect the guests. They arrived an hour later. Lady Edith and Clarissa greeted them all in the wide front foyer, and the staff escorted them to their bedrooms in the guest wing. Soon the whole party was assembled in the large reception room, and Basil, the butler, served cocktails. Clarissa and the Ladies Edith and Anne sipped French 75s, while the men savored Gin Rickeys. The kitchen sent out some delicate hors d'oeuvres which they nibbled hungrily.

Clarissa sized up the young men as she chatted merrily to them. Bruce, the younger son of Sir Anderson and Lady Anne, was very good-looking with thick, wavy, dark brown hair and large brown eyes. He was quite tall and well-built, and he had a ready, infectious laugh.

Chauncey Chelmsford was a smaller man, closer to thirty than either she or Bruce. His hair was too pale and thin and his nose too pointy to be good-looking, but there was a kind intelligence in his blue eyes that made Clarissa warm to him. He had a smart, dry humor about him that made her recall the writings of Oscar Wilde and George Bernard Shaw from her school days. She was thoroughly enjoying herself and although she admired Chauncey very much, she set her sights on Bruce. It shouldn't be difficult, she reasoned. He was so easy to talk to and kept touching her arm in a familiar and affectionate way.

"I wish the weather would clear," sighed Clarissa. She and Bruce were standing in front of the big window. Chauncey had gone in search of more cocktails. "If only it would stop raining, we could take a ride out to see the old walled garden. It's very romantic! You do ride, don't you?"

"Of course. Rather well, I should say. Both Chauncey and I belong to the West Kent Hunt, you see."

"Do you keep a horse, then?"

"I do, yes. Chauncey's family has a country home there. His father is Master of Hounds. I keep my hunter there. Being in London in the banking business is such a drag! I mean, it can make a bloke downright grumpy!"

"And that's why we try to visit the countryside as often as possible," chimed in Chauncey, coming up behind them. He held three drinks and extended his hands toward Clarissa.

"Thank you so much, Chauncey," she said, taking her French 75, that delicious concoction of champagne, lemonade, and gin.

Chauncey handed Bruce his Gin Rickey, and both men raised their glasses to Clarissa.

"A toast," offered Bruce jovially. "A toast to our new friend Clarissa, and a capital time in the countryside!"

"Here! Here!" said Chauncey.

Clarissa smiled and managed an attractive flush of her cheeks.

By next morning, the skies had cleared. It was a beautiful, warm day, and the world was dew washed and just waiting to hand Clarissa her next adventure on a silver platter. She dressed eagerly in her riding clothes. She knew she looked absolutely fetching in her gabardine jodhpurs, white linen shirt, and shiny black field boots. She would draw Bruce out for a ride alone together after breakfast. Yet, there was still the problem of what to do with Chauncey. Clarissa consciously cleared the scowl from her forehead as she entered the breakfast room just ahead of Bruce.

Her problem took care of itself. Clarissa, having seated herself at Lady Edith's right, made up her mind to ask both boys to join her. It was the only way, after all, to start her plan. She dabbed at her lips with her napkin and spoke up.

"I say, would you two gentlemen like a tour of the estate on horseback this morning?" she said. "I know that you would love to see the walled garden, and I am absolutely desperate to get outside and astride a horse! Please, humor me!"

"Capital idea, Clarissa!" Bruce answered immediately. "I should very much like a hack around the old farmstead on this gorgeous morning! That is, if Lord Terrence has a quiet old nag he'd lend me."

Lord Terrence laughed. "We have a stable of eight top-notch hunters. Tommy, down in the barn, will help you. Thanks for playing the hostess, Clarissa. You are becoming almost another daughter!"

Lady Anne giggled. "Clarissa, how lovely of you! I must warn you, they are two of the most eligible bachelors in London! You will be hard put to it to choose."

The company around the table laughed heartily.

"Well, you shall have to do without old Chauncey," said Chauncey nonchalantly. "Lord Terrence and I have some business to attend to." He looked at Clarissa and smiled. "Some of it has directly to do with Clarissa. Lord Terrence has promised to show me some social observations you have written down. That is, if you don't mind."

"Why, thank you, Chauncey! I don't mind a bit!" said Clarissa, secretly thrilled that she would at last be alone with Bruce.

The breakfast group disbanded. Clarissa waited impatiently while Bruce ran up to his bedroom to change into riding clothes. He looked elegantly heart stopping as he descended the stairs dressed in boots and jodhpurs, a white shirt, and tweed hacking jacket. Together, they strolled down to the stables.

They had a wonderful ride. Bruce was so complimentary.

"I say, Clarissa, you are quite the equestrienne! You're a capital girl all round. You really are! Why, you should see what I have to put up with in London! All manner of girls who prey upon me!"

"Prey upon you! Whatever do you mean?"

"Well, they hear who I am. The son of Sir Anderson Tallman, wealthy war hero and appointed peer of Parliament. Nice place in London. Nice place in the countryside. They're all over me! Sharking about." He hung his head dejectedly. "Makes things very awkward." He raised his eyes to Clarissa's. "Nobody wants to be just friends!"

Clarissa processed this bit of information. She did not exactly want to be "just friends," either, but she was careful with her words. There was more to this story than had been revealed. Perhaps his heart had been broken. She would tread lightly.

"Well, that seems very impolite to me," she said.

"I know! Then, they seem so disappointed when I tell them I'm the younger son, you see. Everything goes to my brother, of course. Well, I do have my inheritance, but I need my career, too. Why, everybody has told me to watch out for the American girls, but I find you especially straightforward and delightful to be around! Come, let's have a canter! Then you can tell me about your life in America. I hope to visit there one day!"

He leaned forward in the saddle, and the tall bay leaped eagerly forward. Clarissa squeezed Pimpernel with her thighs, and they galloped together up the lane.

They returned to the house just in time for the midday meal. Basil met them at the door, saying, "Go right into the dining room, please. They are all there. Tina will serve you directly."

Clarissa peeled off her soft leather riding gloves and stuck them into the waistband of her breeches. Bruce took her lightly by the elbow and escorted her into the dining room. Clarissa thought this was a good sign. Rather of a show of one's territory. It would be interesting to see how Chauncey would react.

"Ah, there you are, you two!" Lord Terrence boomed from the end of the table. "Take your seats! Tina, luncheon for the just arrived, please!"

Clarissa took a place at Lord Terrence's right and across from Lady Anne. "I say, did you have a grand gallop?" he asked.

"We did," replied Clarissa. "We did indeed."

"Mr. Chelmsford and I had quite the discussion about you, young lady."

"Really!" exclaimed Clarissa. "Do tell!" She looked right at Chauncey.

Chauncey smiled at her. "I have read your little article on Annabelle's wedding, Clarissa. It is uniquely charming, I must say! I would like your permission to publish it in the social pages of the *Tribune*. It will set the *Times* back some, I wager."

"Oh, indeed!" gasped Clarissa. "Surely it can't be that good! Why, I was only documenting it for Mommy, who was so sad as to have been unable to attend. I wanted her to be able to picture it in her mind."

"You did an excellent job of that!" continued Chauncey. "I am the editor of the social pages of the *Tribune*. We take on all the births, deaths, weddings, appointments, food, drink, music, and any other social trends that loom on the horizon. I am always desperate for talent! So it's a go? I can publish it?"

"Of course," said Clarissa. "I am truly humbled. Thank you very much."

Lady Anne Tallman suddenly spoke up eagerly. "And the other thing, Chauncey. Ask her about the other thing."

Chauncey eyed Lady Anne as a loving parent eyes a mischievous child. "Well, I suppose now is as good a time as any."

"Ask me what?" questioned Clarissa curiously.

Chauncey cleared his throat and said, "I know you are planning to return to America in the near future. Just after Annabelle and William return from their honeymoon, I believe. Well, I was wondering whether you might not reconsider. Whether you might consider a move to London instead. At least for a while. To write for the *Tribune* on different social issues and different assignments. Be a reporter for a bit, you see. What do you think?"

Clarissa was speechless. All the eyes at the table were on her. This was more than she could possibly have hoped for! Another adventure! London! Perhaps the Continent! And Bruce lived in London! She smiled broadly at Chauncey, her eyes dewy with giddy anticipation. "Oh yes, Chauncey! Why not! What fun!"

"Capital!" shouted Bruce and began to clap. "Here! Here!"

"Where should I stay?" asked Clarissa, looking at Chauncey. "I don't know anybody in London."

"You may stay with me. I have a whole house in Kensington where I positively rattle around, so there is plenty of room for you."

Lady Anne spoke up again, this time more seriously. "Oh, dear, Chauncey. Oh, dear! I do not think that would be at all proper, even in this extremely confusing age. We shall have to find her another place."

Chauncey looked taken aback for an instant, and then Bruce piped up. "I have it! Yes, I do! I shall stay with Chauncey, and Clarissa can move into my flat in Mayfair! I have the Duttons. Mrs. Dutton is my housekeeper and Mr. Dutton, the manservant, so Clarissa won't be alone or unchaperoned! What do you say, Chauncey, old chap?"

Clarissa looked from one man to the other. Something passed between them. Something she couldn't identify off the bat. She would have to think about it.

Chauncey smiled. "Capital! Positively brilliant, old man! What do you say, Clarissa? Bruce's flat isn't too far away from my house, so we should be close. What do you say?"

Clarissa grinned. "Why not!"

Over the next few days, Chauncey, Clarissa, and Bruce planned the details of Clarissa's new career (however temporary, she told them) as a journalist. She was not sure Daddy would go for the idea of her actually working for money, but he would just have to adapt to the modern times! She would go with them to London on Monday next, ensconce herself in Bruce's flat, get to know the neighborhood, and report for her first assignment on the Monday after that.

On Sunday night, the night before they were to depart for London, Clarissa lay in her bed, tossing and turning. Things had not progressed with Bruce the way she had planned. They had ridden together, played tennis together, even walked hand-in-hand together. He seemed quite fond of her, kissing her cheek when they parted, confiding in her about his career and his passion for painting. However, he always stopped just short, thought Clarissa, remembering Andrew in the hayloft. Andrew had needed no special encouragement! What was she doing wrong? Then it struck her. Chauncey must be in love with her, too! Yes, that had to be what was holding Bruce back! Chauncey must have confided his feelings for her to Bruce, unaware that Bruce was also in love with her. Of course, Bruce would never cut in on his best friend's love interest.

Clarissa let out a huge sigh. So now it was stalemate! What to do? Finally, around midnight, she worked out a plan. She would go to Bruce's room and hide behind the screen in the corner. When he was safely in bed, she would tiptoe out, climb right into bed with him, and force him to show his hand. Honesty would have to be the best policy. Bruce was a gentleman and would feel compelled to tell Chauncey the truth.

Silently, she got out of bed, slipped her silk robe over her shoulders, and tiptoed out of her room. The guests were in another wing of the house. Clarissa was nearly turned around and headed for the scullery before she found the proper hallway. She had accompanied Lady Edith when the guests had arrived and helped show them to their rooms, so she remembered that Bruce had the room off the far end of the upstairs gallery.

She put her ear to the door. She could hear water in the bathroom. He was undoubtedly getting ready for bed. Slowly, she pushed the door open, hoping it wouldn't creak. Bruce was humming in the bathroom. Clarissa slipped through the door and shut it carefully behind her. She quickly ducked behind the oriental screen in the corner of the room and waited, her heart pounding.

The room was very dimly lit by a small lamp on the bedside table. Clarissa heard Bruce humming as he came out of the bathroom. She peeked through the narrow slit between the panels of the screen. Bruce stood beside the bed, holding a towel. He was completely nude. Clarissa saw with a thrill that her suspicions were indeed true. He was beautifully proportioned, with long, clean limbs, and clearly defined muscles. A powerful chest smoothed into a taut stomach and groin. His cock, at ease, was, again to Clarissa's delight, more than ample.

Suddenly, Clarissa heard a light tap at the door. She held her breath, still peeking out the slit. She watched as Bruce approached the door.

"Who is it?" he said softly. Somebody mumbled something from the other side. Bruce opened the door, still stark naked.

"Is everybody asleep?" Bruce asked.

"Yes. The house is quiet." It was Chauncey. Clarissa's heart beat furiously. What could Chauncey want at this hour? Perhaps to discuss her! She waited, her eye glued to the slit between the panels. She saw Chauncey step through the door and lock it behind him.

"My dearest," he said.

Clarissa's blood ran cold! How could they have seen her? She froze, waiting for them to step behind the screen. Then, suddenly, what she saw left no question in her mind as to the nature of the situation. Chauncey took the naked Bruce in his arms and kissed him, long and deeply, on the mouth. Bruce's back was toward her, and she followed Chauncey's hand as it slipped down Bruce's ribcage and came to rest on his firm buttocks. Chauncey gave a gentle squeeze.

Bruce began to unbutton Chauncey's shirt. "It seems to have worked out beautifully," he said.

"What is that?"

"The situation with Clarissa. We now have a legitimate reason to live under the same roof on an at least semi-permanent basis!"

"We do, indeed! She's a rather capital girl, Clarissa is! Hurry, my dear. Jones is positively straining to be free!"

Clarissa watched, half shocked, half mesmerized, as Bruce unbuckled Chauncey's belt and tugged his trousers down to the floor. Chauncey's cock, of impressive size, sprung forward, erect and eager. Bruce went down on his knees. Taking the formidable member in his hands, he massaged and stroked it and at last wrapped his lips around it.

A gasp of delight issued forth from Chauncey. He thrust back and forth a bit, in and out of Bruce's mouth. Clarissa had a clear view of the whole proceeding. Bruce's hands were wrapped around Chauncey's buttocks, stroking and squeezing them. He worked his fingers between Chauncey's tight cheeks, exploring and prodding. Out of courtesy, Clarissa wanted to look away, but the growing warmth and tingling between her legs kept her focused on the unfolding scene on the other side of the screen.

Bruce stood up, and Chauncey led him to the bed. They lay side by side, gently caressing each other's cocks. Bruce slid down in the bed and once again took Chauncey's cock into his mouth. He began to slide his lips up and down the stiff shaft.

Chauncey moaned and writhed. "Faster!" he whispered. "Harder!"

Bruce teasingly chuckled and just licked around the tip. Chauncey heaved his hips. "Make me come!" he begged.

Now Bruce began to suck in earnest, all the while his one hand tight was wrapped around Chauncey's cock as the other was fondling between Chauncey's legs, pushing and prodding. Chauncey spread his legs wide to allow Bruce access to the tight sphincter throbbing there. Bruce buried two fingers, kneading and pushing. Suddenly Chauncey gave a great gasp and moan. He shuddered. Bruce sat up, his fingers still working in Chauncey's arse.

"Come! Come for me," he urged Chauncey. "I want to see it!"

Chauncey moaned and bucked on the bed, and ejaculate spewed out of his rigid cock onto his chest and belly. He lay panting. Bruce bent down and tenderly kissed him.

"I want to come inside you now," Clarissa heard him say.

This is what Eleanora had told her about. Anybody could love anybody they chose. Two men, two women, a man and a woman. It made no difference. The passion between these two lovers was every bit as intense as it had been between Clarissa and Andrew or Clarissa and Roger Downs. More, perhaps, thought Clarissa guiltily, because she did not truly love either Andrew or Roger.

Chauncey raised himself and, bending forward, took Bruce's erect cock in both hands. Reaching into the bedside table, Bruce brought out a small jar and handed it, smiling, to Chauncey. Chauncey opened it and dipped his fingers into it. Clarissa watched as he rubbed Bruce's cock shiny with the ointment. Then he handed the jar back to Bruce, turned over onto his stomach and opened his legs. Bruce knelt between them and spread Chauncey's buttocks wide. He took a big dollop of the salve and rubbed it all around and into Chauncey's already worked arse.

Clarissa clenched her cunt in anticipation. She reached down into her pajamas, finding the sweetest spot with her finger as she watched. Bruce placed the head of his cock between the cheeks of Chauncey's arse. Playfully, he spanked the man.

"Ask for it," he whispered. "Ask for my cock in your arse."

"Give it to me. Fuck me," begged Chauncey.

Bruce pushed. Chauncey gasped as Bruce's cock entered him. Bruce began to thrust. He held Chauncey's hips, pushing and pulling his cock in and out.

"Oh, you're divine!" he moaned ecstatically. "I live to fuck you!" Bruce fucked faster as Chauncey moaned more loudly and gripped the coverlet of the bed.

Clarissa was caught up in the excitement and began to fuck herself with her fingers. She rubbed her clit, squeezing and pulling it.

At last Bruce cried out and fell forward onto Chauncey's supine form. He jerked and moaned and finally rolled off onto the bed. The two lay panting together, holding hands.

"I love you," Clarissa heard Bruce whisper.

And Chauncey whispered back, "I love you, too. Dearly!"

Clarissa gave a little spasm, coming at her own touch. She gasped and immediately regretted it. They heard her!

"Who's there?" barked Bruce. Both men struggled to pull the coverlet around them.

Hanging her head, Clarissa crept out from behind the screen. She gazed at them sitting on the bed, the coverlet pulled around them, making them look like a two-headed man.

"Clarissa!" Chauncey could barely get the word out. He and Bruce looked at each other.

Clarissa began to cry silently. Tears she couldn't stop trickled down her flushed cheeks.

"Forgive me!" she begged them, "Forgive me! I didn't intend to intrude. Truly I didn't! I had no idea! I had no idea! I was hiding in here to…well, to try to get Bruce into a compromising position."

"Explain yourself!" demanded Bruce.

Clarissa's face felt hot. Her hands began to sweat. She talked faster. "I-I well, you see, I had rather a bit of a crush on you, Bruce. Dear Bruce. I thought you liked me back. I never presumed for a moment…" Clarissa stopped. The truth hit her hard. She blurted out, "I never presumed for a second that you and Chauncey were-were so in love! Oh, dear! Oh, dear! I am so, so ashamed of myself!"

Chauncey rose from the bed and slipped into a silk robe, tying it about his waist. Bruce reached down, picked up his discarded bath towel, and pulled it around himself.

Bruce was the first to speak. "Come sit by me, Clarissa."

Obediently, she went and sat beside him on the edge of the bed, then stared at the floor. Had she alienated two jolly new friends for the sake of relieving her boredom? She felt so utterly selfish. Chauncey sat on the other side of her.

"What will you do?" he asked her in an odd, flat tone.

Clarissa did not understand. Her brow furrowed with the effort of making sense of the situation. "What do you mean?" she asked.

Bruce spoke softly, as he put a gentle hand on her arm. "Clarissa, please do not speak of this to anybody. Awful things could happen to us. We could be separated. Chauncey and I could very well end up in jail!"

Clarissa met his eye with horror. "Oh, dear! Of course I won't mention it to a soul. This is your love, and you are so very fortunate to have each other." She whimpered a little at the thought of herself being alone and unloved. Chauncey patted her hand.

"There, there," he said, "no harm done. Bruce and I have been in love since we met at Eton." He gazed off into space. "Remember, Bruce? I was in my final year and you were a fresh-faced first year!"

Bruce said, "I followed you to Oxford." He looked at Clarissa. "It was there we made our love known to each other. We have been inseparable ever since."

"How wonderful!" sighed Clarissa. Then she ventured, "Does this mean I won't be going with you to London?"

Spontaneously, Chauncey threw both arms around her and hugged her to him. "Oh, my dear, darling girl! You are the answer to our prayers! With you in residence in Bruce's flat, it is the perfect cover for us to at last share a domicile! And the reporter's job is very sincere. You are a talented girl, and now, we find, compassionate as well!" Bruce wrapped them in his arms, and they both hugged her tight.

Clarissa, filled with warmth, could not deny her feelings of affection for both of them.

By ten o'clock the next morning, Clarissa had risen, dressed, and finished her breakfast. Lizzie had packed her belongings in her trunk and overnight bag. She stood on the front steps in her smart little traveling suit with Lord Terrance and Lady Edith, Sir Anderson and Lady Anne.

"Where are those boys?" asked Lady Anne, fidgeting.

Lady Edith bent toward her and said with a sly smile, "And they say women are always delayed!"

As if in answer to her concern, Bruce suddenly appeared, followed by Chauncey and two boys carrying their luggage.

"Good morning, Mother," said Bruce, kissing Lady Anne on the cheek. "Where's the car?"

Lord Terrence spoke up. "It'll be around shortly. So sorry to see you young people go! You should stay another week, until Annabelle and William return."

Lady Edith chided him. "Oh, my dear, they are young and the city calls!"

Just then, the Bentley rounded the corner and came to a halt in front of the little group.

"Well, here we are," said Bruce.

"And here we go," laughed Chauncey.

Good-byes were said all round, the chauffeur opened the door, and the traveling trio climbed aboard. Clarissa settled herself between her two gentleman escorts and positively beamed at the prospect of the adventures that awaited her.

PART FIVE
Clarissa Closes Her Eyes and Does It For England

The flat in London was adorable. Clarissa gave little squeals of delight as Bruce and Chauncey gave her the tour and helped her settle in. Art Deco prevailed, with a nod here and there to modernism. A bronze greyhound, nearly as tall as Clarissa, sat in the foyer. Bruce flung his fedora expertly as they passed the statue and the hat settled upon the head of the dog.

The foyer was ample, with a large coat closet. Four stairs led down on one side and four up on the opposite side. The floor was covered with the latest linoleum design of black and white geometric shapes, and a gilt mirror hung on the wall opposite the front door over a darling little crescent table upon which sat a shallow, shell-shaped silver dish.

Bruce led her up the stairs, chatting excitedly. Chauncey brought up the rear.

"Oh, my dear girl," gushed Bruce, "you will love it here! I do, but of course, I am ecstatic to be moving in with Chaunce! Righto, Chauncey, old chum?"

Chauncey heaved a sigh as he followed them up the stairs. "I only hope I did not make a terrible error in judgment!" he said sarcastically to Clarissa. "I do value my private time! Even though I love you to pieces, dear!" He winked at Clarissa as he shot this last barb beyond her to Bruce, who was opening the door at the top of the stairs.

"Have no fear! Your house is big enough for the both of us. And we are lovely big blokes, if I do say so myself!" He turned to Clarissa. "You should see Chauncey's house! Which you will. Syrie Maugham did it. It's fantastic!"

Clarissa and Chauncey both followed him through the door. Clarissa was charmed. There were two reception rooms, both with fireplaces, on either side of a center hall. The Art Deco theme prevailed. Besides the reception rooms, there was a small office at the end of the hall, replete with a typewriter and a beautiful view of the neighborhood. Through the arched glass doors of the smaller reception room was a spacious dining room lit with a crystal and brass chandelier and crystal wall sconces. Beyond the dining room were three bedrooms. The biggest bedroom had its own en suite bath. Across the hall were two more bedrooms with a bath in between. There were parquet floors and Persian carpets throughout.

"This will be your bedroom," said Bruce, gesturing to the large en suite room. "You will love it. It faces east, so the sun smiles in every morning, and the view of the city is fabulous!"

Chauncey was carrying Clarissa's small duffle. "Bruce's man, Dutton, will bring up the rest of the luggage."

Bruce took her by the hand. "Yes, yes," he said. "Let's go downstairs. It's the domain of Dutton and his wife, who keeps the house, but you should know where to find them. They have a small apartment down there off the kitchen. They're capital folks! They'll tend to your every need and you won't be alone here. Of course, you may call for me or Chauncey at any hour of the day or night."

Clarissa followed the boys downstairs and met the Duttons. Mr. Dutton was a tall, lean, gray-haired man, quite distinguished looking. He was dressed in an immaculate black suit with a crisp, snowy white shirt. Mrs. Dutton was a very attractive woman, about fifty. Despite her conservative dress in a gray frock with starched white apron and high collar, her voluptuous figure was very evident. She wore her gray hair in a bun at the back of her head, secured with two ornate hair sticks. She gave Clarissa a big smile.

"Welcome! Welcome!" she said. "You just make yourself to home, dearie. Mr. Dutton and I will see to anything you find yourself wanting." She wrapped Clarissa in a warm hug and kissed her lightly on the cheek. She smelled heavenly.

Taking Clarissa's hand, she pointed to what appeared to Clarissa to be a complicated electrical panel on the wall by the kitchen door. "There's a button on the wall beside your bed, dearie. When you wake up in the morning, just press that button and I will bring you your tea and breakfast."

"Why, thank you," said Clarissa.

"You will also find a similar button in the office," put in Mr. Dutton. "If you need any sustenance or assistance while you are working, simply press the buzzer."

It was all very satisfactory, thought Clarissa, as she stood in her new bedroom an hour later and looked around. Bruce and Chauncey had departed for Chauncey's house. Clarissa had kissed them both good-bye and promised to show up at seven o'clock for cocktails and dinner. Chauncey promised there would be some people there from the paper whom she must meet, perhaps even the editor himself.

"I would have invited people from the bank," quipped Bruce as they walked out the door. "Unfortunately, they are so frightfully dry!"

Clarissa's first week was so busy, she felt absolutely swept up into another world. The city was intoxicating. The pulse of the *Tribune* offices appealed to Clarissa's sense of adventure. There was so much going on. The clatter of typewriters and the rise and fall of voices. Phones ringing, doors slamming, the more than occasional curse word.

Because of the nature of her assignments, Clarissa did not have to appear every day, but she chose to go in anyway. The energy of the offices rejuvenated and excited her. She was also eager to meet new people and embark on new adventures. She longed to have somebody special to share adventures with. She thought suddenly of the handsome stranger from the wedding, whom she had not seen since. Somebody like him, or at least, whom she perceived him to be. However, Chauncey was always available, checking on her during the day, making sure she was happy and settling in to the chaos of the newspaper. She had yet to meet editor-in-chief Adam MacLaren. Assignments were apparently devised in meetings between MacLaren and the editors of the different departments. Hers were delivered to her via the ever-attentive Chauncey, editor of the Social Pages.

Clarissa also found herself fortunate in Chauncey's choice of assistants for her. Clarissa's assistant was a tall, rather athletic girl by the name of Kitty Brown. Kitty was a bit older than Clarissa and did not have bobbed hair. She wore her thick brown locks in a bun at the nape of her neck. She also wore black rimmed glasses. Clarissa thought they were too heavy and gave her a harsh look that she needn't carry. Kitty was pleasant, but kept her distance, sticking to her job as copy editor and researcher, rather than trying to become friends, but Kitty was nothing if not capable, and Clarissa was grateful that she made her look good in this new position.

Clarissa had been at the *Tribune* for four weeks. Her pieces on different aspects of the British social climate had indeed proved popular. Chauncey was well pleased with her and said so. The summer was waning. One afternoon, as Clarissa sat daydreaming at her desk in the apartment, the telephone rang.

"Yes, hello, Clarissa here," said Clarissa into the mouthpiece.

"I say, Clarissa, dear!" It was Chauncey. The telephone gave his voice a metallic sound. "I say," he repeated, "Bruce and I are headed to the countryside. My father has organized a pre-season hunt, just to get the horses in working condition. Would you care to accompany us? I didn't assign any big stories to you for the Sunday edition, did I?" He chuckled.

Clarissa had yet to write a feature article for the Sunday edition. She knew Chauncey knew she longed to do so, but this invitation was at least a diversion. She would love to meet Chauncey's family and see the incredible estate the boys talked so much about.

"Oh, Chaunce!" she cried. "Why, I would love to! Just love to! When are you leaving?"

"In about an hour, darling. Bruce and I will pick you up in the automobile. Throw some things a bag and we'll be there shortly!"

He rang off and Clarissa pushed frantically at the call button near her desk until Mrs. Dutton appeared at the door.

"What is it, miss?" she asked.

Clarissa explained her predicament and the two women hurried into Clarissa's bedroom together. Clarissa began to rifle through her closet and dresser drawers, throwing articles of clothing and undergarments onto the bed. Mrs. Dutton, the very picture of reason, remained calm as she picked up the things, one by one, folded them expertly, and tucked them tidily into Clarissa's small brown plaid suitcase.

"This will be so exciting, Mrs. Dutton! I hear the estate is breath-taking! Have you ever been there?"

"No, no, I haven't, dear. Mr. Dutton and I have gone several times to Sir Anderson and Lady Anne's country home. It's quite magnificent, but Chelmsford Manor is said to be exceptional!"

"Well, I am very excited!"

The next thing Clarissa knew, she was flying along the open road in the backseat of Chauncey's roadster. They traveled most of the morning. At last, Bruce turned round in his seat, holding his hat on in the open car.

"Now get ready to see Chelmsford Manor as we round this corner! It's too splendid for words!"

Hardly had the words left his lips, than Clarissa, her eyes glued to the vista ahead of them, saw the great house rise above the horizon. It was spectacular. Surely, it was the most wonderful dwelling Clarissa had ever seen. As they approached, Chauncey gave her a quick history of the place, ending with, "And then, when my poor old dad died back ten years ago, I found myself heir to all this! Thank goodness Mummy is still hail and hardy. She really runs the place! Keeps trying to get me to return to live here round the clock, but we'd miss the city, you see, so we come out frequently. My younger sister, Eunice, and her husband help immensely with directing the household and farming operations, and now that Eunie is…well, expecting, Mummy has quieted down some!"

Clarissa was delighted. The moment Chauncey brought the auto to a stop in front of the great front entrance, an attractively dressed older woman descended the broad stone steps followed closely by a short, stocky man on whose arm clung a jolly-looking fat little blond woman.

Clarissa found Lady Winifred Chelmsford, "Mummy" to Chauncey, and the Nigel Restons, sister "Eunie" and her husband, to be most charming. They were rather colorless in appearance, like Chauncey, but like him, they were good tempered and always ready for a cocktail. Clarissa's heart leaped with the anticipation of a wonderful weekend in the countryside.

That is, until Theodore, the aged butler, interrupted a perfectly wonderful dinner.

They were all seated in the opulent dining room, gossiping over their mushroom bisque when Theodore entered the dining room.

He went straight to Chauncey's side, bending down and whispering something in the young man's ear.

Chauncey folded his napkin, saying, "Please, my friends, an urgent telephone call from London. I will return immediately. Please, go on with your dinner. It is too delicious to interrupt." He bowed graciously and exited on the heels of the butler.

He was absent for about ten minutes and when he returned, he put his hands on Clarissa's shoulders, announcing as he did so, "I am sorry to steal our darling Clarissa from the table, but the afore-mentioned telephone call involves her. We shall return as quickly as we can."

Clarissa followed Chauncey, her heart in her throat. When they were out of the room, she managed to gasp, "Oh, Chauncey! What is it? Is it Mommy or Daddy?" Tears were beginning to form at the corners of her eyes.

Chauncey put his arm around her and guided her into the small library. "Fear not, my dear. It is simply a rather bothersome call from our all-powerful editor-in-chief! He insists you return at once to the city."

Clarissa was aghast. "Whatever for?"

"He is lacking in material for the Social Pages, he says. He wants you to polish up the piece you did on Claridge's, the 'Fantastic Flap-per' piece. He's sent the photographer over there tonight to get some good shots. He wants you to come in tomorrow so it can hit the press for the Sunday edition."

Clarissa was astounded. "I don't believe it! I simply won't believe it! What a nasty, vindictive man! Oh, Chauncey, can't you do some-thing? Can't you say I can't come?"

"My darling, I tried. Truly, I did! You know, I've bankrolled that paper personally, just because I love newspapers and I rather thought I liked MacLaren. Straight shooter, he is. I tried to threaten him with that salient point, but the truth is, MacLaren is a straight shooter. He said he was editor-in-chief and he was doing his job. He wore me down. You've got to go back if you want to stay employed by this circus! It won't be so bad. We love having you there, and in London. And Chelmsford Manor will be here for at least another four hundred years, so you've plenty of time to return."

And so it was, after tearful apologies and good-byes and promises to return as soon as possible, Clarissa found herself on the evening train back to London. When she reached the station in the city, she hailed a cab to her flat. The cab driver carried her luggage to the door. Clarissa paid him and then buzzed the doorbell. She had not had time to call to tell the Duttons she was returning unexpectedly tonight.

The door opened. Mr. Dutton stood there. He looked rather pale.

"Dutton, are you feeling well?" asked Clarissa.

Dutton cleared his throat. "What are you doing here, Miss Hardy? I thought you accompanied Bruce and Mr. Chelmsford to the countryside."

Clarissa hung her head. "I did. Mr. MacLaren actually called me at Chelmsford Manor and summoned me, under no uncertain terms, to return to the city and rework an article for publication in the Sunday edition." She sighed.

Dutton still stood firmly in the doorway. Why wouldn't he move aside and let her through? He seemed preoccupied, somehow.

"Will you grab my bags, please, Dutton?" she asked. Suddenly, Clarissa heard the tinkling of crystal and muffled conversation.

"Dutton, who is here?"

Dutton looked extremely uncomfortable. "Well, you see, Miss Hardy," he began.

"Dutton! I shall see for myself! Please stand aside!"

Dutton made a desperate move and took her arm gently in his gloved hands. "Please, miss, come with me."

"Dutton! What are you doing? Dutton! My bags!"

Dutton proceeded to lead Clarissa down the stairs to the kitchen. He pushed her through the swinging kitchen door and latched it behind him.

He called, "Fannie!" The inner door opened and Mrs. Dutton entered the room. Clarissa saw with confusion that she was dressed in a beaded and fringed gray silk frock, as if she was planning on attending the opera or a play in the West End.

Clarissa looked from Dutton to Mrs. Dutton and back again. They exchanged furtive looks. Finally, she said, "Now tell me what is going on here and tell me now! Who is in my home?"

Mrs. Dutton approached her. "Sit down, my dear. We will explain." She sat at the table and gestured to Clarissa to sit also. Clarissa sat uncomfortably on the edge of one of the wooden chairs. Dutton remained standing.

"You see," started Mrs. Dutton, "periodically, we give very exclusive and very fancy dinner parties here for Mr. Tallman's father, Sir Anderson."

"Sir Anderson is in the dining room?" questioned Clarissa.

"Well, actually, he is in the sitting room at the moment, having cocktails with his friends. He always brings two or three friends. Tonight, he brought two foreign statesmen. Quite important guests, my dear."

Clarissa, still somewhat confused, said, "Bruce didn't mention anything to me about this."

"Bruce, the dear boy, has no idea about these dinners. Oh, he is aware, of course, that his father sometimes uses the flat when he is absent, or when Sir Anderson has extended business in the city, but beyond that, he is in the dark," went on Mrs. Dutton. "Let me explain. Lady Tallman has no idea of these dinners, either. These are strictly limited to Sir Anderson's guests only, and they are secret. The security of the government could suffer if the, ah, delicate nature of these dinners were to be made public." She paused. Clarissa's brow knit together as she tried to make sense of the information Mrs. Dutton had given her. Mrs. Dutton continued. "Our assignment is thus: Sir Anderson lets us know the date and time he would like to dine and the guests he is bringing. It is up to Dutton and myself to serve a sophisticated meal and provide gentlemen's entertainment."

The fog began to clear a bit for Clarissa. "What do you mean by gentlemen's entertainment?"

"I mean we provide an evening of superior food, drink, and music. We also provide temporary companionship in the form of attractive young ladies. It is but a brief evening of relaxation for the men who must juggle our national security on a constant basis."

Clarissa's hands flew to her cheeks. "Oh, my!" she gasped. "You mean to tell me you procure young ladies who will bestow…um… favors? Sir Anderson requests this?"

Mrs. Dutton nodded. "He does, indeed. It was Sir Anderson who procured this position for Dutton and myself. Sir Anderson has come to rely upon us to arrange these dinners. His peers appreciate it! Why, nearly everybody in the House of Lords and the Cabinet covets an invitation to one of Sir Anderson's dinners. Mind you, we have had royalty here, also. Most of the time, these dinners are Sir

Anderson's way of rewarding specific individuals, but occasionally they have a more, well, political side. Such as tonight. Tonight, Sir Anderson entertains the French ambassador and a visiting Prussian statesman. He has come to trust Dutton and me unconditionally. We would never betray that trust, and I must ask that you not betray it, either. For the sake of Sir Anderson. For the sake of Lady Anne. For the sake of your dear friend Bruce. For the sake of the Realm."

Clarissa sat as one turned to stone, trying to sort through this astounding enlightenment. Suddenly, the buzzer at the service entrance in the alley went off.

Dutton sprang to attention. "That would be the girls," he said, going off down the hall. A moment later, he returned, followed by two attractive young women. "We seem to be missing one," he said to Mrs. Dutton.

"Oh, dear!" She rose from her chair. "What is the meaning of this, Lucy? You promised Abigail and Hilda. Where on earth is Hilda?"

The girl called Lucy, a pretty little thing with just the hint of freckles on her turned up nose, wiggled uncomfortably. "Well, you see, Mrs. Dutton, she wasn't feeling up to it. She's at her time of the month, you see, and just can't make it."

"Well, couldn't you procure a decent substitute? I need three this evening! Oh, this is devastating!" Mrs. Dutton wrung her hands.

"Why, who's that?" asked the blond curly haired girl, pointing to Clarissa. "What's she doing here? How about her? She's quite adorable!"

"Oh, my, no!" sighed Mrs. Dutton. "Clarissa wasn't even supposed to be here. She's never done anything like this before."

Clarissa was beginning to pay attention. It was all quite exciting, even titillating. Spying and seducing and all. "Anything like what?" she asked.

Mrs. Dutton stared at her and then looked at her husband. Dutton shook his head. "Sir Anderson would recognize her," he said.

Clarissa stood up. "Wait," she said. "Why not! I can do it! Do you have a masquerade? A black mask, to hide my features?" It had been so long since Clarissa had had any real excitement.

Mrs. Dutton began to smile. "Indeed I do! I believe I do! Not long ago, Mr. Tallman had a fancy dress party here! I should be able to find the masks in the spare closet!" Mrs. Dutton paused and looked carefully, searchingly, at Clarissa. "Now, Clarissa, you know what this means? You have some experience? You are not…not… naïve, are you? You understand…the ways of men?"

Clarissa smiled knowingly. "I am perfectly adept in the ways of men."

Dutton spoke up. "You do know they will expect a certain intimacy with you. You must understand you are to comply to their wishes or it will embarrass Sir Anderson permanently and tarnish his reputation as a host. We have no idea what type of dinner this is. It may well involve our national security."

"I understand," said Clarissa. Secretly, she was very eager to embark on this new adventure. She was especially curious to meet Sir Anderson incognito. It would give a whole new perspective to the man.

"We will make no mention of how you have helped us to any person, my dear," Mrs. Dutton assured her. "And we will compensate you generously, as we are."

"There is no need to compensate me, Mrs. Dutton. You and Mr. Dutton are so kind and solicitous of me. It's the least I can do!"

"Well, it is time to join the gentlemen. Ladies, you shall all wear a black velvet mask tonight. It will add to the mystery and excitement of the evening. Into the back, change to fancy dress, back here in five minutes!"

In five minutes, the three girls were back in the kitchen, in fancy dress, each carrying a black velvet, sequined mask. Clarissa was dressed in a number that had white lace and beading, a drop waist, and a peach ribbon round the hips. Lucy had advised her in the choice of foundation garments, so she wore only a garters to hold up her white silk stockings. She wore peach colored slippers on her feet and a rhinestone headband.

Dutton escorted them into the sitting room. "Gentlemen," he said, "I present to you your companionship for the evening, the Misses Lucy, Abigail, and…ah…Gabrielle."

The gentlemen stood and bowed. Dutton melted out of the room.

Clarissa took in her surroundings. The room was dimly lit, and a fire blazed in the fireplace to dispel the chill of the early September evening. One by one, the gentlemen approached to greet them. Of course, she recognized the handsome visage of the older Tallman immediately. The French diplomat was a small, very neat little man with a thin, dark goatee. The Prussian statesman looked the part.

He was a big bear of a man, his well-fed stomach preceding his erect and pristinely attired form. Clarissa guessed him to be about fifty years old. He had a carefully dressed mop of thick gray hair and a large, full gray mustache. He bowed deeply to Clarissa and taking her hand in his huge beefy one, he lifted it to his lips. She felt the prickling brush of the mustache as he kissed it.

Sir Anderson presented each of the girls with the drink of their choice. The six of them made small talk in the sitting room until it was discreetly decided which girl would accompany which gentleman. The Prussian statesman had clearly chosen Clarissa, which she felt was fortuitous, because he had not met her previously. She drank her cocktail rather rapidly. Sir Anderson brought her another.

She was beginning to feel quite bouncy when Sir Anderson suddenly came up behind her and whispered discretely in her ear. "May I speak to you privately? The Prussian has excused himself temporarily. Over here, by the balcony."

Making sure her mask was tight to her face, Clarissa followed Sir Anderson to the balcony. Had he recognized her? It was a beautiful evening and the western breeze billowed the sheer white drapes around them.

"You appear to be quite a bright young thing," he said quietly, looking her up and down.

Clarissa said, humbly, "Why, thank you, sir."

"The Duttons always hire the most sophisticated companions. I have it from Mrs. Dutton that you can be counted upon to take seriously whatever responsibilities might be tossed your way."

"That is true, sir."

"You have a rather odd accent. Are you American?"

"Yes, I am," replied Clarissa. "I've picked up rather of a British way of speaking, so my accent must sometimes seem confused!"

Sir Anderson chuckled. "I shall get right to the point. Things are not as peaceful as they seem. The French ambassador and myself suspect this bloody Prussian to be up to no good. Stealing state secrets, things like that. We're on to him, but we need the name of his accomplice, you see." He did not wait for her to respond, but continued. "Now, here's where you come in, my dear. The man wears a key round his neck. It's small. We believe we know the location of the vault the key opens. What we need to do is make a copy of this key. It shall be up to you, my dear, to obtain an imprint of the key, so that we may continue our mission. Do you think you are up to the task?"

Clarissa was rather appalled by the responsibility suddenly thrust upon her. "How on earth shall I accomplish it?" she asked. "Should I steal the key and bring it to you?"

Sir Anderson shook his head. "Any overt attempt such as that would be immediately detected, I'm afraid. The man is a boor, but he's not stupid."

Clarissa took a long puff on her cigarette to calm her nerves. She had never been a spy before. She watched as Sir Anderson reached into his trouser pocket and brought forth a rather large, life-like phallus, replete with balls.

"Oh!" gasped Clarissa, wide eyed.

"We have heard that the baron is rather playful and likes his toys. This phallus, if you will, is made for that purpose. However, it has a higher purpose. It is made of a special material. All you need do is press the actual key between the testicles, here, like so." He squeezed the rubbery testicles around his cufflink. "Then, viola, as they say, you have the imprint!" He pried the cufflink from between the balls and revealed the imprint firmly embedded inside. "The French are sometimes more ingenious than we give them credit for."

"Oh!" gasped Clarissa again, but she had begun to be very interested. Reaching out, she gently took the apparatus from Sir Anderson and examined it carefully.

"From there, we will have a reliable tool by which to construct a second key. Are you game?" Sir Anderson took the phallus back, smoothing and pulling it until the impression of his cufflink disappeared.

Clarissa took a deep breath and gathered her strength. She held her head high and said, clearly, and with a smile, "Why not!"

"Capital! I shall deposit this weapon, as it were, in a carved box on the library table. You are to take the baron there and carry out your mission." He started to go, then turned to her. "I say, where are you from in America?"

Clarissa said, offhandedly, "Why, near Boston. Yes, the Boston area."

"Hm," mused Sir Anderson, looking at her carefully. "You look somewhat familiar. Probably remind me of somebody I once met."

"Yes, probably," reiterated Clarissa, hoping he would not guess who she was.

She waited for more questions, but he only said, "Good luck to you, then." He turned abruptly and left.

Clarissa returned to the dining room.

"Ah," said the husky Baron, approaching her rapidly from across the room, "There you are, my little thing! I have been seeking you."

"I only stepped out on the balcony for a breath of fresh air," explained Clarissa.

"You are a breath of fresh air," said the baron through his bushy mustache, his eyes crinkling with amusement under his thick eyebrows. "My dear, may I entice you to sit by me at the meal? They are serving it now."

"I would enjoy nothing better, sir," said Clarissa.

The meal was a delightful repast of, among other things, oysters on the half shell, asparagus, stuffed game hens, plenty of wine, and for dessert, chocolate covered figs. The room was dim, lighted only by the candles. About halfway through the dinner, Clarissa felt the baron's hand in her lap. She acted as though nothing was happening as he discretely groped about, trying to hike up the hem of her dress. Clarissa could feel his heavy, fat fingers squeezing her thighs through the material. Unobtrusively, as she laughed gaily at something the French ambassador was saying, she opened her thighs just enough for the baron to feel the bare skin above her stocking. It did the trick. She heard his breath shake.

Turning slightly toward him, but keeping her eyes on the company, she put one foot on the rung of the chair and allowed him access under the frock. She wore no drawers. His fingers reached deeper and Clarissa was surprised at the beating of her heart as she succumbed to the titillating feeling. She could feel the dampness growing between her legs. It had been a long time since she had experienced pleasures of a physical kind. The baron was certainly not somebody she would have chosen for a tryst, but, she reflected ruefully, it was for the good of England. She might as well make the best of it.

Clarissa leaned over and whispered into the baron's ear. "Oh, Baron, you make me swoon!"

Her words seemed to have the required effect. He dabbed at his mustache with his napkin, and whispered back. "Let us retire to a more private area for some champagne, and, ah, conversation." He then addressed the rest of the company. "My dinner companion is feeling a bit light-headed. If the company will permit, I shall take her into the library while she recovers."

The company, of course, spoke up eagerly with remarks of, "Please, enjoy the quiet" and "It is getting late. Perhaps a nap." Or a "By all means."

The baron stood up and bowed to the table. Then he took an unopened bottle of champagne in one hand and Clarissa's hand in the other and led her out of the room. Clarissa followed the baron down the hall and into the cozy little den. A fire was burning brightly on the grate, the curtains were drawn, and there were two glasses on the low table beside a beautifully carved wooden box.

"I was made aware that this was a particularly comfortable room and should be quite adaptable to our purposes," said the baron, as he locked the door and turned to face Clarissa, whose heart was now thumping as she imagined those meaty hands groping her between her legs. She gulped and recovered her resolve.

"It is a particularly cozy room. Quite romantic, actually," she said in a low voice as she seated herself on the leather sofa.

"Allow me to help you to some champagne," said the baron, and, with a flourish, he popped the cork from the bottle. He poured quite expertly into the glasses and handed Clarissa hers. She lifted it daintily to her lips. The bursting bubbles tickled her nose. "One moment!" commanded the baron. Clarissa lowered her glass as he continued. "Let me propose a toast. To you, my dear, and a brief respite from the constant bombardments of everyday responsibilities!"

Clarissa smiled coquettishly, and they clinked their crystal together. Clarissa took a large sip of the champagne and found it quite lovely. She finished her shallow glass in two more gulps, being as ladylike as she could manage. She was hoping that the lively liquid would boost her courage.

"My dear!" exclaimed the baron. "You delight me! You are ready for more so soon!" He filled her glass again. Clarissa took another large sip. The bubbly was beginning to work its magic. Clarissa was starting to feel a bit sassy.

"There is nothing like champagne, Baron, for igniting the fires of romance!" she said coyly, batting her eyelashes at him over the rim of her glass.

The baron sat down on the sofa and crept in close to her. Soon his hand was on her thigh and his heavy face was inches from her own. "And do you enjoy romance, my dear?"

"I do indeed," replied Clarissa truthfully. "I have always thought that the human body was a thing to enjoy!"

The baron chuckled softly and slid his hand up under the hem of Clarissa's beaded dress. "Then I am sure you would not mind removing your frock and allowing me to see this enjoyable thing!"

"Why not," said Clarissa gaily. She stood and reached around, unclasping the back of the dress. It dropped softly to the floor around her ankles. She stood before the baron in a short slip of frothy white lace and her rolled and gartered white stockings.

"Do you like what you see, Baron?" she asked.

"Indeed, indeed," answered the baron somewhat huskily. He reached out with both huge hands and caught her round the waist, drawing her to his lap. He kissed her full on the lips, shoving his tongue into her mouth. Surprisingly, Clarissa thought, he did not taste bad. A combination of good cigars and fine champagne. She sucked on his tongue. Finally he pulled away and looked down at her breasts. The nipples were straining against the silken lace. The baron fondled them, pulling and pinching. At last he tipped Clarissa back against one large arm and pushed up her shift with his free hand.

"Ahh," he said. "A fine young cunny. May I have a closer look? Spread your legs, my dear."

"Oh, Baron," breathed Clarissa as she opened her thighs. Instantly, the fat fingers were fumbling between her legs, prying and prodding, eager to gain entrance.

"Lie back across my lap," ordered the baron, "and spread your legs wide."

Clarissa did as she was bidden. The baron spread the folds of her cunt, examining every inch of her. He took her clit between thumb and forefinger, pinching until she moaned. His fingers at last found her hot opening, and he slid two into her. "You are very wet, my dear."

Clarissa gasped, "You are very persuasive, Baron."

This seemed to please him very much, and he began to pump his fingers in and out of her, all the while pinching and rubbing her hardened clit with his other hand. Clarissa began to gyrate her hips.

She could feel her body flush with the impending climax. Suddenly, the baron pulled out his fingers.

"Stand up in front of me and turn around," he ordered. Clarissa was somewhat disappointed with the interruption, but did as he beckoned.

The baron raised her slip again, baring her buttocks. "A lovely fanny," he commented. "Lovely round buttocks. Lean forward slightly, my dear. I need to explore you."

Clarissa leaned forward. She felt the baron's hands, one on each buttock, squeezing and kneading. He spread her and ran a finger down the valley between her buttocks, over her tight little bung hole, and once again buried it in her cunt.

"Lean farther," he ordered. Clarissa complied. The baron spread the folds of her wet cunt and began to lap and suck at her clit. She gasped as she felt her clit grow more and more engorged. His mustached tickled and pricked her. It was not an unpleasant feeling and she wiggled her bottom into his face. Again, just as she was about to collapse in climax, he stopped.

"Oh, Baron," she implored. "You indeed are teasing me!"

Clarissa stepped away from him. She was remembering her duties. "I should see and explore you now," she said, holding up her slip and fingering herself lasciviously.

"I think not, my little minx," he said, standing. "Not yet, not until I give the order. I am not yet through with my exploration. Now kneel on the sofa, face over the back. Yes, like that. Pull up your slip and bare your ample buttocks. You need to be spanked for your impudence! I give the orders."

"Oh, do be gentle," said Clarissa, her voice shaking.

The baron stood behind her and began to pinch her bottom. He bent his head, licking her buttocks, and then biting them until Clarissa squealed.

"Ah," he said, "you will learn to listen to the baron!" The he smacked her with his open hand. Clarissa felt the sting. She had been spanked before, of course, but this was different.

The baron began a rhythmic spanking, harder at every blow. Clarissa began to flinch and squirm. Heat spread out from her bottom into her voracious cunt. She longed for his cock in there. In fact, any cock would do. Then she remembered.

"Baron, please! I beg you, please may I speak?"

The baron stopped spanking, now soothing her pinkened cheeks with both hands. "What is it?"

"In the carved box you will perhaps find something you may want to employ for your pleasure."

Clarissa looked back over her shoulder and saw the baron, still fully clothed, open the carved wooden box. He took out the large phallus, and a smile spread across his face.

"Why, you surprise me, my dear! I shall fuck you twice over. First with this rubber cock. It is quite large. We will see how you take it. Lie down on the sofa and spread you legs. There. Wider!"

Clarissa opened her thighs as wide as she could manage on the sofa. The baron reached back in the box and brought out a small jar. It was filled with oil.

"Spread your twat for me," he ordered.

Clarissa spread the lips of her cunt with her fingers and the baron poured the oil between the folds and into her throbbing orifice. He fingered her well to make sure she was properly prepared. Then he poured oil over the dildo.

"Pull your legs up and prepare for a rousing fuck," he chuckled. And without pausing, he quite roughly shoved the dildo into Clarissa. She yelped with the shock, but as he moved it in and out, fucking her faster and faster, while simultaneously pulling and pinching her clit, she felt the heat grow within her. Her hips bucked in rhythm to the fucking and at last, the luscious waves of ecstasy broke over her and she writhed in her climax, gasping and biting her lips. She felt the dildo being pulled from her.

The baron lowered his head and began to lap her streaming, throbbing cunt, pricking her ruthlessly with his mustache. His fingers were in her again and he was groaning. Clarissa was lost in the waves of her orgasm.

When she opened her eyes, the baron was standing over her. He had at last freed his own cock. It was huge and turgid and he rubbed it on her face. "Take it in your mouth. Suck me. Make it slippery and hard. Now!"

Clarissa wrapped her lips around the swollen head and tickled it with her tongue. Then she reached up and took the erect member in her hands, holding on as she sucked and tongued it. The baron moaned and groaned and shoved his cock as far into her mouth as he could. Clarissa sucked hard and squeezed with her hands.

At last the baron drew back, and gasping, ordered, "Face me! I will enter you now!"

This was Clarissa's chance. Instead of obeying the baron, she leaped up, and scooting around him, picking up the dildo from where he had dropped it.

"Now I say!" he bellowed, holding his cock in his hands.

"You must do something for me," said Clarissa, "or I shall run as I am straight out of the room. I want to see your body. I want to see your powerful chest over me as you hammer me with your impressive cock. I shall play with the dildo whilst you fuck me. Perhaps I can take two cocks at once! Come, my Baron, you are not shy, are you?"

In answer, the baron tore frantically at his coat, flinging it down upon the floor. In the next instant, his white linen shirt followed, and then an undershirt. Now, Clarissa saw the prize. Around his thick neck, the baron wore a heavy gold chain, and nestled in the thick black hair that covered his chest was a gold key, about an inch and a half long.

The baron struggled with his breeches, finally stepping out them, his enormous cock at attention. "You test me, my dear," he said ominously. "If you were not so skilled at what you do, I should make short work of you!"

Clarissa waved the dildo at him and giggled. "Show me, then, Baron. Show me how you would make short work of me!" She placed herself again on the sofa and slid the dildo into her cunt. The baron thundered across the room.

"Take the phallus out. I will show you a fucking as you have never had!"

Clarissa laughed and spread her legs. Breathing hard, the baron knelt between her legs. She brushed the dildo across his chest and made fencing moves at his cock. With meaty fingers, the baron spread the lips of her cunt wide and shoved his hard cock into her. Clarissa had to admit to herself it felt good. It was a large cock, hot and rock hard. The baron's ample stomach rubbed on her own as he ground into her. Then the fucking began. He rode her hard, jarring her to her core, but transporting her at the same time. It took all of Clarissa's resolve not to give in to the climax that tingled within her.

She took the phallus in hand, rubbing it over the baron's heaving chest. The key flopped like a fish on its chain. Clarissa squeezed the baron's nipples with both her hands, then unobtrusively spread the testicles of the dildo and tried to catch the key as it flew in time to the baron's thrusts. Once he climaxed, once he stopped, it would be too late. Clarissa made a desperate smack at the key and pinned it between the balls against the baron's chest.

"Oh, Baron," she cried out, "fuck me! Show me more! I will beat you with the dildo! Your cock is filling me! Oh! Oh!" She rubbed the dildo against him, pressing it with her fingers, manipulating it for the best impression. What with being rocked and jarred, it was hard to accomplish. Suddenly the key was pulled free and the baron collapsed with a loud groan on top of her, his cock pulsing within her. As he recovered his strength, Clarissa reached over to the low table and replaced the phallus in the carved box, hoping she had been successful.

At last, the baron raised himself from her and withdrew his cock. He laughed and gave her clit a good pinch that made her jump. "I warned you, my dear!" he said, pleased with himself.

Clarissa feigned exhaustion. "Oh, my dear Baron. How shall I be with another man! None can compare! You have certainly proved your claims!"

The baron was pulling up his breeches. He sat on the sofa and pulled Clarissa across his lap. His fingers found her tingling cunt and sought out her turgid clit. He began to work it and rub it, until she gasped and writhed. Quickly, he flipped her over, spanking her buttocks lightly and fucking her with his fingers at the same time. Clarissa could bear it no longer. She gave in to her climax and let it encompass her. Finally, she lay gasping across the baron's lap.

He laughed and lifted her to a standing position. "I will ask for you again, my dear," he said. "I've had a very good time. A very good time indeed!"

The evening was finished. The baron and Clarissa dressed and went into the sitting room. Sir Anderson was there with Lucy, and the French ambassador joined shortly with Abigail. They made pleasant conversation over a nightcap poured by Dutton. Sir Anderson looked at Clarissa. Clarissa nodded, almost imperceptibly. Dutton looked at Sir Anderson, who nodded back at him.

Sir Anderson said, "Thank you, Dutton. That will be all."

Dutton bowed and left the room.

After the nightcap, Sir Anderson saw the French ambassador and the baron to the door. A car was waiting and whisked them away. Lucy and Abigail left the sitting room with Mrs. Dutton, but Clarissa was bid stay and wait for Sir Anderson. Clarissa sat primly in a wingback chair and waited. Before long, Sir Anderson returned, followed by Dutton who carried the phallus.

"Bring the instrument here, Dutton," said Sir Anderson. "Here, hold it under the electric light. My dear, please join us. We shall see whether or not you were successful."

Clarissa rose and joined the two men, who peered at the phallus as Dutton held it under the light for inspection. Her heart pounded. She did not want to fail Sir Anderson.

There, revealed by the piercing light of the electric lamp, was a perfect imprint of the key.

"By George!" Sir Anderson exclaimed. "I do believe we have it! Yes! Yes, your mission was a success!"

"I say!" remarked Dutton, which was excited as he ever got.

"Dutton, you will take this to Headquarters tonight. We must have the imprint as soon as possible."

"Yes, sir," answered Dutton.

"Oh, Sir Anderson!" said Clarissa, clasping her hands together. "I am so happy! Indeed I am! I did not want to disappoint you."

"And you have not, my dear! You have been a tremendous asset to the Realm. We must commend you on a valiant and successful effort!" Sir Anderson bowed low to Clarissa, then took her hand and kissed the back of it. "I am personally in your debt. You may reach me through Dutton at any time should you need anything. And now, I must be off." He bowed again, then smiling in the most debonair way he added wryly, "Locksmith to visit, you see."

The next afternoon, Clarissa was sitting at her desk working on her article for the Sunday Edition. Mrs. Dutton suddenly appeared at her elbow with a cup of tea and some lovely biscuits.

"I thought you might enjoy a cup of tea, miss," she said. "You've been at it all morning."

Clarissa said, "Oh, thank you, Mrs. Dutton. I would most assuredly love a cup of tea. I need to turn this in this evening, you see."

Mrs. Dutton turned to leave, but Clarissa heaved a heavy sigh. Mrs. Dutton said, "What is it, miss?"

"Are we spies, then, Mrs. Dutton?"

"Well, yes, I suppose we are. On occasion."

"It's sad the occasion comes up, isn't it? That people cannot seem to find a common ground. That they must continue to try to hurt each other."

"It is sad indeed," replied Mrs. Dutton somberly. "My own brother is up north in one of the big convalescent homes. Gassed, he was. It's why I do what I do for Sir Anderson. It's continuous surveillance. Not all battles are fought with guns."

Clarissa felt her eyes prick, and she fought to keep back her sudden tears. Mrs. Dutton spoke up brightly, then, "Well, I will tell you something good. It's a good thing there are brave young women like yourself, miss. You completed a difficult mission successfully. Who knows how many lives were saved just by your participation last night. My hat is off to you, miss. That is, if I was wearing one."

Clarissa had to laugh. Mrs. Dutton laughed, too. She took Clarissa's face in both hands and kissed her fervently on both cheeks. "You are indeed a girl of extreme courage and mettle!"

"Thank you, Mrs. Dutton. And actually, between you, me, and the lamppost, it turned out that I had some jolly good fun pulling the mission off, if you know what I mean!"

Mrs. Dutton chucked her affectionately under the chin. "You are scandalous, my dear!" Then she laughed and left the room.

Clarissa bent her head back to her work, warmed from the inside out.

PART SIX
Clarissa in the Dungeon of Desire

After the incident with the baron, a certain patriotic flame for her temporary country ignited within Clarissa. She turned out several more articles concerning the care and convalescence of veterans, the effect of the fluctuating economy on the country still trying to repair its finances, and the political aftermath smoldering on the Continent. Due to the immensely positive acceptance of her first Sunday edition piece, she was now writing the feature Social Pages article every Sunday. Adam MacLaren had sent her a note commending her on her good work but had yet to speak to her personally.

She was sitting at her desk at the offices of the *Tribune* one Friday morning with Kitty Brown when Chauncey approached from Adam MacLaren's office.

"I say, I've been talking with Adam about you," he said.

Both girls looked up. They were deep in the copy edit stage of the latest article.

"What did you say, Chauncey?" questioned Clarissa.

"I have been talking about you with Adam," repeated Chauncey.

"Good things, no doubt," said Kitty, somewhat sarcastically.

"Well, yes, for the most part."

"What do you mean by that?" asked Clarissa, putting down her pencil.

Chauncey pulled up a chair. "Adam feels you're getting too political for the Social Pages. He loves the work you do. Says it's magnificent reporting, but he's hired you for the Social Pages and you've gone Politics on him."

"Then have him publish me on the front page instead," pouted Clarissa. Both girls looked at each other and laughed rather sardonically.

"Not as simple as that," persisted Chauncey. "We need something with a little more fun in it for this Sunday's Social Outlook. You can come up with something, I'm sure. Isn't there a wedding? Or maybe music? Food? Drink? How about drink? With Prohibition upsetting the natural balance in the States, you can certainly write a popular piece on the state of wine, or ale, or gin here in Britain!"

"Capital!" exclaimed Kitty suddenly. "I know just the thing! I have a friend who distills gin. Yes, and he's a wine collector, too. Has a beautiful country home with a wine cellar you wouldn't believe! Turned the pig sty into a distillery. I could telegraph him. He'd be happy to show us around. I was going there this weekend anyway. He is having one of his famous parties. Quite the partier, he is! Would you go, Clarissa? I think you'd have a good time. I go as often as I can. It's very invigorating!"

She seemed so eager that Clarissa could not refuse.

"Why not! I think that's a fantastic idea! I would love to come!"

"Sounds like a capital idea to me. Adam will love hearing about it. Can you have the piece ready for next week? We'll use the design piece this week." Chauncey was busy taking notes.

"I'll have it ready in plenty of time," Clarissa assured him.

"Fine, then. It's on!" Kitty looked happier and more animated than Clarissa had ever seen her.

Kitty stayed the night with Clarissa, and the next morning found the two heading out of the city in Bruce's little runabout. It was a beautiful early autumn day. The trees were beginning to go russet, even though the grass was still emerald green. The sun was shining in the bluest of skies, warm on their faces.

Kitty held a map on her lap and guided Clarissa out of the city, along the river, and at last, into the narrow dirt roads of the countryside. They drove for miles, sometimes passing donkey carts or having to stop for flocks of sheep, but they rarely saw another automobile. Tall hedgerows grew on either side of them. They made a turn at almost every sign post.

"Are you sure you have the proper directions?" asked Clarissa after they had been on the road for fully three hours.

"Oh, yes," replied Kitty confidently, "I've been out here before. We are almost there! Just round this glade, and we should see it."

"If you say so," said Clarissa as she soldiered on.

After another mile or two, Kitty exclaimed, "Here! Go up this way! There's the gate. We're here!"

Clarissa felt her companion's excitement as she turned up a tree-lined drive. The trees were very old and nearly blocked out all the sunlight. Clarissa slowed her speed. A few more yards and they were forced to stop in front of a huge iron gate which bore a weather-beaten sign with the words "Melbourne House" on it.

"What now?" asked Clarissa, her foot on the clutch, but the words had barely left her lips when the door of the gatehouse opened. A tiny man, bent and bony with age, shuffled to the gate.

"Ye wait right there, misses," he croaked. "Ye wait right there. Aye, I'll be opening the gate for ye. Here for the new vintage, ayre ye? Well, the master has just had it delivered from the train this morning!" He didn't seem to expect any reply. He dug into an ancient canvas bag that hung from his shoulder and brought out an enormous key which he inserted into the lock on the gate. Using both hands, he turned the key. There was a metallic rattle and the little man pushed with his whole being upon the gate, which swung open, clearing the way for Clarissa to proceed up the winding drive.

Clarissa looked around her dubiously. Obviously, this estate was not like Chelmsford, or even Annabelle's pleasant home. The hedges that lined the roadway were tall and untrimmed. Grass grew up the middle of the narrow drive.

As though she could read Clarissa's thoughts, Kitty said, "Don't be put off when you see Melbourne House for the first time. It's rather imposing. Almost looks deserted. Brom doesn't spend too much time outside. He's much more interested in keeping up with his wine cellar and developing new distilling techniques."

"Brom?"

"Yes. Brom Von Kessler. He is the master of Melbourne House."

"The master of Melbourne House!" Clarissa exclaimed with a laugh. "Why, it sounds like a rather dark romantic novel!"

"Yes, it does, rather."

"Von Kessler is not an English name," pointed out Clarissa, trying to pry for more information.

"He came here a few years before the War," said Kitty, picking at the fabric of her tweed skirt. "He undoubtedly could see the writing on the wall, and left to where he perceived to be a safe place. He bought Melbourne House from a distant relative, and as far as I know, he's been a gourmet, distiller, and wine connoisseur."

"And he's not been married?"

"Not to my knowledge. He, ah, has specific tastes."

"And he puts on these parties?"

"Oh, yes, quite regularly. Some people come to all of them. A different crowd, actually, from all walks of life. He will be most interested in you doing a piece on his wine collection. He has many very valuable vintages!"

Clarissa continued to drive at a snail's pace over the rutty road until she came to a corner.

"When you round this bend," said Kitty, leaning forward in her seat, "you will see Melbourne House."

Clarissa turned the corner and see Melbourne House she did. It rose fully four stories on a small hilltop, alone and austere, a turreted tower at each corner. A hedgerow of some black branch brambly bush was the only growth around the massive structure. It appeared to be deserted.

"Oh, my!" gasped Clarissa. "It looks like an insane asylum! Or at the very least, haunted."

Kitty laughed heartily. "I assure you it is neither! I've had quite jolly times inside! And the wine cellars are incredible!"

"Who else will be there?" asked Clarissa cautiously. She was feeling a bit doubtful about this assignment.

"Brom has the oddest assortment of people, but very interesting, too. Some come here a lot, but there are always new faces, too. All different nationalities. From the Continent, from India. Why, once, he actually had a couple from South America! She was about six feet tall, very beautiful, and wore a fine leather collar set with precious stones! Brom is well traveled, you see."

"Collar?"

"Here is Hugo," interjected Kitty. "Hugo will take the car round to the back. Madam Sarkoff will show us inside. Look, there she is! Hello, Madam Sarkoff!"

Clarissa stopped the car in front of the two huge wooden doors at the imposing front entrance. The doors were open, dwarfing a thin woman wearing a black dress and starched white apron. Her gray hair was pulled back from her face rather severely, and she wore a white pleated cap. Kitty was waving madly to her.

A young man with a stoic look on his face opened Clarissa's door and helped her out of the automobile. Then he went round the car and helped Kitty.

"Good day to you, Miss Brown," he said. "I shall bring in the luggage directly and take care of the car."

"Thank you so much, Hugo," said Kitty, stepping out of the vehicle. "This is my friend, Miss Clarissa Hardy. Clarissa, this is Hugo. He takes care of our every need!"

Hugo bowed deeply to Clarissa and went about the business of unloading their luggage. Kitty took Clarissa by the hand and led her up the wide steps to meet the woman who stood silently at attention.

"Hello, Madam Sarkoff!" exclaimed Kitty happily. "It's so nice to be back at Melbourne House! And look, I have brought a friend. Miss Clarissa Hardy. She is to write a feature piece on the master's wine cellars."

Madam Sarkoff did not smile, but her tone was surprisingly warm. "You have not been to Melbourne House in some time. Welcome back. And welcome, Miss Hardy. You are sure to find the master's cellars most interesting."

"Is anybody here yet, Madam Sarkoff?" asked Kitty.

"Some people have arrived. We have a most interesting group here this time. The master has been traveling and so has not had guests here for some weeks. So, you see, it is a bit of a reunion! You remember the Santiagos, from Brazil. Yes, of course you do. They are here!"

"Oh, how lovely! I was just telling Clarissa about them!"

"Come inside, ladies," said Madam Sarkoff. "I will take you to the library and bring you some refreshment."

"Where is the master?" asked Kitty as they followed the ramrod straight Madam Sarkoff into the house.

"The master went to fetch some guests from the rail station. They are bringing a special vintage from Rhone. He is quite eager to try it!"

Clarissa looked around as they made their way down the wide hallway into the very bowels of the house. The ceilings seemed at least twenty feet high. The floor of the hallway was a dark, almost black marble, and their footsteps echoed. Gargantuan paintings hung on the walls, depicting scenes of feasting and celebration. Many of them had an ancient Grecian theme, portraying nude men lounging on couches, waited upon by lithesome maidens in diaphanous togas. There were small tables along the walls, holding ancient jugs of different sizes and shapes. Some were beautifully decorated. Clarissa stopped to look closely at one.

"The master collects wine vessels of all kinds. These in this hall are from ancient Greece and Rome," explained Madam Sarkoff, who stopped to let Clarissa examine the decoration. The neck of the tall jug was ringed with naked youths cavorting wildly amongst groups of girls who were also naked. It was very beautiful.

Madam Sarkoff took an abrupt right turn and the girls found themselves in a small room with a lower ceiling. Bookshelves lined one wall, and the same array of art, sculpture, and antiquities decorated the rest of the room. A cheery fire burned on the grate.

"Sit, please, ladies," said Madam Sarkoff. "I shall be back presently."

Clarissa sat down on one of the overstuffed sofas. It was very comfortable, and she suddenly realized how tired she was. The room was very welcoming. Clarissa closed her eyes for a moment to let the warmth sink into her bones. Kitty was talking to Madam Sarkoff.

"When is the master due?" Clarissa heard her ask.

"He will be returning very soon now, and I am sure he will want to greet you personally and meet your friend."

"I am eager for Clarissa to see the cellars," said Kitty.

"Yes. She looks like a good friend. Somebody who will appreciate what the master offers."

Something in her tone made Clarissa open her eyes. The two women were just parting at the door and what did Clarissa see! It happened so fast, she was not quite sure, but she thought she had seen Madam Sarkoff's hand sweep along Kitty's firm backside. Clarissa blinked, but by the time she looked again, Madam Sarkoff had gone, her footsteps echoing down the hall.

Clarissa sat up, basking in the warmth of the fire. "Why, I almost fell asleep!" she exclaimed.

"Isn't it lovely?" said Kitty.

"It's much nicer inside than out," remarked Clarissa.

"What did I tell you?"

"It's all very mysterious, though."

Kitty laughed. "Oh, it just seems that way. The master is really very hospitable. He loves to entertain. It's only a very special person who appreciates him. I hope you will have a wonderful time, Clarissa. You seem so adventurous and eager that I thought you might just be the kind!"

"Well, I certainly do love wine! And adventure!"

At that moment, Madam Sarkoff entered the room again, this time bearing a silver tray fairly overflowing with little plates, glasses, bottles, and pots. She set it down in one elegant movement on the low table in front of the fireplace.

"A bit of refreshment," she stated. "I will let the master know you are here."

Clarissa watched her carefully this time but Madam Sarkoff exited the room without a backward glance. Kitty plopped down beside Clarissa.

"Look at this absolute feast!" she exclaimed.

Clarissa had to admit it did look appetizing. There were little finger sandwiches of cucumber and radish, egg, smoked salmon, and capers. There were olives and tiny pickles. There were adorably decorated petit fours and a pot of steaming black tea. And there was a bottle of a Riesling which was almost dessert-like in its sweetness.

They had nearly finished their late afternoon feast when the door flew open.

"Welcome! Welcome!" A tall, slim man strode into the room. Clarissa was reminded of a ringmaster. He was blond, about forty-five years old, and dressed flamboyantly in a white linen shirt with billowy sleeves. When other men would have worn an ascot, this man sported a long, bright silk scarf, and his legs from the knee down were sheathed in shiny black leather boots.

He smiled broadly at the girls, crossing the room in two strides. He kissed Kitty on both cheeks saying, "Ah, Kitty! Kitty, you are back! We shall have to do something especially to honor you!"

Clarissa stood and steeled herself as the man approached her. He took her hand and kissed it.

"And you, my dear, must be the famous Clarissa Hardy! Yes, yes, I know who you are. Forgive me, but I have done my research and

I know all about you. I have read every column you have written and enjoyed every one! Welcome, my dear, to Melbourne House! I cannot wait to show you the cellars and include you in the fun that takes place there!"

"It's so wonderful to be here again," said Kitty, smiling from ear to ear. "Clarissa plans on doing a Social Pages feature on your amazing wine cellars and the vintages you have there."

"What fun! And, I say, my dear Clarissa, are you game for a party as well? You can work all you want during the day, but in the evening, you must let yourself go and partake with us the pleasures of the flesh! What do you say?"

This speech struck Clarissa as a bit odd, but she was a good sport, after all, so she smiled her most brilliant smile and said, "Why not!"

The master threw back his head and laughed. Then he said, "Kitty, I do believe I shall enjoy your friend immensely!"

That evening, Clarissa and Kitty joined the other guests for dinner in the enormous dining room. Brom Von Kessel sat at the head of the table, Clarissa on his right and Kitty on his left. The Brazilian Santiagos sat on Clarissa's right and across from them were two Dutch women with pretty, round faces and stocky, strong bodies. After that, Clarissa rather lost track. There were about twenty people, including a young couple from the local neighborhood, and a single man from the Rhone Valley who had evidently been instrumental in acquiring the special new vintage that would be featured at the celebration the next night. The table was abuzz with conversations of all kinds. Brom Von Kessel proposed toast after toast, welcoming each person separately.

At last, the meal was over. The merry company dispersed to their rooms, and some of the men retired to the library where Clarissa and Kitty had been served their afternoon refreshment. Clarissa was exhausted from the drive and the constant stimuli, and she intimated so to Kitty.

"I am ready for some sleep, also," Kitty assured her. "I shall ask Madam Sarkoff to show us our room."

Madam Sarkoff was duly summoned. "Come this way, please." She motioned the two young women to follow her. Clarissa paid attention to the hallway as she followed the older woman. She needed to notice a few interior landmarks so she would know where she was. The house was vast.

Madam Sarkoff showed them to a darling little bedroom. There were twin four-poster beds, ample room to unpack their clothing and make themselves comfortable, and a well-appointed private bathroom. No sooner had Madam Sarkoff bid them a good night's sleep and shut the door behind her than Clarissa rifled through her overnight bag and plucked out her silk pajamas. She washed her face, brushed her teeth and tumbled into bed. Kitty was already snoring in the bed next to her. Clarissa thought it might be the most comfortable bed she had ever slept in, but before she had time to think about it, she was fast asleep.

The next day proved interesting indeed. Clarissa and Kitty woke early, refreshed, and made their way down to breakfast. They sat across from the young local couple. Soon, the Dutch women joined them, as well as the Santiagos. Clarissa noticed that today, the woman, who was extremely beautiful, wore around her long neck, a soft leather collar set with precious stones. The buckle and ring were gold.

Breakfast conversation was animated and light, mostly getting to know little personal details about each other. The local couple were a chemist and a school teacher. They had met the Dutch women at Melbourne House on a previous occasion and introduced them to Clarissa and Kitty. At last, just as Clarissa was finishing her cup of tea, Brom Van Kessel entered the room with a flourish. He addressed Clarissa directly.

"Miss Hardy, my dear! Have you finished your breakfast? Oh, excellent! You must follow me now. We shall tour the cellars and the distillery, and you shall have the meat for your feature. We will get the work out of the way early, yes?"

"Oh, yes," agreed Clarissa, dabbing at her lips with her napkin.

Brom Von Kessel pulled her chair out for her and took her arm. "Come, my dear," he said. "Everybody, Miss Hardy, and I have work to do. Make yourselves completely comfortable. Madam Sarkoff and Hugo will attend to you." He pulled a large gold watch from his watch pocket. "I ask that you are ready for play at eight o'clock this evening." He bowed with a great flourish, all the while holding on to Clarissa's hand. "I bid you adieu." Then he led Clarissa away.

It was a fascinating day. Brom took Clarissa first to see the distillery. Clarissa was awed by the huge steel tank and the copper tubing, the beautiful glass bottles, and the most pleasant scent.

"Got rid of the pigs, I did," he said. "Yes, yes. Sold them to a farmer right here in town, and glad enough he was to pay the price. They were fabulous pigs, you see, but I saw that this quaint little building, cleaned and shined, would be a most wonderful distillery. And so it is!"

Clarissa was scratching away in her little notebook with her pencil, taking down the most interesting things the man was saying. She followed him back inside through a door at the back of the house. Across this entryway was another door, huge and wooden with great wrought iron strap hinges.

"Come this way, my dear," he said, swinging the giant door open and flicking a switch. A low, yellow light illuminated the room.

Clarissa gasped. It was a spectacular room, long and built of brick. Each wall was a series of arches and inside the arches were the wines on wooden shelves. Hundreds, no, thousands of bottles of wine of every imaginable vintage.

"I am indeed impressed, Mr. Von Kessel," remarked Clarissa honestly. "This is the finest collection of wine I have ever seen!"

"I assure you, it is. And later this evening, you will get to taste some of the elegant flavors stored on these shelves. Come, let me show you."

He took Clarissa slowly down the long room, stopping to explain this vintage and that, telling the most charming stories about some of them, where they came from, how he came to have them. Clarissa was ecstatic. So much fodder for her article. Surely, this would impress Chauncey and Adam MacLaren like nothing she had written before.

"And now, my dear, would you like to see where I shall host my party this evening?"

"Why, yes, I would."

"Come right this way." And with that, Brom Von Kessel pulled a ring on one of the wine casks. The whole end wall, wine bottles and all, swung slowly aside. Clarissa was wont to gasp again.

Brom turned to her proudly. "Quite impressive, no?"

"Quite impressive!" exclaimed Clarissa.

"Follow me."

Clarissa followed Brom somewhat apprehensively into the room. It was cavernous, with brick walls and vaulted ceilings. Chandeliers, hung at various heights, washed the room in a shimmering light.

Low couches were grouped here and there around low tables, and thick Persian carpets covered the floor. Despite its being underground with no windows, the room was warm and dry, albeit a bit spooky.

Clarissa looked round her. There were various wrought iron rings in the brick walls, and scattered here and there were odd machines and what seemed to be equipment one would find in a high school gymnasium. At the far end of the room were two great chairs, almost like thrones.

"Why, what an interesting room," remarked Clarissa diplomatically. "It really is a private place for a party."

"It is, isn't it!" agreed Brom. "We have had as many as a hundred people here. Tonight will be a small collection of my favorites, about thirty all told. We do themes. Do you like themes, Miss Hardy?"

"I'm not sure what you mean by themes," said Clarissa slowly, trying to figure out what all the machination was. "Do you mean fancy dress?"

"Well, it's similar. We do ask that you dress to fit the theme. Appropriate dress will, of course, be provided. Would you like to know tonight's theme?"

"Why yes, I would!"

Brom made a flourish with his arms and a bow. "Tonight's theme will be Ancient Greece. It's one of my favorites! We have had *A Thousand and One Nights*, Asian Dynasty, things like that, but Ancient Greece remains the most fun! I think it might be because of the wine and the food. We do authentic food, you see, and music. Tonight we will have minstrels playing the lyre and the harp."

"Oh, it sounds lovely!" said Clarissa, enchanted.

"I hope you enjoy yourself," said Brom, suddenly taking up her hand. To Clarissa's surprise, he bent forward and kissed it. "I think you will be much admired at this party." He released her hand. "Now, it is getting on toward afternoon. Let us rejoin the world above. You will find your party clothes in your room. Kitty has been to parties before. She will instruct you. Rest well this afternoon because we party until dawn and our games can get quite—how should I say?—rowdy!" With that mysterious remark, he bade her follow him out of the room and up the stairs.

It was later than Clarissa had guessed. After Brom had bid her a temporary adieu in the hallway upstairs, she turned to go back to her room and ran headlong into Madam Sarkoff.

"You should watch where you're going, young lady!" said the woman sharply.

"Oh, dear! I am so very sorry, Madam Sarkoff!"

Madam Sarkoff's face softened imperceptibly. "Yes. Well. I believe Kitty is in the library with Mrs. Santiago, Hilda, and Ursula. You should join them. I shall see you again later tonight."

"Thank you, I will! And I am very sorry I was so clumsy!"

Madam Sarkoff smiled shrewdly. "Don't worry, my dear. You shall have ample opportunity to make up for it." She laughed softly and continued down the hall.

Clarissa pondered this mysterious remark, but the thought evaporated from her thoughts as soon as she entered the library. It was a gathering of a few of the women who had been at dinner the night before. They were drinking wine or sipping tea while munching on the most delicate of cakes and candies. They greeted Clarissa with a cacophony of good cheer. Kitty patted the sofa next to her, and Clarissa seated herself comfortably. Ursula, one of the Dutch women, poured her a glass of wine, and the rest of the afternoon passed quickly in a melee of good humored chatter.

Finally, Kitty stood up and said, "I think we had all better go to our rooms for a short beauty nap. The festivities tonight are looking promising, and you all know they can last until the sun rises!" She took Clarissa by the hand. "Come, Clarissa, we need to rest. Good afternoon, ladies. Enjoy your cleansings! I'm looking forward to seeing you all tonight!"

Kitty led Clarissa down the hallway and continued past the door to their room.

"Where are we going, Kitty?" asked Clarissa. "I thought we were taking our rest."

"We have an appointment for our cleansing and then back to our rooms for our rest."

"Cleansing?"

"Yes. You shall see. We go to the baths and are cleaned inside and out. It really is quite invigorating and helps one to enjoy the food, drink, and festivities to the maximum."

"Why not!" said Clarissa cheerfully.

Kitty led the way down a flight of stone stairs. At the bottom, Hugo stood in front of a large wooden door.

"Good afternoon, ladies," he said. "Are you here for your appointments?"

"We are indeed, Hugo," answered Kitty.

Hugo swung the door open, and Kitty and Clarissa walked through. The door shut behind them. Clarissa found that they were face to face with two women dressed in white smocks and trousers. Their heads were swathed in snow white turbans. One of them spoke to Clarissa. "Follow me, miss," she said.

Clarissa glanced at Kitty. Kitty said, "Have no fear, darling. Trust me, you will enjoy it. I shall meet you back here in a little over an hour."

Clarissa nodded and followed the woman into a room that opened off the reception area. The woman closed the door behind them. Clarissa looked round the low lit room. There was a deep stone bath, filled with steaming water. The air was permeated with warm, relaxing steam. In the middle of the room was a sturdy table, upon which lay a soft mattress swathed in brightly colored cloth. Shelves on the walls held towels, bottles, and jars.

The woman said to Clarissa, "I work silently, only speaking to you when I need to. You will do the same. It is part of the cleansing. First you must undress fully."

Clarissa felt a slight stab of apprehension, but, as she was curious and did not feel particularly threatened, she did as she was bid. When she had disrobed, the woman handed her a towel.

"Wrap this round your hair," she said, "and step into the tub."

Again, Clarissa obeyed. As she stepped into the tub, the woman poured something into the water. The air was suddenly awash with the most intoxicating fragrance. Clarissa sat down and let the warmth and aroma of the water sink into her skin.

"Stand for a moment, please," ordered the woman.

Clarissa stood. The woman slipped oversized gloves on and poured something on them. Then she began to wash Clarissa. At first, Clarissa was mildly shocked, but, as the washing felt so good, she obliged. The gloves were of a material just rough enough to be extremely pleasant. The woman soaped Clarissa from top to bottom and everywhere in between, using a gentle, circular motion. She had Clarissa sit on the edge of the tub and suds her hands and feet as well. Finally, as Clarissa stood there, she parted the lips of her pouting cunt and washed it tenderly.

When she had finished, she said, "Turn your backside to me." When Clarissa obliged, the woman spread her buttocks and washed between them, including her tight little sphincter.

"Now stand while I rinse you." The attendant took a small tube with a shower head and sprayed Clarissa all over with the steamy water. "Come lie down upon the table, front side up."

The attendant had been right. She said no more than was absolutely necessary. Clarissa made herself comfortable on the soft mattress. The woman brought down from the shelves a small pot and a straight razor. She gently spread Clarissa's thighs and proceeded to foam Clarissa's thick growth of hair with shaving cream.

"I will shave your cunt," she said. Clarissa lay quietly while the woman worked industriously, shaving all the hair from Clarissa's mons. She even skillfully shaved Clarissa's labia, and, after turning Clarissa onto her stomach, removed any stray hairs that might have been around the little pinky-brown sphincter.

"There. A fine looking bottom you have, indeed! Stand up and I shall rinse you."

By this time, Clarissa was relaxed and beginning to feel aroused. She struggled to ignore the tingling between her newly exposed labia as the woman directed the spray of water between her legs.

The attendant finished rinsing Clarissa and patted her dry with a large towel.

"Now, we have one more step. You must be cleaned inside as well as outside. Please, return to the table and kneel at the end of it, with your knees apart."

Clarissa's heart was thumping as she obeyed the woman. The attendant rolled in a pole from which hung a large rubber bag. A long tube with a cylindrical attachment was connected to it. The attendant held the cylinder in her hands.

"Have you douched before?"

"Why, no. I have not," answered Clarissa.

"There is no need to worry. It is quite pleasant." The woman stepped behind Clarissa. Clarissa felt her hand between her legs and then felt the woman's finger working its way between the lips and into her cunt. "Ah," she heard the attendant say. Then Clarissa felt the cylindrical apparatus being introduced into her cunny. The next thing she knew, a warm wash of fragrant water was filling her inside.

The woman worked the cylinder gently in and out. The water began to come out, streaming down Clarissa's legs.

"Pay no mind," comforted the attendant. "This is the cleansing. Water in, water out, taking all the impurities with it."

At last she withdrew the cylinder. "Stay right where you are," she instructed Clarissa. She proceeded to massage Clarissa's cunt with a fragrant oil. Clarissa nearly came.

"We are now ready for the final procedure. Lean forward on your elbows. Put your bottom into the air." Clarissa, breathing more rapidly, again did her bidding.

The woman refilled the bag and hung it back on the pole. Then she spread Clarissa's nether cheeks. Clarissa felt her dribble warm oil directly onto her bung hole. The attendant massaged with her finger round and round, and finally worked it into Clarissa. Clarissa groaned. The woman left her finger in Clarissa for what seemed like at least five minutes.

"Do not move," she said. When she withdrew her finger, Clarissa felt loose and relaxed. The woman quickly inserted the cylinder, working it in and out, and round and round. "I will now fill you with the cleansing water to remove any impurities. It will feel warm. When I am done, you may evacuate in the water closet."

Clarissa felt herself filling with warmth. The attendant moved the cylinder inside her as deeply as she could go, then withdrew it slowly. She moved it in and out rhythmically until Clarissa felt she might come then and there. At last she removed it.

"Now, evacuate and return to the table."

Clarissa went into the water closet and let nature take its course. When she returned to the table, it was entirely remade with a soft, clean mattress.

"Lie down, facing up."

Clarissa obeyed.

"Would you like to have an orgasm?" asked the woman clinically. "I am allowed to do this for you, as it relieves the tension that the procedure often arouses in the recipient."

"Oh, yes, please," gasped Clarissa. She was mad for her climax.

"Bend up your knees and spread your legs."

The attendant spread Clarissa's wet cunt as wide as she could and inserted a heavy dildo of thick proportion. Then she began to work it in and out, all the while pulling on Clarissa's clit. Clarissa writhed in ecstasy.

Finally, the attendant bent her head and began to lap Clarissa's taut, stiff little clit. Faster and faster she lapped and sucked until Clarissa gasped and moaned and gave a little shriek as her climax exploded over her.

The woman allowed Clarissa to lay on the table until her heartbeat returned to normal. Then she helped her dress. "You were a pleasure to cleanse," she said and gave a little smile as Clarissa left the room.

Kitty was already in the anteroom. She smiled at Clarissa. "How do you feel?" she asked.

"Surprisingly light and energetic," answered Clarissa.

"Then you enjoyed the experience?"

"Oh, yes. I was confused at first, but now I feel so good! It does cleanse one!"

"I knew you would enjoy yourself! And if you enjoyed that, you will certainly have fun at the party!"

Clarissa followed Kitty to their room, and both girls lay down on their beds.

"Why is everybody so excited about the party?" asked Clarissa, as she gazed up at the ceiling. "I know parties are fun, but how is this different? Brom told me that we wear specific clothing, as the party is themed after an ancient Grecian feast."

Kitty giggled. "More than that," she said mysteriously. "Brom's parties are very special. You'll not find many fancy dress parties as interesting as his parties! Perhaps I should explain a little bit about this evening."

"Please do," encouraged Clarissa, pulling a cozy quilt up over herself and settling in to listen.

"Well, the people who are invited to attend are selected very carefully by Brom and Madam Sarkoff. Only very specific people are sent the exclusive invitation. Most of the attendees at this particular affair have attended previously. Only you and the Dutch women are invited for the first time. It is a very exclusive honor."

"Tell me more," said Clarissa.

Kitty laughed. "We call the room where the party takes place the Dungeon of Desire."

"Really! How…original."

"We dress up according to the theme and then the attendees are divided into masters and slaves. Because it is your first time, you will be designated a slave. You have to earn the role of master, and you can be demoted back to slave at Brom's whim."

"Masters and slaves?"

"Oh, do not be anxious about it," reassured Kitty. "It is capital fun. And you must leave your inhibitions at the door. The frolicking can become rather intense!"

"I am not particularly inhibited. I'm sure I will have a wonderful time."

"I am sure you will. You must give yourself over to the theme. It's almost like playacting. You become the character you are assigned and pleasure ensues! And of course, the food and wine is beyond compare!"

There was a gentle tap, tap at the door. Kitty raised herself off the bed and opened it. A maid stood in the hallway and handed a parcel to Kitty. Kitty thanked her and closed the door.

"These are our costumes," she announced. "You shall see how truly beautiful they are. Now let us get some rest."

Two hours later, Clarissa was being gently shaken by Kitty. "Wake up, dear," said her friend. "It's time to get ready for the party."

Kitty unfolded the garments she had received earlier and handed one to Clarissa.

"Oh, it is beautiful indeed!" exclaimed Clarissa. The short toga was made of gauzy linen and cotton with a girdle of blue. Gold wrist cuffs and a gold collar were included. Kitty helped Clarissa to dress.

"There are no under garments allowed. It must all be authentic, you see." She slipped the toga over Clarissa's head and tightened the blue girdle about her waist. Then she snapped on the cuffs and collar, making sure to attach a small ring to each one.

"Feet remain bare," she instructed. "And don't worry. The Dungeon is always very warm and pleasant." Clarissa waited until Kitty was clad in her own toga, cuffs, and collar. Then they went together toward the Dungeon of Desire.

The sound of lively conversation filled their ears as they walked through the huge door. Clarissa looked around at the animated scene. It was the same room Brom had shown her earlier in the day, but now low couches were everywhere, upon which men and women alike lounged with wine glasses, eating bread, cheese, and a myriad of fruits from gold plates. At one end of the room, Brom sat in one of the big chairs. He was dressed in a long, white toga and wore a wreath of leaves around his head. Clarissa was surprised to see Madam Sarkoff sitting in the chair next to him. She looked almost beautiful, Clarissa noted. Wearing a long white toga similar to Brom's, her thick gray hair had been freed from its customary chignon. It tumbled down over her shoulders, held away from her face with gold cording. Clarissa saw that she wore makeup and seemed to be carrying on a spirited exchange with Brom. They both held silver chalices and ate tidbits from a gold plate which sat on a table between the chairs.

Clarissa's observations were interrupted by Hugo, who approached them, wearing a short white toga that revealed long, muscular legs. His handsome face was lit with an uncustomary smile.

"Ladies," he said, "please follow me. Brom has instructed me to show you to a special lounge, near the front. The Santiagos are also there, as well as Mr. Humbolt, the gentleman who brought the master the rare Rhone vintage. And of course, myself." He smiled particularly brilliantly at Clarissa.

Hugo led the way, and they soon found themselves at their designated table. "Ladies, make yourselves comfortable. Eat, drink, for the festivities are soon to begin." Hugo gestured to the couches. He lay down on the large one occupied by the Santiagos, resting his head on Mrs. Santiago's exposed thigh. Mrs. Santiago giggled and fed him a piece of fruit which he took gently enough with his lips and then proceeded to bite her finger. She squealed and buried her face in her husband's arms.

Clarissa and Kitty assumed a similar posture on the soft couches after being gaily greeted by the others. Clarissa nibbled on a grape and continued to observe the scene around her. An assortment of about half a dozen young men and women whom she did not recognize circulated throughout the room, pouring wine from large pottery carafes and refreshing the food platters. A winsome girl smiled shyly at Clarissa as she filled Clarissa's silver wine goblet. Clarissa noticed all the servers were rather scantily clad; the girls wore short, sheer togas, and the boys were dressed only in loin cloths. All of them wore collars around their necks.

Suddenly, their small talk was interrupted by Brom, who stood up from his chair, and, raising his goblet, called for attention. The room became instantly silent.

"Welcome, welcome, my friends," he said. "Madam Sarkoff and I welcome you all once again to our humble gathering." Madam Sarkoff beamed at him, quite uncharacteristically, thought Clarissa, and bowed to the guests. Brom continued his speech. "And now it is time for the toast!"

At this announcement, the six attendants entered the room bearing trays laden with small crystal glasses filled with green liquid. They began to circulate, offering the tray to the guests, each of whom took a glass.

"Is it like a stirrup cup?" whispered Clarissa to Kitty.

Kitty giggled. "You shall see. It is very fun! Here, take a glass and wait for Brom to toast us."

Clarissa picked up one of the lovely cut crystal cups and waited.

Brom raised his glass. "A toast," he called out, his voice booming throughout the room.

"A toast," echoed Madam Sarkoff, standing up beside him and raising her own glass. "Everybody, a toast! Raise your glasses! To masters and to slaves! Shout it, my friends!"

The whole room responded in kind. "To masters! To slaves!"

"Now, drink!" commanded Brom Van Kessel. "Drink together to the night ahead and pleasures untold!"

Clarissa followed suit as the whole room raised their glasses to their lips and swallowed the green liquid in unison.

The instant the liquid touched her lips, Clarissa was aware of a tingling sensation, first on her lips, and then spreading up into her cheeks. She took it into her mouth. It felt like liquid velvet, and the taste was indescribable. It was something akin to warm strawberries fresh from the sunny field, with perhaps a hint of mint, but there was something heavier and seductive there, something like honey. Clarissa swallowed it down. She immediately felt the pleasant tingling wash through her whole body. A distinct warmth, not least between her legs, quite surprised her.

"Oh, my!" Clarissa exclaimed when the initial burn began to die away. "What on earth is that?"

Kitty laughed. "Isn't it fantastic? It's Madam Sarkoff's special concoction to get people in the party mood!"

Clarissa found herself wanting more, but the servers were collecting the crystal cups. She found herself staring at Hugo's powerful arms and thinking what it would be like to be imprisoned by them. Madam Sarkoff was speaking again.

"I would like to announce that we have three newcomers, all slaves, with us tonight. Miss Clarissa is lounging with the Santiagos, and Misses Ursula and Greta are at the far table with the Samuels. As usual, the master has his pick of slaves first, and I have a feeling I know just who that will be!" Her large, dark eyes looked directly at Clarissa with an intensity that made Clarissa blush.

There was an amused titter that rippled through the crowd, along with several exclamations of "Ooohhh!" and "Teach her well, master!"

To cover her embarrassment, Clarissa took a sip of wine from her goblet. She watched Brom Von Kessel rise from his chair on the dais. He stood straight and tall, looking at Clarissa. He held out his hand and one of the serving slaves laid a long gold chain across it. Brom stepped down from the dais and walked across the room to stand right in front of Clarissa!

Clarissa sat, dumbly looking up into his face. The tingling had not left her body, and she was mesmerized by the sensation. Kitty pinched her arm and hissed into her ear. "Stand up, Clarissa! He has come for you! You are quite fortunate, darling!"

Feeling a little bit dazed, Clarissa stood up. Brom stepped up to her and clipped the gold chain to the loop on her collar. Everybody in the room let out a rousing cheer. Brom turned and pulled on the chain. Clarissa was not quite prepared and she lurched forward.

Brom stopped in his tracks and turned. "Collect yourself, slave. Do not speak. You shall come and sit by my chair. After the inspection."

Clarissa was feeling almost panicked. She cast an eye toward Kitty, who nodded at her. Well, thought Clarissa, I was warned. Brom tugged at the chain again, and this time Clarissa followed meekly. Brom led her to the brick wall of the room where four chains hung. He backed Clarissa against the wall and snapped one of the chains to the cuff on her wrist. Then he attached the other chains to the cuffs on her other wrist and each of her ankles. Clarissa found herself chained to the wall, spread eagle.

Brom turned to the crowd. "As with all my new slaves, I seek the approval of my guests," he said. "Let me have your opinion of this fine young thing. Is she worthy to be slave to the master?"

Brom opened the front of Clarissa's toga and exposed her breasts. He took each one in his hand, squeezed it, and pulled the nipples.

"Breasts?" he asked the guests. Everybody applauded vigorously. A few cheered. Clarissa shivered. Brom smiled as he turned back to Clarissa and lifted the skirt of the short toga, exposing her naked cunt. The guests burst into applause.

Brom pulled the lips of her cunt apart and flicked her clit with his thumb and forefinger. "She appears to have a fine clit. Small and alert. Now, the finger test." Clarissa gasped audibly and wriggled as Brom inserted a finger into her cunt.

The guests shouted, "One!" Then Brom inserted another finger. "Two!" shouted the people. Then a third finger. "Three!" The crowd applauded. Clarissa forgot all about the voyeurs who surrounded her as Brom moved his fingers in and out. Clarissa felt her clit harden and grow hot. Just when she thought she might climax, Brom began to unclasp the chains that bound her to the wall. She assumed she was to be released, but the tall man turned her to face the wall, securing her again with the chains. She could not see him, but she felt him as he lifted the skirt of the toga and exposed her plump bottom.

"Behold!" he announced to the guests. "Quite pink and firm, don't you think!" There was raucous laughter. Brom squeezed her cheeks in his large palms. Then suddenly, Clarissa heard him cry out, "The paddle!"

The first strike stung Clarissa, and she yelped in surprise.

"Be still, slave!" the master commanded. "You need your bottom smacked, and good!" Now he began to spank in earnest, but instead of getting more painful, Clarissa felt the burning smooth into a heat that spread throughout her entire body. She squirmed, not knowing whether she was squirming to get away or to get closer to the offending paddle.

At last the spanking stopped. Brom reached between her legs, poking into her cunt with his finger. "Very wet!" he announced. "Very wet indeed!" She felt his hands skim gently over her throbbing buttocks. He grasped them firmly and spread them. "Do we all see the back door?" he asked the crowd.

"Yes! Yes!" Clarissa heard the crowd's response. She felt Brom's finger circling her sphincter. The cleansing had made the orifice loose and relaxed. She groaned as he pushed his finger into her. Now she was on the edge of her climax. The crowd was laughing and clapping. Brom toyed with her, but not long enough. He withdrew his finger and released her from the chains.

Taking up her leash once more, he said, "Take a bow, slave. The guests have approved!"

Clarissa had no choice other than to curtsy to the crowd and accept their approval. Brom then led her back to his chair.

"Sit at my feet," he commanded. Clarissa sat on the floor as he seated himself in his chair. Her cunt was throbbing. "Let the festivities begin!" shouted Brom Von Kessel as the most amazing sights filled Clarissa's eyes. All around her, people were drinking, laughing, and engaging in explicit and erotic behaviors.

Clarissa watched Madam Sarkoff rise from her seat. She, too, carried a leash of gold chain, but she also carried a riding crop. She walked to the group with whom Clarissa had been seated and snapped the leash on Kitty's collar. Then she gave Kitty a sharp smack with the crop across her bottom.

"What do you say to that, young lady?" asked Madam Sarkoff.

Kitty murmured, "Thank you, Madam."

Clarissa caught her breath as Madam Sarkoff began to stroke up under Kitty's toga with the crop.

"Expose yourself," said the Madam to the slave. Kitty lifted her toga to reveal her own shaved cunt. Madam Sarkoff gave her three quick slaps across her naked mons with the riding crop. Clarissa heard Kitty groan. Then Madam Sarkoff pulled Kitty's toga down over her voluptuous hips, letting it fall to the floor. "I like you naked and vulnerable this evening," she said.

"Down on your hands and knees!" ordered the older woman. Kitty dropped to the position, and Madam Sarkoff pulled on the leash, leading her across the floor to an empty couch. "Lay over the couch," directed Madam Sarkoff and Kitty obliged. The older woman began to stroke and tickle Kitty's upturned bottom with the crop and then the spanking began. Clarissa watched as Kitty squirmed and wriggled as her bottom went from pink to red. Madam Sarkoff struck harder and harder. A small crowd of spectators had gathered around. Finally the spanking stopped. Kitty was panting hard.

Madam Sarkoff knelt down behind Kitty and began to kiss and lick her welted arse. Kitty moaned and writhed. Madam Sarkoff buried her face between Kitty's legs and sucked on her naked twat from behind. Clarissa squirmed, and unconsciously moved to touch herself. When she did, she received a sharp tug on her leash. "Do not move!" he ordered. "You may continue to watch the party, but do not touch yourself. You shall have your turn presently."

Clarissa watched as Madam Sarkoff sank her fingers into Kitty's cunt, fucking her hard. When she withdrew, she jerked Kitty to her feet. "Hugo!" she called out. Hugo stepped out of the group. Clarissa could see he was a master, too. He had been toying with one of the Dutch women and his cock was large and hard. "I think my slave needs a good fucking with a stiff cock. Tie her down."

Hugo smiled. He lifted Kitty up onto the couch and placed her on her back. Then he proceeded to tie her securely with leather straps to the corners of the couch, spreading her legs. Madam Sarkoff picked up an urn and dribbled oil between Kitty's legs. "Fuck her, Hugo, and after you, the others."

From her position on the dais, Clarissa watched as six masters tied their slaves to rings on the walls and came to join Hugo. Madam Sarkoff took Hugo's rigid cock in her hand and led him between Kitty's legs.

"Fuck her," she said again. Hugo drove into Kitty with such force she cried out. He thrust his big cock in and out, bending forward over her. Madam Sarkoff twisted and pulled Kitty's nipples. Finally, Hugo shuddered and collapsed as he reached his climax.

When he regained his breath, he dismounted Kitty and said to Madam Sarkoff, "You have a most enjoyable and pliable slave, madam. I thank you for sharing her. I invite you to inspect this new slave I am breaking in."

Madam Sarkoff smiled. "You are most welcome, Hugo. I will visit you later in the evening. Right now, all these masters would like a turn at my slave! I enjoy watching this pleasure."

The next master was already inside Kitty, thrusting and heaving over her, sucking at her breasts. After he finished, Clarissa saw the fresh, hot, viscous ejaculate ooze from between her legs. Another master took advantage of the slippery situation and rammed his hard cock into Kitty. Clarissa watched as each master took his turn. Between men, Madam Sarkoff would kiss or lick Kitty or suck on her nipples. At last, when the final master had had his fun, Madam Sarkoff untied Kitty. She sat beside the exhausted girl, gently stroking her cunt.

Everywhere, people were engaging in delightful pursuits. The young server who had brought Clarissa her glass of green liquid was bent over a padded bar. Mr. Humbolt was inserting a bulbous, phallic-like plug into her bottom while Ursula, her leash held by Hugo, sucked on his cock.

"A fine, plump slave you are breaking in, Hugo," said Madam Sarkoff, coming up on the group.

"Slave," ordered Hugo, pulling Ursula back from the young man's cock, "address the mistress!"

"Have your way, mistress," murmured the new slave.

Madam Sarkoff laughed. "Indeed I will!" Clarissa watched, fascinated, as Madam Sarkoff stripped the toga from the ample form of Ursula. She hefted the huge breasts in her hands and then sucked on the large, brownish nipples. Ursula groaned.

"Lie on the floor," ordered Madam Sarkoff, "and spread your legs wide."

Hugo laughed and bore down on his new slave until she lay supine on the floor, rolls of plumpness jiggling with anticipation and some fearfulness.

"You are indeed ample," said Madam Sarkoff, and she sat on the woman's upper thighs, so that their cunts came together. Madam Sarkoff rubbed her cunt against Ursula's, then slipped down between her legs. "I feel her wetness, Hugo," she said. "Whip her into wantonness."

Hugo brought forth a small leather thong and began to whip the large girl between her legs. Her shaven mons grew redder and redder. Madam Sarkoff spread the girl's cunt and pulled at her clit.

"Enough," she said, bending her head. She began to suck at the reddened twat. Clarissa's arousal was heightened as she watched Madam Sarkoff sink her fingers into the bare, plump cunt. Hugo handed her the leather thong, the handle of which was shaped as a phallus. Madam Sarkoff plunged it deep into the now dripping cunt. Ursula let out a cry.

"That's it!" said Madam Sarkoff. "Scream out your passion. I mean to have it all!"

Two servers approached and each one attached a silver clamp to Ursula's turgid nipples, twisting slowly. Ursula gasped, "Oh! Oh! Yes! Stop! Oh, fuck me!"

Madam Sarkoff laughed. "You seem confused, my dear," she said, pulling out the whip. "Now, how many fingers can you take up the arse?"

"No!" cried the slave.

"Answer Madam!" barked Hugo.

"I-I don't know!" answered the new slave.

Madam Sarkoff rolled the ample figure over. The two servers spread the large buttocks wide. Hugo poured oil into the crevice.

Clarissa was shocked to see Madam Sarkoff actually lick the slave's bung hole.

Then, she slowly inserted her index finger. "One finger!" she said. The slave groaned and jerked. Another finger followed, then a third. Ursula grunted and heaved her arse. "More?" said Madam Sarkoff. "Tell me to fuck you in the arse, slave. You will enjoy your humiliation!"

"Fuck me up the arse," cried Ursula loudly.

Madam Sarkoff began to move her fingers in and out, and Hugo began to whip. The large girl writhed on the floor, gasping. At last Madam Sarkoff withdrew.

"A pleasurably soft and pliable ass," she said to Hugo. "You are fortunate to have such a slave."

"Slave!" Clarissa heard Brom speak. She looked up. "I think you have seen enough. It is time to join the festivities. Present your arse to me." Clarissa stood and backed up between Brom's knees as he sat in his chair. He separated her buttocks. Clarissa gasped as he inserted a thick plug snugly up into her arse. "You will wear this all evening. It will heighten your senses."

"Yes, master."

"Now, suck my cock. I mean to take you through your paces."

Clarissa turned around and knelt between Brom's knees. The plug moved inside her with her every motion. Indeed, it did as Brom said, heightening her sensations. She pulled aside his toga and was pleased to find that his cock was long and thick. Clarissa's blood was high. She took the cock in her hands and closed her lips around the tip. For half a minute, she simply played with the tip, running her tongue around it, pulling at it with her lips. Then she slipped the throbbing shaft far into her mouth, cupping it with her tongue, sucking and pulling until Brom reached under her chin to pull her face up.

"Enough for now," he said.

By this time, Hugo had joined them. Brom sat down on the couch and pulled Clarissa onto his lap. Grabbing her thighs, he pulled them apart. Hugo was ready. Before Clarissa quite knew what he was about, he drove his rigid cock deep into her. She was caught between the two masters, pressed between their heaving chests. She gasped with shock at the wave of sensation that went through her as he began to pound and thrust, his cock like a jackhammer. Hugo continued until he shuddered and collapsed forward, nearly smothering her as he leaned over Brom's broad shoulder. Finally, he pulled himself upright and slipped out of her.

Brom laughed. "And how do you find the new slave, Hugo?" he asked.

Hugo caught his breath and wiped the sweat from his brow as he stepped back and took a long look at Clarissa, still on Brom's lap, her thighs held asunder.

"She is indeed tight," remarked Hugo. "And fair." He bent forward and parted the lips of Clarissa's cunt. "She has a most beautiful twat and pert little clit. I think she is quite a valuable addition to our stable."

With that, he turned and walked away to attend to the stocky Dutch woman whom he had left cuffed to the wall. Clarissa saw him pick up a length of rope just before she felt the tug of the collar around her neck again.

"You may suck me once more before we proceed," said Brom, and Clarissa dropped to her knees.

"Ah, and how is our newest slave responding?" It was Madam Sarkoff's voice. Clarissa instinctively stopped what she was doing. It was a mistake. Instantly Brom was on his feet.

"I gave no order to stop the sucking!" he said sternly, jerking her collar.

"Recalcitrant, is she?" laughed Madam Sarkoff. "It appears you must teach her a lesson. Who is master. Who is slave."

"She must be humiliated," agreed Brom. Then he said to Clarissa, "On your hands and knees, slave! Follow me."

Brom led Clarissa across the floor as Madam Sarkoff had led Kitty. He led her to a small clot of people bent over a slave. It was the young server. He was lying on a low table, trussed up like a holiday turkey and blindfolded. Bright red ropes went round his neck and over his chest. His arms and legs were secured by the rope behind him. He was utterly helpless. Several people watched as Mr. Humbolt toyed with his slave.

"Suck the cock," said Mr. Humbolt. The slave's mouth opened and Mr. Humbolt inserted his stiff member. The slave sucked heartily until Mr. Humbolt withdrew. Rolling the young man over on his back, Mr. Humbolt took up a small cat-o-nine tails. Taking the slave's balls in his hand, he flicked the man's cock with the whip. The slave writhed and groaned.

"Silence!" ordered Mr. Humbolt. "I want you hard! And I will whip you until you grow hard!" Flick, flick, went the whip. Clarissa could see the slave wince, but his cock was indeed growing harder and harder, larger and larger.

Suddenly, Mr. Humbolt flipped the bound slave over on his stomach and began whipping his buttocks in earnest. When they were quite pink, Mr. Humbolt stopped.

"Are we quite ready?" he said. There was a cheer from the small group, but not a sound from the slave. "Slave, are you ready?" said Mr. Humbolt. The slave nodded. Mr. Humbolt stroked his upturned ass, then spread the young man's cheeks, exposing his hole filled by a plug. He rolled a plug around and removed it. Another slave appeared silently, bearing a ewer of oil. Mr. Humbolt poured the oil between the slave's buttocks and then onto his own cock. He stroked the sphincter tenderly, gently inserting a finger, then two, then three, stretching the sphincter slowly to make it loose and pliable. The slave groaned and wriggled his arse. Mr. Humbolt reached under the young man and pulled at his cock, all the while fucking him gently with his fingers. At last he released the slave's cock and withdrew his fingers. The slave's back entrance remained quite open and relaxed. Climbing up on the low table behind the slave, Mr. Humbolt slipped his oiled cock into the young man's waiting orifice. Everybody applauded. Mr. Humbolt proceeded to give an excellent fucking, bringing both himself and his slave to climax even as the slave strained against the ropes.

"So you see how it is," said Brom to Clarissa, smiling. "Follow me to the couch. On your hands and knees."

Somewhat apprehensive, Clarissa did as she was bid. What was to happen now? Would she be fucked in her arse, or cunt, or both?

"Now climb up on the couch and drink this." Brom handed her another small glass of the green liquid, and she drank it down. As the wave of warmth washed over her, Clarissa felt much of her apprehension dissipate. Madam Sarkoff appeared at Brom's side carrying bits and pieces of leather and rope.

Brom said, "Why, thank you, my dear. Have you lent out your own slave?"

"She is resting. I saw that I had exhausted her. Now she is resting so she will be ready for what awaits her next."

"A good strategy, my love."

As distracted as she was, Clarissa just barely caught the words "my love" as Brom reached behind her to fasten a wide leather belt around her waist and pull it tight. It was jet black and hung with many rings and hooks. Were Brom and Madam Sarkoff a couple, then? Clarissa wondered, even as Brom threaded rope through a ring in her collar down through a ring at the back of the thick belt. He pulled it tight and Clarissa's head was tipped back, her chin in the air.

"You are a pleasure to watch, my dear," said Madam Sarkoff in admiration.

Brom smiled at her as he took Clarissa's hands, holding them together behind her back. He slipped the rope through the golden rings in the cuffs, knotting the rope tightly so that her hands were held fast.

"Lie down, on your side, slave," he commanded, and Clarissa had no option but to obey. Brom took hold of her legs, one at a time, bending them into a half-squatting position. Once more, he threaded the rope through the rings on her ankle cuffs, pulling the rope as tight as he could and finishing with a flourish of intricate knots. Finally, he threaded the remaining tail of the rope through her tightly bound thighs, tying a knot that lay firmly against her now throbbing twat. Brom finished by tying the end of the rope to the front of the leather belt encircling Clarissa's waist.

Madam Sarkoff clapped her hands together. "You are truly an artist, my dear!" she said and planted a passionate kiss directly on his mouth. "Do you wish an audience? Yes, I think we should invite the others to take part in the slave's initiation to humiliation."

So saying, she rang a little silver bell that hung from a silver chain around her neck. All around, Clarissa noticed the masters as they looked her way. Lying trussed up on the couch, she saw many of them smile, and then tether their own slaves to rings in the walls, sometimes bound and gagged, sometimes spread eagle, or bound much the same as herself. The masters began to collect around her.

Brom leaned down and kissed her lips. "Bring the nipple clamps, my dear," he said, "and the gag." Madam Sarkoff left and returned momentarily with two silver clips which she fastened to Clarissa's taut nipples. The pinch was so intense at first, that tears sprang into Clarissa's eyes, but soon the pain began to fade into a titillating throbbing. Brom began to stroke her all over, slipping his hand between her tightly bound thighs and stroking her slippery cunt. She saw Brom nod to Madam Sarkoff. The tall woman approached Clarissa's head.

"Open your mouth, slave," she ordered. Clarissa parted her lips and Madam Sarkoff inserted a hard leather bar and then strapped it behind Clarissa's head. "You may chew on this, as the sensations you are about to feel may necessitate."

She reached over Clarissa and slowly removed the plug. Brom turned Clarissa from her side up onto her elbows and knees, then he stepped behind her. Her cunt was exposed and he lapped it voraciously. Clarissa tried to cry out in frustration as both the pain and the ecstasy grew dizzyingly, building to a fever pitch, but she was only able to manage a garbled groan. She gnawed at the leather bar. Brom began to spank her with his bare hand. She groaned and flinched with each strike. The spectators clapped their hands.

"I shall finish her now," said Brom to the crowd. The crowd cheered. Clarissa felt the plug as he reinserted it, pumping it in and out. She writhed and then, suddenly, his cock was in her. Brom began to thrust harder and harder, driving his hard cock into her again and again. With abandon, he smacked her upturned bottom, twirled the plug, and even bit her on the buttock again and again as he continued the relentless fucking. Clarissa lost all sense of time or feeling, until, without warning, her climax crashed down around her with an almost sickening intensity. She screamed. The crowd cheered and clapped, and then she felt Brom pull out from her, his rigid cock slapping against her buttocks. Then, as she gasped for breath, she felt his warm ejaculate flood over her bottom and drip down her thighs. The crescendo of the crowd was deafening. Brom collapsed onto the couch and pulled Clarissa over with him.

Madam Sarkoff, brandishing a knife, stepped up and kissed first Brom and then Clarissa full on their lips before cutting the ropes that bound Clarissa.

"The slave has been humiliated," announced Brom, getting to his feet. "And so our little soiree must be ending." He took Clarissa's hand and pulled her gently to her feet. She felt weak in her knees and leaned against him. "However," continued Brom, "there is one more thing that must be done. We have a slave here, who has been so submissive, so willing to please, so devoted, for so long, that today, Madam and I are making her a master! Madam, please bring the slave forward."

Madam Sarkoff smiled and walked to the wall where Kitty was manacled. She unlocked the manacles and led Kitty forward, completely unfettered.

"Congratulations!" "Speech! Speech!" shouted the crowd. Kitty blushed.

"I-I just don't know what to say. I truly don't!" she said softly.

Brom said, "Madam Sarkoff, present our newest master with the long toga."

Madam Sarkoff draped the long, white toga over Kitty's shoulders and tied it with a golden rope. "Congratulations, my dear!"

"Now, your first act as master must be to take your pleasure with any person in this room, slave or master. We will watch."

"I thank you, Master Brom, and you, Madam Sarkoff," said Kitty, looking around the room. Then she smiled slyly, and said, pointing at Madam Sarkoff, "Pick up the silken rope!"

The crowd cheered and laughed and clapped as they crowded around to see Kitty make a slave of Madam Sarkoff, at least for this initiation act.

Kitty tied the silken rope around Madam Sarkoff's neck. She pushed the older woman down on the couch and tied the end of the rope to the couch leg. She reached into the basket and drew out a long phallus with leather straps. The spectators cheered as she buckled the straps around her waist. She was now in possession of a cock and Clarissa saw she meant to use it.

Kitty folded up Madam Sarkoff's toga and pulled her legs apart. Spreading the lips of the woman's exposed cunt, Kitty heaved forward with her hips and drove the rubber phallus deep into the supine woman. Madam Sarkoff groaned as Kitty gave her a thorough fucking, all the while pulling and massaging the clit of her slave.

Finally, Madam Sarkoff cried out and shuddered as she reached her climax. At last, Kitty pulled out, leaving Madam Sarkoff limp on the couch with a faint smile lingering on her lips. Kitty turned and bowed to the assembled crowd, who honored her with cheers and applause.

Shortly thereafter, dressed in the tattered remains of their togas, Kitty and Clarissa ambled down the wide art-hung hallway.

"Everybody became quite carried away, didn't they?" remarked Clarissa pensively.

"I told you," answered her friend.

"It was very interesting…and stimulating," Clarissa pointed out.

"So you had fun?"

"Oh, I did, although, I must admit, I rather surprised myself. I mean, I am not a reticent personality, but I did not imagine myself in some of the situations in which I found myself this weekend!" Clarissa looked at Kitty and gave a little laugh.

"Dear Clarissa, you were amazing! And Brom was very impressed with your sociability. Yet there is a bit of a secret. All the most adventurous parts of us are at once enhanced by the green drinks that we consume throughout the festivities!"

"I thought as much!" exclaimed Clarissa. "I felt the arousal immediately after drinking it. From the inside out! Even before anybody touched me!"

"Yes! It strips away our inhibitions and allows us to experience these adventures most pleasurably!"

Clarissa opened the door to their room. The sun was just rising over the eastern horizon.

"Oh, my, Kitty! It is daylight! Wherever did the night go?"

"We could discuss that forever, my friend! We could discuss that forever!" And so saying, Kitty stepped out of her toga and crawled between the sheets of her bed. She was snoring before Clarissa had finished undressing.

ᛈART SEVEN
Clarissa Falls in Love

It was the end of the day. Clarissa was tired and she said as much to Kitty as she tidied her desk at the *Tribune*.

"I think I shall go directly home, have a cup of hot soup from Mrs. Duncan, and go to bed!"

Kitty laughed. "Well, I am back out to the countryside."

"To visit Brom? Is there another party?"

"Oh, no," said Kitty, quite shyly. Clarissa looked up at the change of tone in her friend's voice.

"What is it, Kitty?"

"I-I…well, I am going out to see Hugh."

"Hugh?"

"Oh, I'm sorry. You know him as Hugo."

"Hugo!" Clarissa searched Kitty's face. "Kitty, please, what is this about?"

A flush lit up Kitty's face. Her eyes sparkled. "I went out to see Brom and Madam Sarkoff, just for a visit. Hugh—that's his real name—and I got to talking and then we took walks. We began to see that we were getting on famously. He-he has been writing me letters. He has invited me back to the countryside for the weekend! Clarissa, oh! I think we are falling in love!"

Clarissa's face lit up with happiness for her friend. "Kitty! That is marvelous! I am so happy for you!"

"I am very happy myself," said Kitty shyly. "Well, dear, I must be off! I am catching the train in fifteen minutes!"

"Have a wonderful time!" exclaimed Clarissa earnestly as her friend turned to leave. Kitty looked back over her shoulder and gave a little wave. Clarissa had never seen her so happy.

It must be marvelous to be really in love, thought Clarissa. Although she had had so many lively adventures, she had never really been in love. Eddie had been just silly. Her liaison with Roger had been physical only. Eleanora was…well, while she had had a good time and learned much, Clarissa really preferred cock to cunt. Andrew had almost done it for her, but there was still something missing. She wanted somebody who took her breath away, who obliterated the memory of all the others. Somebody with whom to build a life and face the future.

One by one, the other reporters locked up their desks, covered their typewriters, and left the big newsroom. All at once, Clarissa was alone. The room, usually buzzing with the clacking of typewriters, voices rising and falling, telephones ringing, people shouting, footsteps hurrying on the bare wood floor, was now entirely silent. Clarissa sat still, and then a lonely feeling washed over her. Everybody had somewhere to go, somebody to see, something to do. Her life was as empty as this room.

Clarissa hung her head and sighed a deep sigh, allowing herself to indulge in a bit of self-pity. While she was truly happy for Kitty, she envied her falling in love. How marvelous it must be! She envied Bruce and Chauncey their devotion to each other. And Annabelle and William. In the end, all the fun and games in the world could not replace true love. Would there ever be anybody for Clarissa Hardy?

The turn of the outer door knob startled Clarissa from her reverie. Somebody was coming in! The door swung open and a man, a tall man, backed into the room. She could not see his face. His back was to her and he was swathed in a raincoat and soaked fedora. He was struggling to fold up his umbrella. Alarmed, Clarissa stood up.

"Damn!" he cursed as he turned around, rain drops flinging this way and that and puddling on the floor around his feet.

Clarissa gasped out loud. It was him! It was the man she had met at Annabelle's wedding. The man who lit her cigarette on the veranda. She could not forget him. She thought of him often, in that time just before falling asleep. Those eyes!

He snatched off his hat and then saw her, standing at her desk. His face lit up.

"Hey," he said, taking a step forward, "I know you!"

"I-I know you as well," said Clarissa softly.

"I know you," he repeated, not taking his eyes off her as he shed his soggy coat, "but I fear I do not know your name — or what you are doing here."

"I am not about to tell you my name until I know yours, sir," said Clarissa, recovering her dignity. "I will tell you I am here because I am a reporter for the *Tribune*. There is no other person here at the moment. May I help you with something?" Clarissa slipped around her desk so that it stood firmly between her and the stranger.

The man's handsome face broke into grin. "I am Adam MacLaren. I am the editor of this rag."

Clarissa felt her knees go weak. She gripped the desk for support. Cold embarrassment broke over her. "Oh! Oh, my!" she murmured. Then, with a supreme effort to remain calm, she said clearly, "I am Clarissa Hardy, and I write a column for the Social Page."

Adam MacLaren approached, holding out his hand and smiling. "So you are Clarissa Hardy! Chauncey Chelmsford thinks the world of you! I quite like your column myself. Very nice. Yes, very nice. It's grand to finally meet you." He reached across the desk with his open palm.

Clarissa took it in a firm handshake. "I am pleased to meet you. Thank you for your compliment to my work."

"You are an American?"

"Yes, as you obviously are."

"Quite right!" He released her hand. "I don't mean to keep you, Miss Hardy. I just left an extremely dull meeting with some MPs who droned on until I nearly had to stab myself with my tie pin just to stay awake!"

Clarissa giggled. He strode to his office door and turned the key in the lock. "I only have to leave off these pages. Then I'm off to my favorite watering hole. I say, do you have an umbrella, Miss Hardy? The weather has gone awry out there!"

"Oh, dear!" Clarissa said, looking about her. "I forgot it today! The morning was so brilliant!"

"Well, then, wait where you are, and I will escort you to your ride. You do have transportation, do you not?"

"Oh, I am afraid I walked this morning, but it's fine. I shall get a cab."

MacLaren was locking his office door. He turned around. "I have a grand idea," he said. "Allow me the honor of your company to the aforementioned waterhole. We shall quench our respective thirsts, and I shall assuage my guilt at not meeting you sooner!"

Without warning, Clarissa's heart leaped. "Why, that sounds divine!" she said with renewed spirit.

He ushered her through the outer door, switched off the lights, and locked the newsroom behind them.

Out on the street, Adam opened his umbrella and held it chivalrously over Clarissa's head. "It's right around the corner," he said. "Hope you're not getting too wet."

"I'm fine, really, Mr. MacLaren. This is really awfully nice of you."

"My pleasure. We can have the interview we never had. I threw that ball to Chauncey, I'm afraid, at the time. Must have been busy with something else. Well, anyway, here we are."

He found them a little table near the window so they could look out on the rainy street. It was a cozy little place, more sophisticated than a pub, more intimate than a restaurant. The table was laid with snowy white linen and a vase of fresh flowers.

A young waiter, garters on his sleeves and a brilliantly white apron tied around his waist, greeted them happily. "Mr. MacLaren! How are you, sir? What would you have this evening?"

"Your best Scotch, with a splash," replied Adam.

"And the lady?"

Clarissa remembered what her father had always told her. *"I don't approve of your drinking alcohol, but, if you must, always sip the best Scotch. It won't muddle your brain."*

"I will have the same," said Clarissa.

"And don't be afraid to bend that wrist when you pour," called Adam after the waiter.

Clarissa laughed. Indeed, she found herself laughing often during the evening as she and Adam discussed all matter of subjects. She told him how she came to be in London. "And you?" she asked. "Why are you playing the expatriate?"

Adam gave a little laugh. "I was in France during the war," he said, tracing imaginary lines in the tablecloth. "When I went home to Boston, my father put me to work in his bank. I thought I would go crazy. It was so dry, so boring, and I felt trapped. I became claustrophobic, you see. I had the jitters. Finally, I packed up and went to Europe. I started at my aunt's place in Edinburgh, then bounced around the Continent before coming back here and meeting Chauncey. Chauncey was the one who got me this position. I started out as a correspondent on the Continent and then the editor-in-chief of this paper up and quit. Before I knew what was happening, Chauncey called me back from Belgium, and I found myself in the editor's chair."

"Just like that?"

"Chauncey has a lot of money tied up in this rag. And we always got along. I honestly don't know why he thought of me. Seems like there were heaps of fellows ahead of me for the job."

"Chauncey told me you were a straight shooter," said Clarissa, sipping her drink.

"I like to think I'm fair," he said, watching the legs of his Scotch slide down the inside of the glass.

And so they talked through two drinks. Then they were hungry. They ordered steak and kidney pie with mashed potato. Clarissa, relaxed by the Scotch and warmed by the food, found herself having a better time than she'd had in months. She could hardly take her eyes away from his. He was so handsome, so funny, so solicitous of her. Finally, when they had finished the last of their dessert, Clarissa forced herself to declare it was high time for her to be heading home.

Adam said, "I will walk you. The rain seems to have let up, and it's really quite balmy outside."

They strolled up the street. There was a mist in the air, sparkling under the streetlights. As they passed under one of them, Adam laughed softly. "The mist is clinging to your hair," he said. "It looks like you are wearing diamonds." He passed his hand ever so lightly over her head.

A delicious shiver shook her to her core. She longed to touch him, to take his hand, to feel his skin next to hers. She knew in her heart how it would feel.

"This is where I live," she said, stopping in front of the wrought iron railing of Bruce's townhouse.

"So this is Bruce Tallman's place. Very nice."

"Yes. How did you know?"

"Chauncey explained the living arrangements to me when you came on board."

"Where do you live? Oh, oh! I'm terribly sorry. It's really none of my business. Please forgive my bad manners."

Adam laughed out loud. "Again?"

"What do you mean?"

"I mean, the last time we met, which was for the first time, you asked me to forgive your bad manners!"

"Oh, I think I did." Clarissa giggled. "I didn't have a match and I couldn't light my fag, and I was trying to avoid Andrew!"

"Something like that. I remember now what I said. I said I thought you were charming."

Clarissa was glad it was the gloom of evening. He could not see the blush that crept up her neck and over her cheeks. "And then Andrew interrupted us!"

"Was…is…Andrew your beau?"

"Far from it!"

"Well, Miss Clarissa Hardy, I still find you charming. Thank you for making my supper less lonely than it usually is. Good night."

"Good night," said Clarissa, realizing for the first time that the evening was coming to an end. She turned and went up the marble steps to the front door. Adam gave her a jolly wave and walked off down the street.

Clarissa pushed the bell, and Dutton let her in.

So began one of the most magical chapters of Clarissa's young life. When she returned to her desk on the Monday following her Friday tryst with Adam, she found she could not take her eyes of his office door. He had evidently not come in, for the lights inside were not on.

Clarissa was so lost in her own thoughts, staring at the door to the editor's office, that she yelped out loud when a voice said, over her shoulder, "He went off to the Continent to see a colleague. He'll be out for the day."

Clarissa whirled around to face Chauncey. "I was thinking it was about time I asked for a tougher assignment," she said grumpily.

"Adam rang me up this weekend. He told me about your little impromptu dinner. He said he was absolutely charmed by you and allowed me much credit for securing you for our paper."

"How thoughtful of you."

"Do I detect a note of sarcasm?"

Clarissa sighed. "Is that what I am? Something to be 'secured,' something to be haggled over or offered up for credit?"

Chauncey's looked at her askance. "My word, dear, you seem rather bitter this morning. And I thought you would be just jolly to know that our esteemed editor found you quite charming. Come into my office for a chat."

"I'm sorry, Chauncey. Really, I am! It's just that here I sit at my little desk writing about dances, or jazz bands, or wine, and there are other correspondents covering the political climates in France and Belgium, even Russia. Russia's in a mess, you know!" Clarissa followed Chauncey into his office, and he closed the door on the rest of the newsroom.

Chauncey's face grew serious. "I know Russia is in a mess," he said, looking into space. Then he said, "So you think you want to cover more serious material? Aren't you having fun?" He took a seat on the little couch facing the window. The newspaper offices were, for the most part, a little seedy, but Chauncey's was the height of style.

"Everything is copacetic, Chauncey! I don't even need to work. Mommy writes me frequently, always asking me when I am coming home! I was only supposed to be gone two weeks and here I am looking into winter! I don't need this job for money, so what good am I doing if I'm not doing something worthwhile? Anybody can cover the fluff that I present week after week."

"Actually, they cannot. Very few people would be able to maintain the quality of work you do, week after week. And don't forget, your pieces are very important because they keep the public engaged. All the papers report on the political climate, the threats left from the war, the brewing undercurrent, the economy. What makes them pick the *Tribune* over all the other rags? Columns like yours!"

"You say lovely things, but I still wish for a more challenging assignment!"

"Well, there is nothing to stop you from discussing it with Adam MacLaren, though I urge you to choose your time carefully. He has a plan for this paper, a way he wants it to run, to appear to the public. I guarantee he has a place in mind for you."

"He can change his mind." Clarissa plunked down beside Chauncey, her elbows on her knees, her face in her hands, just as Bruce burst into the room.

"What, what!" he said. "Chaunce, old man, what the devil is going on with our Little Miss?"

Clarissa looked up at Bruce. She fought it, but her heart felt constricted and tears collected at the corners of her eyes. "Oh, Bruce! I am dejected. I want a more challenging position in the paper. I feel all out of sorts today. I feel all played out and am not myself!"

Chauncey cut in. "I'm afraid that is not the problem."

Both Clarissa and Bruce stared at him.

"Then what is?" asked Bruce bluntly.

Chauncey put a sheltering arm around Clarissa's shoulders. "I am afraid our Little Miss, as you put it, is a woman, after all. And a woman in love!"

Clarissa stared at him. It was no good trying to hide anything from Chauncey.

"Isn't that true, Clarissa?" he asked gently.

Now the tears spilled over and trickled pathetically down her cheeks. She nodded. "It's hopeless," she said miserably.

"What!" exclaimed Bruce, sweeping in and kneeling on the floor in front of her. "Are you in love, Clarissa? Are you?"

Again, Clarissa nodded, wiping away the stray tears. "He hardly knows I exist! At least in that capacity," she said miserably.

Bruce began to get worked up. "Who is it, dear? Who is this person who is summarily dismissing you? Has he compromised you? Has he hurt you? Tell me his name! I will bring him to his senses immediately! He shall be sorry for his behavior!"

"Bruce! Please!" said Chauncey, somewhat irritably. It was true, Bruce could jump the gun.

"It's not like that."

"Well, what is it like? And who is the man?"

Clarissa's lip trembled, but she said softly, "It's true. I am in love with Adam MacLaren."

"No!" gasped Bruce. "Oh, my! How has this come about? Does he know?"

Clarissa shook her head sadly. "He has no idea. That's part of the problem. I am determined to ask him for a more challenging position. It will take me away from this silliness that has gripped me for no good reason!"

Then she turned into Chauncey's shoulder and allowed herself to weep.

The next morning, Clarissa arrived at the *Tribune* early. The lights were on in Adam's office. The newsroom had not reached its typical crescendo of pandemonium. Clarissa took a deep breath and decided now was as good a time as any to knock on the door and pursue her quest for some investigative reporting.

"Why not!" she said out loud, to herself. Squaring her shoulder, she marched forward and rapped with authority on the frosted glass of the door, just under the black letters that spelled *Editor*. She was not her father's daughter if she could not set her emotions aside and concentrate on business.

"Come in," she heard Adam say from within.

Clarissa opened the door and went in. Adam was standing with his back to her, looking out the window. He turned to face her as she entered and, once again, the attraction she felt for him hit her so hard, she felt the breath escape her. She was immediately disarmed.

"Miss Hardy!" His handsome face broke into a friendly grin. Clarissa could detect no guile behind that smile. He seemed truly happy to see her.

"Mr. MacLaren," she said, returning the smile.

"Adam, please."

"Then you must call me Clarissa."

"I would be honored."

"I —" began Clarissa, but Adam was not listening.

"I was going to call you in today," he said almost shyly, looking down at his desk and shuffling some papers around. "I am just re-turned from Paris. I have something to discuss with you."

Oh, no, thought Clarissa, *now I am going to be sacked. Oh, well, Mommy wanted me home anyway.*

However, Adam looked up and said, "I was wondering whether you might accompany me to a function I must attend for communications officials. It is dinner. There will be many MPs there, as well as MI6 officials. It's to be held Thursday evening at Claridge's. Will you go with me?"

Clarissa felt her heart must have stopped. She seemed to be floating inside some sort of bubble, where the only thing she could hear was Adam's voice saying "Will you go with me?" She was rendered speechless and did not seem to be able to move.

"Clarissa?"

"Oh!" she exclaimed softly, when she had recovered her breath. "Am I understanding you clearly? You are asking me to go to a dinner with you on Thursday evening?"

Adam nodded. "Yes."

"Just making sure," said Clarissa, grinning. "Yes, of course I will go."

"Thank you so much," Adam said. "I shall pick you up at your home at seven o'clock. Now what did you want to see me about?"

Clarissa's eyes grew wide. She was loath to upset him with her personal pettiness, but she cleared her throat and said bravely, "I-I came in to ask for a tougher assignment. Even a small one. Please think about it. I am eager to do something investigative. Something important."

Adam looked at her, his expression serious. "I would hate to lose your contributions to the social pages," he said, "however, I understand that a personality such as yours cannot be contained for long. I will consider it, Clarissa. I must be honest. Your move to such an assignment worries me. The forums upon which these issues play themselves out are not as safe as a society wedding."

Clarissa laughed. "I would not be so quick to agree with that!"

Adam smiled. "We will talk about it. And Thursday night?"

"I shall look forward to Thursday evening." And she wandered back to her desk, thoughts of investigative reporting having fallen down a rung or two on the priority ladder.

When Clarissa arrived home that evening, Mrs. Dutton brought her tea in the sitting room, along with a letter on a silver tray. Clarissa thanked Mrs. Dutton and opened the letter as she sipped her tea. It bore a curious stamp and postmark, but no return address.

Clarissa was thrilled to find that it was from Eleanora. Eagerly, she read:

My dear Clarissa,

I am writing to tell you of my latest adventures and where they have landed me! Let me say first I am indeed quite happy, at least for the moment! Since leaving you in London, I have had so many adventures, I will have to sum up most of them and get to the one I am in presently.

I did go to Greece and was successful in exploring many of the lovely ruins built so long ago by the esteemed ancients. It is indeed a beautiful place. I threw my hat into the ring with a young archeologist and traveled with him to many of the scattered islands, including Lesbos, of which I spoke to you during our crossing together. Anthony is a postgraduate student at Cambridge and he was there collecting data for a very significant paper on the culture of ancient Greece. I assisted him in his work and, make no mistake, in his play as well! We had a wonderful time and many laughs together. I would love to send you a photograph of him, as he is simply the most delectable young man! He begged me to return with him to England, but, alas, my wanderlust was not yet satisfied, so he returned alone.

I continued on to Egypt, and then to the Orient. I made significant acquaintances in many lands, sailing from Sumatra, through the Philippine Islands and on to Formosa. In Formosa, I made the acquaintance of a cloistered group of the most interesting women whose sole purpose it is to provide any type of entertainment for gentlemen. The mistress, if you will, of the group was incredibly intelligent and friendly, and spoke our native tongue of English very well. She taught me some of the indigenous language and then asked me to participate in the group's activities for a while. May I tell you, my dear Clarissa, I did learn some very valuable skills from those women!

Everything from lyre playing, to tea service, to bringing a gentleman to his climax by working the muscles in my cunt alone! I can honestly say I was reluctant to leave them, but the world called to me. I thanked them profusely, and finally set sail through the South Seas, stopping at last at this fantastical location from which I write.

My dear Clarissa, it is a wonderful place. Picture an island populated by the most beautiful people in the world. It is an island jewel sparkling in the South Pacific where the air and the water are forever warm to the touch. Perhaps that is why the inhabitants are warm as well! They are indeed free with their love, which pleases me no end, as you can imagine! They lead a polygamous life, the men collecting wives throughout their lives, and all living harmoniously together. I discovered that there was one Caucasian woman actually living among them. Her name is Margaret. She hails from Oxford, where she is a professor of sociology, purportedly working on an important dissertation on the culture of these islands. However, to be frank, I doubt she will ever leave. She is married to a chieftain, a most wonderful, handsome man with large gold earloops. She is his third wife, and he has taken another since her. The family lives together in a longhouse, quite content.

It was to this longhouse that she brought me, to be the guest of her and her husband. And, dear, you would not believe how they welcome guests to their island! It is quite marvelous! The women took charge of me and bathed me. They were most complimentary, admiring and caressing my large breasts and soft skin, smiling and murmuring and giggling together. Margaret translated part of it, saying that the women were betting as to the reaction of their husband when he at last met me. Then they gave me a most beautiful silk sarong to wear. A feast was prepared in my honor, in which the whole village took part. It was at this feast that I met Margaret's husband, Kono. He was so beautiful a masculine specimen that my breath was quite taken from me! We partied into the night, eating and drinking a special alcoholic concoction made from coconut milk.

Finally, I followed the women back to the longhouse and lay down in a most comfortable hammock to sleep. Well, I shall inform you, that I did not get much sleep! Just as I was nodding off, the women, including Margaret, began to stroke and pet me. They stripped the sarong from me and oiled my body with the most fragrant and soft oil. Physical feelings began to awaken in me, yet I dared not interrupt their ritual. They rubbed me from head to foot, helped me out of the hammock, and laid me down upon a thick mat of ti leaves. At that juncture, Kono came in, completely naked. He stood over me, smiling. Margaret took his cock in her hands and another wife covered it with soft licks. Margaret explained to me that the act of sex was sacred to these people, and therefore, the best gift one could bestow upon a guest. I watched with fascination as the big man's cock grew to amazing proportions in response to the caresses it received while in Margaret's hand.

So caught up in the moment was I that I hardly noticed when the remaining two wives, giggling, gently opened my thighs. I was exposed to the chieftain! Margaret murmured something in the native tongue and the wives withdrew and sat around the ti leaf mat. I lay still, mesmerized.

Kono shouted a word and then knelt facing my now wet and shiny twat. He inserted a finger and felt around, all the while smiling. Then, without further ado, slipped me over, hiked my arse in the air and entered me from behind! What a fucking I received! After the disciplined, controlled, and trained sexuality of the Formosa women, which was lovely in its own way, the utter wantonness of these island people is indeed a different pleasure! Most enjoyable!

At this time I would like to invite you to visit me in my new home. I honestly am so content here, I may stay indefinitely. I live in a longhouse with other single girls. Kono is considering me as another wife and tries me out with increased regularity. Other men are at liberty to try me, also, as long as I agree. There is great equality between the sexes, despite the polygamous nature of their marriages. A woman is valued according to her contributions and intelligence, just like the men. Of course, I agree most of the time, and there are always the girls to play with! It is a wonderful place.

I am including the name and location of the port that provides access to these islands. An outrigger would then transport you directly to Kono's island and to me! You would have such fun here, Clarissa dear. Please give my invitation serious consideration. We would love to have you as our guest! At any rate, please answer my letter and post to the address shown at the bottom of this page. It will take some time to get here, but even in paradise, news of the outside world is appreciated.

Until we meet again, with true affection, I am your friend,

Eleanora

Clarissa smiled fondly at the letter with its bawdy story of Eleanora's travels. Under normal circumstances, Clarissa might have seriously considered her friend's offer. A romp on a South Sea island was extremely tempting. However, some of Clarissa's adventurous appetites had been dulled of late. Something was occurring in her, something unfamiliar, that gave her tummy a funny feeling and set her heart to thumping. She folded the letter and slipped it into the pocket of her middy blouse. She must remember to put it into the drawer of her bedside table with the rest of her personal correspondence when she went to bed.

Clarissa waited in the sitting room with Mrs. Dutton.

"You look absolutely smashing, my dear," said the older lady, fussing with the stunning beaded and sequined headpiece that hugged Clarissa's high forehead. Mrs. Dutton had swept her golden bob to the side and up in the back. "Simply smashing!" she said again with emphasis.

"Oh, are you sure?" said Clarissa. "I do so want to be chic. He is the editor, you know. I must try my hardest." Clarissa was wearing a silk and linen beaded sleeveless cocktail dress. The top was beaded ivory linen, and the skirt was just a shade lighter and adorned with glass beading, giving it a marvelous motion when she walked.

Mrs. Dutton laughed out loud. "Oh, my dear, you are certain to be the most beautiful girl in the room. You are très chic, my dear! Mr. MacLaren will see that immediately!"

Downstairs, the bell rang. Clarissa's eyes grew wide as she heard Dutton opening the door. She heard Adam MacLaren say, "Adam MacLaren here for Miss Clarissa Hardy."

"One moment," said Dutton. "I will let her know you are arrived."

She heard Dutton coming up the stairs.

"He is here!" hissed Mrs. Dutton, putting the beaded purple clutch into her hands. Mrs. Dutton kissed her on both cheeks. "Have a wonderful time, dear!"

And, before she could collect herself fully, Clarissa found herself in the backseat of a chauffeured car, next to Adam MacLaren.

"Thank you," he said, "for accompanying me tonight."

"You are quite welcome. It is my pleasure."

"And thank you also," he said in a softer voice, "for taking the time to look so absolutely stunning!"

Clarissa blushed. "We couldn't have the editor-in-chief showing up to an important dinner at Claridge's with any old girl on his arm! I am glad you approve."

Once at Claridge's, they were escorted to the cocktail room. Clarissa was introduced to many people whose names she had heard, but whose faces she had never seen. Then, suddenly, as she stood talking to the tall, bony and stylish wife of a member of the House of Lords, Adam was saying, "And I believe you know Miss Hardy."

Clarissa turned around and there stood Sir Anderson Tallman and Lady Anne Tallman, both smiling at her. Of course, the last time Clarissa had seen Sir Anderson, she was in fancy dress, complete with mask and carrying out a supremely sensitive espionage assignment for him. Immediately, she collected herself, hoping he would in no way recognize her.

"Oh, Sir Anderson! Lady Anne! I am so very glad to see you again!"

"And are you having fun in the city, my dear?" asked Lady Anne.

"I am having the time of my life!" answered Clarissa, quite honestly.

"We are so glad MacLaren was able to lure you here," chuckled Sir Anderson. "He has outclassed himself, I am sure!" They all laughed as the bell rang announcing that dinner was about to be served. "And two others you may know," added Sir Anderson.

Clarissa turned. There were the Duttons, smiling fondly at her.

"Don't be surprised, darling," whispered Mrs. Dutton in her ear as she planted a kiss on Clarissa's cheek. "There is more to us than meets the eye!"

Clarissa had to agree with that as they filed into the dining room. As there were only about fifty or sixty people present, the dining room was intimately set with round tables swathed in the most brilliant white linen. Polished silver flatware, candlesticks, and vases full of white flowers graced the tables, and the cut crystal sparkled in the candlelight. Clarissa was enchanted. She sat at a table between the Tallmans and across from Adam, who was flanked on either side by the annoyingly attentive wives of the MPs also present.

The dinner passed congenially. Clarissa exchanged much eye contact with Adam, but little conversation, as they were seated across a round table from each other. At last, dessert was finished, and an aperitif was served. As Clarissa lifted the drink to her lips, she noticed via her peripheral vision Sir Anderson nodding covertly to Adam.

Adam stood and walked to the podium that stood facing the tables.

"May I have everybody's attention, please?" he said. "We are here tonight, enjoying each other's company, sipping fine wine and liquor, eating excellent food. A pleasant evening for all, I'm sure you would all agree. Yet we are here for a more important, a more urgent reason, a more humble reason, if you will. We are here to honor several individuals who have gone above and beyond in order to assist MI6 not just during the war, but even now. I would like to call Sir Anderson Tallman up to present the medals, by appointment of the Crown, to these brave individuals who have worked tirelessly and courageously behind the limelight. Sir Anderson."

Sir Anderson squeezed Clarissa's hand as he rose and planted a kiss firmly on his wife's cheek, then proceeded to the podium.

"Thank you, Mr. MacLaren," he said. "I shall now waste no more time in honoring these individuals, who, it must be understood, had no idea that they would be receiving these awards tonight. First, we honor Major Nigel Thackery-Johnson. Major, come forward to accept your medal from the Crown. We regret that we are unable to make public the reasons behind the awards. Suffice it to say that each selfless act may have saved the empire. Major, I honor you."

Major Thackery-Johnson was a small, thin man, about sixty years old. He sported a thick mustache and stood ramrod straight as Sir Anderson clasped the medal around his neck. Somewhat overwhelmed, the major thanked the Crown profusely and took his seat.

Next, Sir Anderson called up the Honorable Jacques duPorier, Ambassador from France. Clarissa was surprised to recognize him as the Frenchman who had joined Sir Anderson and the Prussian statesman at her flat the night she took the impression of the secret key. Ambassador duPorier accepted his award with typical French aplomb, bowed, and returned to his seat.

Sir Anderson said, "And now we give our final honor tonight. It goes to a very courageous young lady who put her reputation, her career, and indeed, her life, on the line because she saw the gravity of the situation and understood what had to be done. And although we are not at liberty to reveal the nature of her mission, suffice it to say it was successful to such a degree, it may have averted an end of the Armistice. Miss Clarissa Hardy, please allow Great Britain to bestow upon you our most highly esteemed award with affection and gratitude!"

Clarissa sat as one stunned. She tried to breathe and could not. She tried to move and could not. She tried to speak and could not. Adam crossed the room and took her elbow. She stood and allowed herself to be led to the podium. She felt absolutely numb as Sir Anderson clasped the medal around her neck and the group applauded.

When the applause ceased, Clarissa knew she was expected to say something, as the French ambassador, and the major had done. She cleared her throat and said, clearly and confidently, "I am not British, and that makes this honor all the more extraordinary. For that, I am most humbled. May I say simply that I am an American. Our countries have a long and storied history, indeed, a familial bond, spanning centuries. Were I called upon, I would do it all over again. Thank you all for this most marvelous accolade."

There was vigorous applause again. Sir Anderson conducted Clarissa back to her table.

Feeling quite faint, she whispered to him, "Oh, Sir Anderson, did you know it was me all along?"

"I did," he replied. "No mere mask could disguise your intelligence or your beauty, my dear."

She ventured one more question. "Does anybody else know?"

"Save the Duttons, no. Nor will they. We are most indebted to you, Miss Hardy. I asked Mr. MacLaren to bring you here, but did not tell him for what action you were receiving this award. The details of your mission will forever remain classified."

Clarissa felt a sudden stab to her heart. So he had been ordered by British Intelligence to bring her to the event. It had not been his choice.

Sir Anderson pulled her chair for her. As she sat down, he whispered in her ear. "We are indeed indebted to you, my dear." It was a supreme compliment from a most distinguished member of The House of Lords. Ordinarily, Clarissa would have been thrilled to hear it, but at this moment, she could only feel the ache in her heart. She nodded and smiled at Sir Anderson automatically as she smoothed her skirt.

Adam gave closing remarks and returned to his place at the table. He smiled at her and tried to keep eye contact with her while the dinner ended, but Clarissa was conflicted. She avoided his eye and talked buoyantly with Lady Anne.

In the car on the way home, Adam leaned close to her. "You seem quite subdued, Clarissa. And after an honor such as was bestowed upon you this evening, it seems you should be feeling rather grand."

Clarissa hit it head on, as was her wont. She looked directly at him, and fighting the power behind his large blue eyes to reduce her to a trembling ingénue, she said, "It was not your idea to ask me. You were ordered to do so. You would not have thought of me at all, had the word not come down from Sir Anderson. I should not have expected anything else. It's just that-that I—" and here Clarissa's resolve faltered. She looked down at her gloved hands and fussed with the clasp of her clutch. She felt irritated and disappointed. She had made short work of a high school principal, an amorous young adventurer, and a spy. Why was she having such a devil of a time with a newspaper editor?

Adam let out a sigh. He reached over to take Clarissa's hand and held it in both of his. They were warm and comforting. Inwardly, Clarissa felt her resolve evaporating. It was no good. She had met her match and she was at a loss as to how to proceed.

"Clarissa, while it is true that Sir Anderson asked me to escort you to the ceremony, it is also true that I was most willing and eager to do so. If I may be candid, I have thought about you every day since our little soiree the other evening. No, I retract that statement! I have thought about you ever since I first set eyes on you and lit your cigarette at the wedding! So many times it pained me when I realized my attraction to you and that I might never see you again."

Clarissa's heart was rapidly mending itself from the aforementioned stabs. She lifted her eyes and met his. She smiled. "I should not speak so frankly, Adam, but I have thought of you often since that day also. I am glad to be here with you, no matter the circumstance that brought it to pass!"

The rest of the ride home was a dream. Clarissa's heart, fully recovered, soared. Adam did not let go of her hand.

Just before the car turned up the street where she lived, Adam said, "I think I shall not be enjoying the time we are apart. Would you come out to dinner with me tomorrow night? Can you put up with me two nights running?"

Clarissa laughed out loud. "I would be most happy to go to dinner with you!"

The car stopped in front of the townhouse. The driver opened the door, and they disembarked. Adam walked with her up the sweeping steps to the front door. Without a word, in the glowing light of the streetlamp, he took her by the shoulders and turned her to face him.

Clarissa stood transfixed as he lifted her pert little chin and lowered his face to hers. He kissed her on the lips. Clarissa thought she might swoon. His lips were soft and tender and warm. She awakened to the secret urgency in him, kissing him back.

Adam drew back, looking down at her and smiling. Wrapping his arms around her, he folded her into his chest. Clarissa could hear his heart beating like a song in her ear. At last he released her.

"Thank you," he said. "Thank you for showing up in my life again."

"You are very welcome, sir," she answered with a little laugh. "Thank you as well! Now, I must be going in. It is growing late."

Adam smiled and touched her cheek. He lifted her hand to his lips and kissed it. "Good night," he said. "I look forward to tomorrow!"

Clarissa smiled and slipped inside without another word. Her heart was beating through her breast.

The days swirled by. News traveled fast in the social circles, both in and outside of London. Adam MacLaren was squiring the American social columnist Miss Clarissa Hardy to every event and then some. True, they seemed always to be in company of others, Lord and Lady Tallman, Chauncey Chelmsford, or one or another MP, so perhaps it was just convenience, the papers speculated. Yet they found it fascinating enough to fill their society pages with news of the liaison.

Clarissa obviously could not write about herself, so she sat wrapped in her silk peignoir one Sunday morning, surrounded by the *Times*, the *Daily*, and the *Herald*. Mrs. Dutton had served her breakfast in bed. Outside, the dreary, wind driven rains of late November pelted against the windows, but Clarissa felt particularly safe and warm. She snuggled down deeper into her pillows.

The columns were mostly very complimentary. Clarissa was called "fresh," "American beautiful," "stylishly sporty during the daytime and smoothly chic for evening," and perhaps best of all, "a compliment to the tall and handsome visage of the older editor-in-chief." She liked that.

She liked everything she did with Adam. They were together almost every evening. Sometimes there was a function to attend, sometimes dinner with Chauncey and Bruce, or the Tallmans, or Hugo and Kitty, when Hugo could come to London, and sometimes — the best times — just an intimate supper for the two of them.

She had written as much to Annabelle, who was settling into married life in the countryside, and had issued a kind, and Clarissa thought, perhaps a bit desperate, invitation for Clarissa and Adam to join them for the holidays. *Please come,* she had written Clarissa. *I love my home, but sometimes, especially at the holidays, it can get a trifle boring.*

Clarissa giggled to herself upon reading that statement. William was rather dull, after all. She did hope her lesson to him had had the desired effect. At the memory of that jolly night, Clarissa smiled to herself. Andrew had been great fun, but nothing about him had ever induced Clarissa to feel more than friendship, however genuine. No, she was in love with Adam MacLaren. She sighed, and put down her newspaper.

How odd, she thought. They had been seeing each other for six weeks, constantly in each other's company, and yet they had not slept together. How odd she should have bullied Eddie into it after just a few weeks, jumped aggressively into an affair with Roger in one afternoon, and allowed Eleanora to lead her down a different path altogether, after only being acquainted for four days. How odd she should have been so randy that she first opened her legs to Andrew and then proceeded to take on Andrew and William together. How odd that she should be so adventurous as to throw herself wholeheartedly into a Greek orgy with people she hardly knew and yet she was shy as a virgin with the one man she wanted above all the rest, the man who had her heart.

Clarissa wanted desperately to sleep with him. Every time he kissed her, she felt herself begin to melt. They held hands and she could feel the electricity, the desire, between them, but true love was not to be trifled with. Clarissa was happy to wait for this man. Anything that happened between them was sacred to her and so she was patient, even as he had slipped his fingers down her throat to the cleft between her breasts last night in the car as he kissed her. At that, she had become nearly sick with unrequited desire.

Still, she had no reliable word from Adam that he felt in any way more attached to her than to any pretty young woman who was socially adept and would allow him a kiss at the end of the evening. As much as she as desired him, she must at least wait for him to tell her he loved her. And Clarissa felt that this must happen soon. Even buoyed by true love as she was, her patience would not last forever.

Clarissa was snapped out of her daydream by a tap at her boudoir door.

"Yes," called out Clarissa.

"It's Chauncey and me," said Bruce. "May we come in?"

"Of course," answered Clarissa, smoothing her hair and gathering the bedclothes around her.

Her friends entered. Chauncey took the slipper chair, and Bruce ensconced himself on the bed at her feet.

"I see you are enjoying your Sunday morning," said Chauncey.

"I am, indeed. What brings you here so early?"

The door opened again, and Mrs. Dutton entered with a silver tray laden with coffee and scones for the three of them. She set it down on the table near Chauncey. "Shall I pour?" she asked.

"No, no, that's quite all right, Mrs. Dutton. I shall do the honors myself," answered Chauncey.

"Very well." Mrs. Dutton left the room.

Chauncey handed Clarissa a cup of coffee and then poured one for Bruce.

"Chauncey and I are going away for the holidays!" blurted out Bruce after his first sip.

"What!" exclaimed Clarissa. "I say! Are you really, Chaunce?"

"Yes, we are. We are going to Italy and then to knock about the Mediterranean for a few weeks."

"I am sick to pieces of the bank," explained Bruce. "We haven't been anywhere for so long!"

"What do your families say?"

Chauncey sighed. "They are not keen, but I told them I was doing a piece on the exotic culture of the islands and Bruce was coming along as a sort of scribe. They will adjust."

"Well, I certainly shan't," pouted Clarissa. "You are my best friends! I shall miss you dreadfully!"

"Pooh-pooh, I say to that," scoffed Chauncey. "You have been rather busy yourself and seem to have a new friend, if I am not mistaken. Why, I have to read about you in the papers! Besides, you should have girlfriends to chum about with. You will just get bored rubbing elbows on a daily basis with a pair of old puffs like Bruce and me."

"Speak for yourself, man," snorted Bruce.

"You know what I mean."

"I shall miss you no matter what!" persisted Clarissa.

"And Adam," said Bruce, serious for once, "is he treating you well? Are you happy, my chook?"

"I am deliriously happy," said Clarissa, hugging her knees. Clarissa looked from one to the other. They both wore serious faces. "Is there something wrong?"

Chauncey spoke first. "We just want to make sure you are in good circumstances before we leave."

"Well, I am, I assure you."

Bruce picked at the coverlet. "I ask you this because we love you," he said. "Has there been a…an…well…"

"Has there been a consummation, as it were, of your relationship?" Chauncey finished for him.

Clarissa was taken aback. "If you mean have we slept together yet, the answer is no. My dears, I love this man, and I am willing to wait until he declares himself to me. I feel certain he will!"

Both Chauncey and Bruce seemed to be relieved. Clarissa was feeling a bit peevish. They did get so fussy at times!

"Dear, your business is your own, of course," said Chauncey. "Bruce and I adore you, and I suppose we want to impart a bit of our wisdom to you before we leave."

"Sometimes you are overdramatic," said Clarissa. Instantly, she was regretted her remark and apologized. "I am so very sorry. It was an unfortunate remark. I have been harebrained lately!"

Chauncey was patient. "And that is why we wish to have this little chat." He put his fingertips together. "You must remember that Adam MacLaren is a man of the world. He is probably close to ten years older than you are."

"Chauncey, you know I am experienced for my age!"

"Technically, perhaps. Emotionally, no."

"What do you mean?"

It was Bruce's turn to answer, with the clarity of thought that, though hidden most of the time, was one of the primary reasons Chauncey had come to love him. "We mean, dearest, that you ought to protect your heart. Now, we are not saying in any way that

MacLaren means to seduce or compromise you. We are just saying that the man has been knocking about single, handsome, and full of testosterone for most of his adult life. Things may come up."

"What sort of things?" asked Clarissa, her eyes narrowing.

"I wouldn't have the faintest idea," said Bruce. "We are just telling you to take it slowly. The man is Scottish, you know, even though he was born in America. Sometimes the Scots can be, well, rather harsh. I do not want your feelings hurt or your enthusiasm dampened!"

Clarissa jumped to her knees and crawled down the bed. She threw her arms around Bruce's neck and kissed him on the cheek. "You two are the best friends a girl could have!"

"I will say what I've said in the past," said Chauncey. "The man is a straight shooter. He's honest. We're just cautious, darling. We want the best for you! Things can come up when a man has been single and in the crosshairs for as long as Adam has."

"And by 'things,' you mean other women?" said Clarissa cheekily.

"That's exactly what we mean," replied Chauncey. "The man has not been without female company, I'm sure."

Clarissa was young and, for the first time, truly in love. It made her cocky.

Clarissa crossed the room and bestowed the same caress on Chauncey. He looked up at her and smiled. Clarissa thought his pale blue eyes were a trifle sad.

"Don't worry about me. Go off on your holiday! Have a wonderful time! I shall be thinking of you on your sunlit isles while I am shivering before the fire! And write to me, please!"

Clarissa saw them off that Saturday. They stood on the deck, Chauncey in white linen, and Bruce in fawn colored cotton, madly waving their fedoras. Clarissa was gripped with a sudden loneliness, as though she was facing the world without her protective flank men.

That evening, over drinks at their favorite little pub where they had had their first tryst, Clarissa confided to Adam. "I was very sorry to see them go," she said. "You know they are my closest friends here in London!"

Adam peered at her over the rim of his glass of Scotch. "And sometimes, I am jealous of that. In fact, I am jealous of anybody who takes you away from me."

"Why, Adam! Whatever do you mean? Jealous of Chauncey and Bruce? That's silly!"

"Is it? They have your ear. Do I have your ear? You discuss everything with them. Do you even care what I may think about anything? It is hard to gauge your emotions, Clarissa. Especially those emotions directed toward me. You are always blithe and charming to me, but you are always blithe and charming. It seems you enjoy our times together, but who is to say? I may simply be an entertainment." He stopped and gave a rather shuddering sigh. "I speak from my heart, Clarissa. Don't invalidate me."

His remark hit home. Clarissa felt awful. "Oh, dear! Oh, Adam, I did not intend to trifle with you. Truly, I didn't. Anyway, I do not kiss Chauncey or Bruce!"

He smiled at that, but said, more seriously, "Who do you kiss, Clarissa? Do you kiss Andrew, or would you, if he were here? I am quite a lot older than yourself. Do you wish you were escorted about by a younger sort, like Hugh squires Kitty? How can you not understand how I feel about you? I wake up each morning thinking about you. I go to bed each evening thinking about you. Have you stopped to think about why I haven't given you an assignment outside the society section?"

Clarissa shook her head silently, letting him talk without interruption.

"It is not because I don't think you wouldn't make a marvelous success of it. No, I am sure with your pluck, you would have the Communists eating out of your hand. No, it is because I have no desire to lie in my bed at night, while you are cavorting about the Continent, or the Balkans, or mushing through the icy wastes of Siberia. It would worry me sick on two fronts. I would be in constant fear of your physical safety. And, more acutely, I would be in constant fear that you would be swept off your feet by some king or prince, and forget all about lowly newspaper editors."

His voice has risen slightly. Clarissa recognized the gravity of the situation. She set her drink down and tucked her hands into her lap to hide the fact that they were shaking. She said, as calmly and quietly as she could manage, "Adam, what are you saying?"

Adam cleared his throat and leaned forward across the small table. He reached out and traced the line of her cheek where her hair swung jauntily forward. "I am saying, Clarissa Hardy, that I love you. I am saying that you have captured me, heart and soul, and that I have no wish to escape. I am saying that I sit here in fear that you might not feel the same about me, and what shall I do if you don't? Do you feel the same, Clarissa? Even in part?" His large blue eyes smoldered darkly.

Clarissa's heart soared. She threw back her head and laughed with true happiness. "Adam! This is the most wonderful declaration. I have yearned to hear you say this! I have yearned for it! Oh, Adam, I do love you, too! I have been living in a quandary, wondering where your true emotions lay, wondering whether I had a place in your heart! I have been keeping my own emotions under wraps, quelling them, so as not to have my heart broken!" She clasped her hands together, but Adam took them and pulled her forward until their lips met across the table.

Then, keeping hold of her hands, he sat back and heaved another sigh. "Well, I am safe, then," he said. "My heart's desire desires me as well. Clarissa, I want to take you to my aunt's home in Edinburgh for the holidays. It will be from Christmas through the New Year. My mother and father will be there. You must meet them. You must meet my family. What do you say?"

With all the hope and happiness in her heart, Clarissa said, "Why not!"

Clarissa began to plan in earnest as Christmas grew closer. Adam told her that the weather in Scotland could be quite brutal. She bought new clothes in preparation against the cold and packed them carefully in her traveling trunk. They would be taking the train, an overnight from London. They would be met at the station by Aunt Caroline's butler. As the day approached, Clarissa grew more and more excited. She did so want to make a good impression.

The week before they were to embark was frantic. Adam had meetings with his editors, as well as a quick trip to France to meet with a sister newspaper there. Clarissa had to turn out several columns which would then be published daily during her absence. They would not see much of each other until they stepped aboard the train.

Clarissa came back to the paper one evening to finish a column and found a note on her desk from Adam. It read:

DARLING, SORRY ABOUT THE SHORT
NOTICE, BUT WILL BE CROSSING THE
CHANNEL AND MAKING FOR PARIS FOR
MEETING WITH THE HERALD. I WILL MISS
YOU DREADFULLY! CAN'T WAIT UNTIL WE
ARE ALONE ON THE TRAIN AND I CAN
TAKE YOU IN MY ARMS. ADAM.

Clarissa's heart leaped. She smiled and tucked the note into her purse. She sat down at her typewriter and clicked and clacked merrily.

The next morning, she was the first person in the newsroom. Or, at least, that was what she thought. There were lights on in Adam's office. *My,* she thought, *that was a quick trip! He must have decided not to go.* Eagerly, she crossed the newsroom and opened the door.

There was a woman sitting at Adam's desk. A woman Clarissa had never seen. She looked up when Clarissa entered the room.

"Yes?" she asked.

Clarissa said, "Where is Adam?"

"Mr. MacLaren is away on business. He will not be returning soon."

"Who are you?" asked Clarissa.

"I beg your pardon!" said the woman harshly. She stood up. She was tall and thin, with dark, shoulder length curled hair held back from her angular face with combs. She wore a severely tailored wool suit, cut beautifully, obviously expensive. She was older than Clarissa and had she smiled, she might have been attractive.

Clarissa was not to be cowed. "I asked who you were. What are you doing in Adam's office? I shall call the watchman."

The woman smiled with one side of her mouth. "Perhaps you have heard of me. I am Amelia Southerton. I am a personal friend of Mr. MacLaren. I needn't say more to you, except that you may leave at once."

Amelia Southerton! Clarissa had heard of her! She was a famous independent foreign correspondent, connected to the highest sources, and sought after by all the established news agencies.

"I am also a close friend of Adam's. Closer than yourself, I am sure. I work here at the *Tribune* writing the social column," said Clarissa, holding her own.

Amelia Southerton laughed harshly. "Ah. I see! I understand now. You must be Clarissa Hardy." She walked around the desk and sized Clarissa up with glaring eyes. "So you are Adam's little entertainment! My, my. Well, I will give you this. You are quite as attractive as he says, but I am back now, and for quite some time, so I do not think you will be seeing him in any other context other than as your boss."

The breath left Clarissa's body. The room swirled around her. She thought she would faint and made a valiant effort to regain her composure.

"You stand there as if nobody told you of the relationship between Adam and myself. I am sorry to be the one to inform you. I thought he had done it. Men! Well, you never know with them, do you?" She laughed again and the sound sliced through Clarissa's heart like broken glass. "Yes," she continued, "we have been an item for a long time now. Of course, we are apart a good deal of the time, so we have rather of an understanding, but I am thinking we will not be apart much longer now." She approached Clarissa.

Clarissa's wits seemed to have deserted her, as well as her ability to move. Clarissa wanted to run from the room, to keep on running. For the first time in nearly a year, she wanted to be home with her mother and father. However, the courage that had brought her grandfather across the Atlantic to build a better life in America and the courage that saw her mother's family through near starvation to earn doctorates from America's best universities and prosper in the new land had not been diluted. It coursed through the blood of the young woman, even as she stood facing an incomprehensible situation.

Clarissa said clearly, "I am nobody's entertainment. I am Clarissa Hardy. You are not even in the employ of this newspaper. If you do not leave immediately, I shall ring Scotland Yard and have you escorted out and arrested. I will file charges myself."

Amelia Southerton grinned nastily. "Do not put yourself out. I see how Adam must have found you amusing indeed. I shall leave. Adam will return tomorrow night and I will meet him at his home."

She stalked past Clarissa. Clarissa did not move until she heard the outer door slam. Then, panic seized her. It was a complete and consuming panic. She saw her dreams pop like so many soap bubbles. She saw no past, no future. The pain in her stomach was unbearable. She had to get out. She had to leave now. Blindly, she turned and ran out the door, stopping only to grab her purse.

Arriving at the townhouse, she fled upstairs, only to collapse on her bed. The hurt was too acute for tears. She lay on her back, staring at the ceiling, seeing nothing. What was she to do? She called for Mrs. Dutton, who appeared seconds later, it seemed.

"Clarissa, are you not well?"

Clarissa gave a little, pained laugh. "No, Mrs. Dutton, I am not well, but not in the medical sense. Would you bring me a whiskey, please?"

Mrs. Dutton made no reply, but returned in a flash with an old fashioned glass half full of whiskey. It wasn't even on a tray. She handed it to Clarissa. "Do you need me to stay?"

Clarissa took the whiskey and sipped it. "Not at the moment, Mrs. Dutton. I need to think things through."

"I understand." She melted out of the room.

Clarissa gazed into the whiskey glass as though into a crystal ball. Still, the tears would not come. They were jammed in her throat, aching, hurting her. She reviewed her options. She could accept Annabelle's invitation. The holidays would be jolly there. Andrew might even be there. No, that would not do. That is where she first met Adam. She could stay where she was. No, that would not do. If she ever saw Adam and Amelia together, she could not be responsible for her own actions. She could catch a liner back to the States, back home. Return to Mommy and Daddy and Michael. No, that would not do, either. She would be surrounded by Bonnie, happily married, Mommy and Daddy, still in love after twenty-five years, Eddie, probably married by now, and Roger, after her for a good fuck, and nothing else. What to do? What to do?

Then, the epiphany. Of course! Clarissa, even in her pain, had to give a little smile, and thank the Powers That Be. Eleanora. Dear, dear Eleanora, with her outlandish behavior, her honest pursuit of life, her true friendship. Clarissa made up her mind. She would book the next itinerary available to the South Seas and join Eleanora in paradise. She could nurse her wounds there. Eleanora would see to it. Clarissa rang for Mrs. Dutton.

"Yes, dear?" Mrs. Dutton's brow was furrowed with worry.

"Mrs. Dutton, I am ringing the agent and booking passage to the South Seas. I…I need to work on a particularly absorbing column about…about the geographical cure, as it were."

"I understand."

"I need you to pack my trunk and to ask Mr. Dutton to withdraw considerable cash from my account. I may be able to leave on the morrow, so these things must be accomplished today."

"I must ask you…" said Mrs. Dutton.

"Yes?"

"Are you sure? Is your mind made up?"

"I appreciate your concern and your help, as always, Mrs. Dutton. You have been my mainstay! Yes, my mind is made up."

Impulsively, Mrs. Dutton swooped in and hugged Clarissa to her ample bosom. "I shall see to it immediately."

When she had left the room, Clarissa took pen and paper in hand.

Dear Adam,

I am leaving for the South Seas. I have a dear friend on a remote island there. There is no need for me to seek explanation from you. Miss Southerton was quite clear with her own explanation and the very fact that this situation has come up is reason enough for us to part. I have nothing I wish to say or to hear from you. Please extend my apologies to your family. If you have the courage, you may tell them what a cad you are. If you do not, you may tell them I was called away to the States due to a family emergency.

As always, Clarissa

The next morning, the household was awakened before the sun had fully risen by a loud pounding at the front door. Clarissa leaped out of bed, wrapped herself in her peignoir and rushed to the top of the stairs. Dutton, unbelievably dressed in his customary livery, was opening the front door.

"Dutton! I say, Dutton," yelled a familiar voice from outside. "Let me in! I must see Miss Hardy on a matter of the greatest importance!"

Dutton opened the door, and Adam MacLaren practically fell into the foyer.

"Miss Hardy is indisposed," said Dutton coldly. "She is still in her bedroom."

"Then get her out! I must," Adam gasped for air, his voice shaking, "I must see her!"

"I'm sorry," Dutton continued, but Clarissa interrupted him, standing at the head of the stairs. In her hand, she held the note she had written the night before.

"It's fine, Dutton, thank you," she said calmly. "I will talk to Mr. MacLaren."

Dutton looked up and saw Clarissa. He said, without a glance at Adam, "I will be in the kitchen if you need me."

Adam stood at the bottom of the stairs dressed in a rumpled white shirt and dark trousers. He looked as though he had slept in his clothing.

"Clarissa, I—" He started to climb the stairwell toward her.

Clarissa spoke low, through her teeth. "Stop where you are. If you take one more step toward me, I will lock myself in my bedroom and Dutton will throw you out."

Adam stopped. "Please," he begged, "hear me out. Be fair, Clarissa."

"Fair? Fair!" Clarissa had to control the timbre of her voice, lest she sound like a shrew. Even in extenuating circumstances, one must keep one's dignity. "Was it fair that I found out about Amelia Southerton on my own? Why didn't you tell me? You knew she was coming. You let me walk into that-that bloody arena uninformed. Misinformed, actually! There she was, all high and mighty, spewing innuendos about the two of you and attempting to dismiss me as entertainment! Is that how you treat a person you said you loved? My heavens, Adam! You are a cad and a liar and a schemer!"

Her hand on the banister was beginning to shake. Her knees were weakening.

"I did not know she was coming. And I thought it was over between us! The last I knew of her, she was in Paris. I went there especially to tell her that I had fallen in love with you. She wasn't there, and unbeknownst to me, she had started back for London. She seemed determined that we should start up again."

"Well, maybe she'll get her chance. You told me you didn't want a woman who was cavorting around the Continent!"

"Clarissa, please—"

"I have nothing more to say. I want you to go. I don't know where the truth lies. I don't know who you are. Straight shooter? Bah! Please leave."

"All right, I'll leave, but promise me you will not do anything rash. Promise me you will think things through and give me a chance. That woman is nothing to me. Please, promise me."

"Oh, I will not do anything I am not completely sure of," said Clarissa. "I will give my every move extreme consideration and do what is best for Clarissa Hardy." She held the envelope in her hand and, impulsively, threw it down the stairs. "You may read my note after you leave. Good-bye."

Clarissa's resolve was dissolving. Mustering all her remaining courage, she turned and walked back to her room. It was only after she heard the front door shut that she collapsed in uncontrollable sobs.

PART EIGHT
Clarissa Hardy in the South Seas

Dutton himself drove Clarissa to the steamer. The boat was a trifle seedy, but it had been the most direct route, sailing to Egypt where Clarissa would pick up a freighter bound for eventual harbor in Australia, but carrying several passengers to be dropped off through Indonesia and the islands of the southern seas.

Once on board, Clarissa wrote letters. She wrote to Mommy, explaining her new assignment. She wrote to Bonnie and told her the truth. She wrote to Eleanora, in hopes that it would reach her before she herself did. The swift little boats that zipped in and out of the island nations often delivered the mail, along with daily supplies, and even contraband.

Clarissa also wrote in her journal, documenting her journey and her life aboard the deadly boring steamer. It was therapeutic and, despite her shattered soul, Clarissa once more began to see beauty in the sunsets and the undulating sea.

One afternoon, Clarissa climbed to the uppermost deck to stroll, trying to amuse herself watching the seabirds that followed the ship. She felt trapped on the ship. It was small, as freighters go, and there were no activities. Clarissa's naturally social tendencies needed an outlet. The other passengers aboard were exceedingly dull: a couple of academics and a team of three marine scientists who spent their days testing samples of the seawater for new species of krill.

Clarissa's stroll became a walk, and the walk, a pace. She was like a caged animal. She must find some outlet to relieve the tedium.

"Passengers are not allowed on this deck," said a deep voice from behind her.

Clarissa jumped, startled, and turned around to see the captain of the vessel standing in the open doorway of the bridge. Clarissa had seen him when she boarded in Egypt. He was a tall, lean man, with sandy colored hair and pale blue eyes. Not at all unattractive, Clarissa noticed.

"Oh, Captain," she said, "you startled me."

"You must return to the lower decks," he said, ignoring her remark. "This is the domain of captain and crew only."

"I was seeking a wider vista," said Clarissa in a friendly manner.

"Plenty of vista exists on the decks below," said the captain. "I must insist you leave immediately."

"Please forgive me, Captain — I am sorry, but I don't know your name," said Clarissa stubbornly. She approached him, extending her hand. "I am Clarissa Hardy."

Begrudgingly, the captain took her outstretched hand. "I am Captain Erik Larsson."

"I am glad to meet you."

"Likewise," said Captain Larsson abruptly. "Now I must ask you again to return to the lower decks."

"At once," said Clarissa. She was not going to spar with this taciturn man any longer. A thought had occurred to her.

Clarissa skipped down to her cabin. *How do you replace a man you've lost?* she thought. *Why, you simply replace him with another!*

It was nearly dinner time. Most days, the captain ate at seven o'clock, about an hour later than the rest of the crew and passengers. Tonight, Clarissa would be late as well. She prepared well, picking a sporty little number with a short skirt and a low, boat neck top to wear.

At seven o'clock, she appeared at the door of the galley. She called in to the cook.

"I say, I am so sorry, but I missed dinner at the usual time. Is it too late to get something to eat? I am quite famished!"

The cook grunted and motioned with his ladle. "Take a seat. No skin off my nose. Plenty of food."

The dining room was actually part of the hallway off the galley. It was furnished with two long tables, perpetually set for the next meal. As soon as one shift finished eating, Spud, the cook's helper, would whisk the dishes away and reset the place.

Clarissa sat primly at one of the tables. Spud, a lanky young man with pimples, brought her a bottle of beer.

"Captain's dining late tonight, too," he offered eagerly as he set the beer in front of her.

"Why thank you for the beer, Spud," said Clarissa sweetly. "Perhaps the captain would enjoy some company with his meal. Where does he usually sit?"

"Captain don't enjoy much, miss, but you're welcome to try. He sits over here, his back to the galley."

"Why, then, I will sit opposite him. Thank you, Spud."

Clarissa took her beer and resettled herself next to the captain's seat. A moment later, Captain Erik Larsson entered the room. He glared at her. Clarissa pretended not to notice.

"Please, sit with me, Captain," she said, patting the table next to her. "I must say, I am glad to see you. I hate to eat alone. You are late this evening."

Clarissa had always been a willing accomplice, but never a full on aggressor. This was quite a fun challenge.

"I usually eat alone," he grumbled, taking his usual seat nonetheless. "It gives me private time to think."

"Well, you have plenty of private time in that stuffy little bridge of yours," said Clarissa, daintily sipping her beer. "I should say this would be a welcome change for you."

"Humph," grunted the captain.

Spud came in carrying two plates of chipped beef and gravy on toast points.

"How did you come to captain this vessel?" asked Clarissa.

"I was born in Norway," he said. "I captained on the Great Lakes in America, and I grew sick of the cold and ice and snow. I worked all the time until I could buy this boat and I set off for warmer waters. I have been sailing the South Seas ever since. That is my story."

Clarissa laughed charmingly. "Imagine! A Viking in the South Seas!"

Spud came out, this time with a tray, bearing hot tea and pound cake topped with canned peaches.

The captain sipped on his third beer, which must have been softening him up, for he offered, "I enjoy the warm seas. It is lonely at times, but this boat is my home, wherever I want to be."

"And you don't miss female companionship?" Clarissa asked winsomely.

"There are plenty of females in every port."

"Ah, a true sailor! Now, to change the subject, I wonder if you could take me to the top deck? You see, I am a reporter and I would very much like to chronicle your life aboard this vessel."

"I am not in the habit of entertaining the passengers."

"Please, Captain. I assure you it is not entertainment. Besides, I see no reason why you should be so rude. Who do you take me for, I ask you? Do I frighten you in some way?"

Captain Larsson snorted. "Do not flatter yourself. I am not afraid of anything."

"I am happy to hear that, Captain. It's a good quality in a man with your responsibilities. Now take me to the bridge."

The captain met her eyes. Clarissa waited. She knew she looked cute. She watched his jaw work. Obviously, he was wrestling with himself about something. Then he blinked. "Follow me," he said shortly and exited the room, Clarissa close behind him.

"As long as you are so eager to see how things work, we will take the captain's way to the bridge," announced Captain Larsson over his shoulder. He strode to the end of the hallway and opened a thick metal door. Inside was a narrow, spiral staircase. "This staircase gives me access to every deck and below decks as well. Can you climb?"

"Of course," said Clarissa. "However, will you let me go first? In that way, if I misstep, you will be there to catch me."

"Go ahead then." Captain Larsson stood aside, and Clarissa entered the silo staircase. It was damp and musty. The only light was from dim sconces at every deck level. Clarissa looked down and saw the staircase spiral into the black depths below. She shivered and decided to concentrate on upward motion. Grasping the railing, she began to climb the stairs. She heard the door slam and looked down. Captain Larsson was a few steps below her, looking up.

Clarissa wondered whether he had noticed yet that she was not wearing underwear.

Up and up they went, finally reaching the top. Clarissa yanked and pulled at the door handle, but it refused to budge.

"It is difficult," said Captain Larsson, coming up behind her. "Allow me, please."

In order to be able to reach the door handle, the captain had to come closely up behind Clarissa until he was wedged in the tight space, his body squashing hers against the recalcitrant door. She gave a slight wiggle.

"Please excuse my close proximity," muttered the captain as he reached over her shoulder to force the door open.

The door flew open with a bang, and Clarissa was catapulted through the opening by the weight of the captain behind her. She stumbled into a small room and fell full length on the floor. Her skirt billowed up in the process, exposing her firm buttocks. Feigning demureness, she pulled the renegade clothing back into place, regained her feet, and turned to face the captain.

The look on his face betrayed the fact that he had seen the territory heretofore hidden beneath her skirt.

"Oh, I am so clumsy!" exclaimed Clarissa dramatically. "Please forgive me!"

"Are you quite all right?"

"Yes, yes, I'm fine. I have only scraped my thigh a bit. Let us continue with our tour."

"Ah, well, yes," stammered the captain. "As you can see, it is not a big place. There is the wheel, and the navigational instruments—"

Clarissa had hiked her skirt up and was trying to examine the backside of her upper thigh. She heard Captain Larsson cough.

"Oh, my!" she laughed. "I am so sorry, but my scrape is stinging a bit. I can't seem to see it and I would hate to get blood on my dress. Would you mind assessing the damage?"

"Me? You want me to look at your leg?"

"If you would, yes. I want to see whether it is bleeding or whether it is only an abrasion." She backed closer to him, raising her skirt and bending forward slightly.

"I see nothing," said the captain. "Where do you feel the pain?"

"Up further. Get closer. Feel free to raise my dress, Captain. You are the captain and the law on this ship. I put myself in your hands." She glanced back over her shoulder.

The captain stood motionless for an instant, then bent forward, his long nose close to her leg. He raised his hand and tentatively touched her thigh. "Does that hurt?"

"No, not at all," remarked Clarissa.

"How about this?" Captain Larsson ran his finger up her thigh, just under the hem of her skirt.

"No, nothing."

"And this?" His hand was up under her skirt at the top of her thigh.

"Oh, Captain. Why, why that feels rather good, I must say," purred Clarissa. She took a step backward and his hand slipped between her legs. He withdrew it immediately. Clarissa laughed. "I understand completely if you need to examine me more closely, Captain. Please, it would relieve me to know I was not injured."

Clarissa leaned forward, bracing herself with her hands on her knees. "I am ready," she announced. She glanced back and saw that he had succumbed. The pale blue eyes had clouded over and he was licking his lips. Slowly, he raised her skirt and exposed her buttocks. With his big hands, he stroked both of her thighs, working from just above her knees to just brushing the lips of her pouting cunt.

"Spread your legs," he said huskily.

Clarissa stood wider. The captain slipped a hand between her legs and squeezed her cunt. "Everything appears as it should be," he said. "However, sometimes there can be damage done inside. I must check."

"Oh, please do. I want you to be thorough," gasped Clarissa, giving in to her carnal desires.

"It is best to be sure," agreed Captain Larsson. He spread the lips of Clarissa's cunt, stroking them. At last, he found her clit and pinched it between his roaming forefinger and thumb. Clarissa groaned.

"Is there pain?" he asked.

"No. None at all."

"I am not done. There is more to examine." So saying, he slipped a finger into her wet cunt, turning it round and round, reaching as far inside as he could. "At sea, we do not see women for months sometimes," he muttered. "I must get a better look. Stand up."

Reluctantly, because her throbbing cunt craved the attention, Clarissa stood up, his finger still deep in her. He gave a couple of thrusts and withdrew it. Opening a box mounted on the wall, he took out some blankets and said, "Follow me out onto the deck. There is room to lie down there and I can complete my examination."

Clarissa followed him, waiting while he made a makeshift mat with the blankets. He motioned to her, and she lay down on her back. He knelt beside her and unbuttoned her middy blouse.

"I had crushed you against the door. I must examine your breasts for bruising and tenderness." With that, he opened her blouse, freeing her naked bosom.

A deep breath escaped him. He squeezed her breasts in his hands, pulling at her nipples. At last, he bent down and sucked them.

Clarissa gasped, "Oh, Captain! Oh, my! How do you find them?"

"I find them alert and delectable. Perfectly normal. Now I must go below." Clarissa heard him chuckle at his own remark.

"Spread your legs," he said, and when Clarissa did, the captain opened the lips of her cunt and flicked her clit with his tongue. Clarissa's back arched. The captain began to lap her cunt and to sink his tongue into her as far as it would go. Clarissa wriggled. He put a finger into her again, fucking her slowly with it, then another finger, and another. With his other hand, he rubbed her cunt until she thought it might catch fire. She cried out as her climax broke over her, twitching and rolling.

"Ahh," he said. "The proper response! I pronounce you unharmed by your fall."

Clarissa lay heaving on the blanket. When she had caught her breath, she sat up, facing the kneeling Captain Larsson. "Now, may I examine you?" she asked coyly. "I would like to make sure you are not injured. Please, take off your trousers."

Captain Larsson needed no urging. He peeled off his trousers, freeing a magnificent cock, standing at attention amongst a forest of gingery curls. Clarissa leaned in and placed a tender kiss on the red tip, then rimmed the shaft with her tongue. Captain Larsson moaned aloud.

Clarissa took the shaft in both her hands, squeezing and rubbing it until it reached an amazing degree of hardness. Though she longed to impale herself on it, she felt she owed the captain a good time. Who knew when a woman last held his cock in her mouth?

Clarissa sucked and licked. Captain Larsson cradled her head in his hands and gently fucked her mouth. Clarissa relaxed her throat and took the whole shaft. With her hands, she fondled his balls. Then, reaching a curious finger between his buttocks, she traced his arse, playing and poking at the opening while she sucked his cock. His ball sack grew tight and Clarissa did not want him to come in her mouth. She needed to ride that cock!

Drawing away, she lay back, spreading her legs wide to give him access, but instead of entering her in that position, he sat down, his cock standing rigidly upright. Grasping her firmly by the hips, he brought her down on the object of her attention with not a little force. Clarissa felt pierced to her core, and she cried out in ecstasy.

Clarissa was prepared for short duration, due to the fact that Captain Larsson might not have had a good fuck in some time, but he proved her wrong. He kept up the vigorous thrusting and pumping for what seemed like forever. He was very strong and turned her in all sorts of contortions, stabbing into her with his cock as far as it would go, lapping her periodically to keep her moist. Clarissa was transported as, almost violently, another climax hit her.

Still the captain pounded away with a nearly unbearable intensity. Suddenly he pulled out and taking her by the arm, bent her over the railing. Standing behind her, he buried his cock into her once again, resuming his actions with renewed lustiness. Clarissa felt his tight stomach banging into her bottom, his cock deep within her. At last, when Clarissa thought she could no longer stand but would fall over the side, he let out a roar and gripped her about the waist. They crashed down upon the blanket, locked together, his cock pulsating within her.

Captain Larsson began to laugh. It was a strangled sound, as though he wasn't used to laughing, but as he laughed, it became stronger, and jollier. Clarissa found herself laughing as well.

"I must say, Captain, you have quite done me in!"

"Well, you may have eighteen hours to recuperate, for I shall need to examine you again! I feel my strength returning! It has been quite a long time, but you are a very decent port in a storm!"

After that, the voyage was much more interesting and she was almost sad when at last, in the early evening hours of what had been a lovely day at sea bidding the captain a rigorous good-bye, Clarissa's ship docked at a surprisingly modern port city on an island unknown to Clarissa.

The deckhand, who had also done double duty as a steward, informed Clarissa that he would be unloading her travel trunk on the dock and that word had been sent to the island of her planned destination. However, he said, in a strange accent Clarissa did not recognize, she would be well advised to book a room in the hotel, since her transport would probably not arrive until morning.

Although her heartbreak resurfaced at the knowledge that she was again on her own, Clarissa remained unfazed. She disembarked and booked a room in the hotel as the steward had suggested. She found it hard to care, but she did notice that the hotel was quite a bit more luxurious than she had anticipated. She ate a fine dinner and retired.

At dawn, she was awakened by a knock at the door. "Miss must rise. Outrigger is waiting. Miss must rise!"

"I will be ready immediately," called Clarissa through the door. "And I will need somebody to transport my travel trunk."

Twenty minutes later, Clarissa walked down to the docks, followed by two sturdy boys hoisting her travel trunk between them. Four tall islanders stood on the dock above a large outrigger canoe. They were bronze of skin, very handsome, and dressed only in colorful cloths that swathed their loins. Their black hair swept back from their smiling faces and was plaited with colorful seashells. One of the men approached her, smiling. He bowed to her and handed her an envelope. It was a note from Eleanora, assuring her these men would take good care of her.

"You come. You come now," said the bronze man, holding out his hand.

The dalliance with Captain Larsson had only been Clarissa's attempt at a salve for her wounded spirit, but, at the thought of joining Eleanora on her island, she smiled to herself. For the first time since she had confronted the interloper in Adam's office, Clarissa felt her spirits rise. She took the man's hand. He immediately pulled her to him, took hold of her round the waist, and lifted her down to the next man standing in the outrigger. The second man laughed at her.

"You need eat more," he said jovially. He set her down gently on the floor of the outrigger. Then, more quickly than Clarissa could comprehend, the men had taken their places, plied their oars, and set the outrigger for the open sea.

It was a rigorous journey. At times, Clarissa was unable to see beyond the next swell, but the men were not only resolute, they were happy. They smiled and talked to her in their native tongue, which was a lovely sing-song language that Clarissa found quite reassuring.

Three hours later, Clarissa could make out the far-off landscape of an island. When at last the men drove the outrigger through the surf and up onto the white sands of the beach, Clarissa felt hopeful. There was a crowd gathered to meet her, and front and center was Eleanora, waving madly beside a stout red-haired woman who must be Margaret. She ran to Clarissa, clasping her in her arms.

"Oh, my friend! My dear friend! I am positively ecstatic!" Eleanora stepped back and all the women from the crowd approached her shyly, placing leis of fragrant tropical flowers around her neck. By the time all the leis were bestowed, Clarissa was heady from the scent.

And now, at last, Clarissa felt the tears. She began to weep and wept uncontrollably. The women swarmed around her, patting her, murmuring tenderly. Eleanora led her gently off the beach to the village. Margaret was on her other side.

"There, there, dear," whispered Margaret. And Eleanora said over and over again, "The cad! The wretched cad!"

Clarissa was ushered lovingly through a village of longhouses shaded by coconut palms and all manner of tropical foliage. Eleanora and Margaret guided her into one of the longhouses and laid her down in a most comfortable hammock.

"There, there," said Eleanora. "Sleep, my dear. You are overwrought now, but in this place, not for long! Let the island breezes lull you to sleep. We will return with food."

For a week, the women of the island nursed Clarissa tenderly. She was cloistered in the longhouse, only coming out to go for therapeutic walks on the beach with Eleanora and Margaret. Clarissa found Margaret to be jolly indeed and an effective antithesis to Eleanora, who, while very dear to Clarissa, could tend to be a trifle clinical and over-analytical. It was at Margaret's urging that Clarissa talked through her whole ordeal. There were more tears, but they came less frequently. The daily food was refreshing and clean tasting, mostly fruit and fish.

At last, Clarissa began to feel well enough to join the community. She helped prepare meals, look after children, and dig shellfish. Her complexion began to get very brown, and Eleanora teased her that, but for her blond hair, she should look like a native!

It was at this juncture that Clarissa was to be presented with her sarong. It was a beautiful piece of clothing, tangerine colored with bright yellow sunbursts woven throughout. One of the young women had shown Clarissa the garment and Eleanora had explained.

"This evening, you will be bathed, cleansed of sorrows. In front of all the women of the village, you will don your sarong and become one of us. It is then you will meet Kono, the chieftain of this island and husband to Margaret, Moya, Tika, and Pi. Now, Clarissa, there is the distinct possibility Kono may wish to welcome you in the traditional way. Are you ready for it?"

Clarissa smiled. It was nearly her old smile. "Why not!" she said.

The day was exciting. The women ran hither and thither, preparing a great feast. The men brought in huge batches of fish and shellfish and seaweed. Others decanted the coconut alcohol into large coconut vessels and prepared the fire pits where the fish would be wrapped in seaweed and steamed along with mango and papaya and all manner of different and exotic fruits.

As the day drew to a close, the women took Clarissa to a secret freshwater pond. Here she was stripped of her Western clothing, which had dwindled since her arrival to a khaki skirt and white shirt. She was thoroughly washed with a fragrant soapy substance, and her hair, which had grown considerably in the six weeks since she had left England, was brushed out until it was shiny and full around her face.

"You are indeed a beautiful young woman," remarked Margaret, patting Clarissa on her behind. "Quite delectable. I would not be surprised to see my husband grow hard!"

Eleanora laughed and said to Clarissa, "You must remember these people live an open life, free with all their emotions and urges. It makes life quite exciting!"

Margaret was speaking to Moya and pointing to Clarissa. Moya was laughing and she circled the naked Clarissa, looking at her carefully. She ran her hands down Clarissa's chest and pulled at her nipples. Everybody laughed.

"They like the way you look," whispered Eleanora. "Although they think you could put on a few pounds!"

Finally, they dressed Clarissa in her beautiful sarong, and singing a light hearted tune, they escorted her back to the village.

The feast was wonderful. Clarissa was guest of honor. She sat between Eleanora and Tika, festooned with flowers and drinking her coconut liquor out of a hollowed out shell. At last the evening began to wane. Clarissa was feeling a bit dizzy, but very cheerful. The crowd began to thin. Many of the men walked up to Kono and spoke in their native tongue, which was followed by guffaws of laughter. A pleasant little shiver went up Clarissa's spine.

Suddenly Kono stood and walked away.

"Where is he going?" whispered Clarissa to Eleanora.

Eleanora winked. "Do not trouble yourself. He will show up when he is most needed!"

"Will he fuck me?"

"Shhh."

The four wives and Eleanora rose. Eleanora took Clarissa by the hand and followed the wives into the longhouse.

Eleanora led her to a thick mat of ti leaves that had been prepared in the middle of the floor. "I will now remove your sarong." Eleanora gently peeled the garment from Clarissa, and she stood naked. Tika approached bearing a coconut shell of warm oil. Margaret was the first one to dip her hands into the bowl. She scooped up some of the oil and began to rub Clarissa down.

"Relax and enjoy the sensation," instructed Margaret pleasantly. "We would have honored you sooner, but for your delicate constitution at your time of arrival." Expertly, she rubbed lightly around Clarissa's nipples. "Ah, I see you are responsive." She playfully pinched each nipple. Clarissa could not help but smile. All the wives joined in, rubbing the warm oil over every part of her.

At last Eleanora said, "You may lie down, on your back, please, on the mat."

Clarissa did as Eleanora instructed.

"Now open your legs."

Clarissa spread her legs.

"A little wider, please, dear." When Clarissa complied, Eleanora knelt down between Clarissa's legs and spread the lips of her cunt. All the women leaned in for a close look, murmuring approvingly.

"A lovely little twat, dear," said Margaret. "May I?" And without waiting for an answer, Margaret reached down and pulled at Clarissa's clit. Clarissa let a groan escape her as she threw herself into the experience. Margaret chuckled and slipped a finger into Clarissa. The other wives giggled.

Tika said, in English, "We must make her feel the wave."

"Yes," said Margaret, "we must."

Eleanora explained. "They want to make you come. Are you willing?"

"Please," gasped Clarissa. Margaret was finger fucking her. Clarissa began to writhe. Eleanora sat at Clarissa's head. Reaching under her arms, she pulled Clarissa onto her lap in a half sitting position.

The quiet girl Pi, who was the newest wife, stepped up and Margaret withdrew her finger. Pi looked at Clarissa and wiggled her tongue. Eleanora reached around Clarissa's shoulders to pinch and pull her nipples. Margaret, Mayo, and Tika began to massage her as Pi bent forward. Clarissa felt the flick of Pi's tongue on her clit. She groaned aloud again. Pi spread the lips of Clarissa's cunt and began to lap her. She licked slowly, dragging her tongue in long laps from Clarissa's tight arse sphincter, all the way up to the tip of her rigid clit. Somebody's hands were squeezing her buttocks, and there were fingers in her cunt as well. Pi intensified her caresses, changing the long, slow laps for quick, hard licking, burying her tongue as deeply into Clarissa's twat as she could. The fingers worked harder in her cunt. Clarissa began to thrust her hips, and Eleanora pulled at her nipples. Pi began to suck on Clarissa's clit until Clarissa thought she would burst with the pent up urges she had carried for so long.

At last, her climax broke over her. She screamed out. The women held her as she jerked and twisted with the power of it. Finally, she lay quietly, breathing softly, satiated.

"It's not over, my dear," said Margaret. Clarissa, still leaning against Eleanora, opened her eyes. Kono was standing before her, completely naked.

"I will fuck with you now," he said. As Eleanora had described in her letter, Margaret stepped forward and took Kono's large cock in her hands. She squeezed and massaged it, holding it out as Moya stepped forward, bringing it to life with sucks and licks. Kono's cock was the longest, thickest cock Clarissa had ever seen. He smiled broadly as he approached her.

Eleanora said, urgently, "They do not fuck face to face, but always from the back. Quick, over you go, arse in the air!"

Eleanora flipped Clarissa over in her lap, holding her fast to her chest. Clarissa felt the heat of the man as he came close up behind her. He made a grunting sound. Clarissa felt him lick her buttocks. He bit her, softly at first, then harder, until she squealed. He laughed and licked her cunt from behind. Eleanora reached over Clarissa and spread her buttocks. Kono inserted his finger into her.

"She is ready," he said.

Clarissa was indeed ready. Her cunt felt hot and throbbing. Kono withdrew his finger.

Eleanora said, "Here it comes. Hold on." Clarissa squealed as Kono shoved his enormous cock deep into her cunt. He began thrusting immediately and vigorously.

Clarissa cried out, "Fuck me! Hard! Oh! Oh!" Faster and faster Kono fucked her. He grabbed her hips, his cock becoming an auger that drilled into her very core. Clarissa cried out with the wanton lust that gripped her.

The fucking seemed to go on forever. At last, Kono stopped, but did not withdraw. He said something and Clarissa felt the warm oil pour down between her buttocks, over her sphincter, and around his turgid cock. Kono tickled her arse, making her groan. Seemingly satisfied with her reaction, he began the fucking again. Clarissa found herself transported into some sort of trance-like state of lust. The heat in her was growing to a crescendo. She felt Kono's arm reach under her, holding her to him. With his other hand, he squeezed her whole cunny in his hand. He squeezed hard. The effect was astounding. Clarissa's climax crashed over her, nearly drowning her in the sensation. She shrieked. The wives cheered and clapped. Kono collapsed over her, bucking in his ecstasy.

They lay quietly, all of them. Kono held Clarissa to his chest, his cock receding from inside her. Eleanora and the wives lounged comfortably, dozing around them. Clarissa slowly recovered her senses. And while she felt nothing could possibly cure her broken heart, she did allow herself to think that this place, at least, could act as a much needed diversion.

PART NINE
Clarissa Teaches a Lesson and Is Fulfilled

Little by little, Clarissa acclimated to the island society in which she found herself. All the people were so kind, and Margaret and Eleanora began to teach her the language. She found that the women went out of their way to include her in their busy days and teach her island skills. They had all heard her heartbreaking story and were extremely sympathetic. He was not worthy of her, they would say comfortingly. What kind of man was he who couldn't even handle two women! Two women! Imagine! Why, the men of their island had multiple wives each and loved each one of them equally! They were even solicitous of the single women until those women became wives.

So they embraced Clarissa and taught her their ways. She learned to wrap the fish that the men caught in ti leaves, soak it, and steam it in a pit of hot coals. She learned to make poi, the odd tasting mush made from the manioc root. She learned the art of making jewelry from shells and flower leis. She helped watch the little children as they ran naked on the beach or scampered up the palm trees to knock down the coconuts at the top.

Still, Clarissa often found herself sitting alone, gazing out onto the wide sea, her heart heavy within her chest. Images of Adam were burned into her brain. Adam smiling at her across a table. Adam walking beside her down a crowded London street, her small hand warm and secure in his large, strong one. And Adam drawing her to him as he kissed her lips.

Her usual interest in the world around her slackened. Clarissa felt her enthusiasm for anything draining away. Alarmingly enough, even physical encounters, which she had heretofore found exceptionally stimulating, with Kono and the other perfectly appealing men of the village, failed to raise her spirits.

One evening as Clarissa sat alone on the beach gazing numbly out across the water at the glorious sunset, she felt a tap on her shoulder. She was far too apathetic to be startled. She turned around to see Margaret and Eleanora.

"Oh," said Clarissa, "hello."

"Clarissa, darling," said Eleanora, seating herself on the sand beside Clarissa, "Kono seeks you. He wants to present you to an esteemed visitor from a neighboring island. His name is Pualopua. He is a powerful chieftain."

Margaret settled on the other side of Clarissa. "We have been concerned for you, dear," she said. "You have seemed uncharacteristically quiet and introverted of late. Are you still pining? Is not this astounding and beautiful paradise enough to lift you from your sorrow?"

Clarissa sighed deeply. "I must admit, I am not in the best of moods. I have been trying to forget Adam MacLaren, yet his face seems always before mine, whether I am waking or sleeping."

"Come with us, then, and for the moment, put your emotions away. Kono is very proud of you and wishes to present you to Pualopua. It is a great honor!"

Clarissa shook her head slowly and said, "I am sorry, my friends. You are so kind to include me, but I would rather sit here with my own thoughts for a while."

Clarissa saw Eleanora and Margaret exchange glances. Margaret spoke, "I'm sorry, my dear. I am afraid you are required to come with us. Kono is, after all, our chieftain, and when he demands something this important, we must comply."

"Just tell him I am indisposed," said Clarissa simply.

Eleanor spoke up. "You do not seem to grasp the gravity, and honor, of this request. Indeed, Kono only requests to be polite because he does favor you greatly, but he will resort to a mandatory edict if he must."

Clarissa blinked. "Mandatory edict?" She felt rather peeved.

"Yes. Your presence is demanded."

"I am able to make my own choices," said Clarissa, making no effort to cover her pique.

"Unless your choice is vetoed," said Eleanora patiently.

"Why that is not what freedom of choice means!" exclaimed Clarissa. "It makes no sense!"

"Kono has the last word on everything."

"Now, come along, please, dear. It will not be a hardship and may help take your mind off your heart," said Margaret, taking Clarissa's arm.

Since Clarissa felt she would do most anything to banish the memories of Adam MacLaren from her mind, she begrudgingly allowed herself to be led back to the village. She looked back over her shoulder to catch a last glimpse at the sunset. She was surprised when she saw a ship, a speck on the horizon.

"Look!" she exclaimed. "A ship! I haven't seen one since I came here!"

Her companions turned and looked. Eleanora said, "A tramp steamer, no doubt. They sail from island to island, trading, bringing mail, ferrying people back and forth. Come along, dear."

As they approached the village center, Clarissa was surprised to see the extent to which the villagers had gone to prepare a celebration honoring their guest. It was dusk, and torches blazed around the huge roasting pit. Women were busy preparing fish and shellfish, wrapping it in seaweed to set upon the glowing coals. They were all dressed in their best sarongs, with brilliant flowers tucked behind their ears. Drums were beating, and the men were chanting softly. It was really quite exciting. Clarissa felt her spirits rise just a bit.

Eleanora and Margaret led her to Kono's hut. He sat inside on his seat of woven cane and smiled at her when she walked in behind Margaret and Eleanora.

"Greetings, beautiful one," he said.

Margaret and Eleanora pushed Clarissa forward in a most unusual way. It all seemed a bit too formal for Clarissa, but she kept a cheerful face as she greeted Kono in return.

"Greetings, my chieftain," she said in the native tongue.

Kono answered her in English. "I wish to make you acquainted with Pualopua. He is a great chieftain and must have a welcome beyond words. I have chosen you because—" He hesitated and looked at Margaret.

"Because of your enthusiasm and exotic looks," Margaret explained.

"Thank you, Kono," said Clarissa honestly. "However, I am afraid my enthusiasm has waned at this point. Perhaps another—"

Kono stood up suddenly, his face clouded over momentarily and he took Clarissa's arm. "It must be you!" he said, it seemed to Clarissa, with unnecessary vehemence. "It must be you! He has requested you. He has heard of you and now he comes, to visit me, chieftain to chieftain. I myself have no choice in this matter."

Clarissa looked up into his black eyes and thought she detected a tinge of panic. She was confused.

Kono did not take his eyes off her, but commanded, "Eleanora!"

Eleanor stepped nervously forward. Clarissa's brow furrowed. Why was everybody so jumpy?

Eleanor said, "Clarissa. Clarissa, dear. Pualopua is the most important and most powerful chieftain in this archipelago. He is also the fiercest, sometimes making war on his otherwise peaceful neighbors. Through the traders, he has heard of you and your beauty. He and a party of several men and women came by outrigger this morning. He and Kono have been in talks all day. As you can see, it has taken quite a toll on our beloved husband and chieftain. He wants to make the best possible impression on Pualopua. If he does, Pualopua will go away and leave us in peace. Otherwise, he will take what he wants by force."

"He sounds like a bully to me," said Clarissa, indignantly. She had dealt with bullies before. "We only need to stand up to him."

Now Margaret joined the conversation. "It is not that simple, dear," she said. "He has the power to—how shall I say this?—bother, yes, to bother us."

"All you need to do, dear," said Eleanora, "is suffer him for this evening while the celebration is going on. He is actually quite good-looking." She winked at Clarissa, but Clarissa felt it was a hasty afterthought.

Then she looked at Kono. He stood, ramrod straight as usual, dressed in colorful material wrapped around his waist. His chest, rock hard and rippled, was bare, save for a necklace of white shells. A similar string of white shells was plaited into his hair. However, Clarissa was quick to note, the usually present happy-go-lucky expression and smile crinkles at the corners of his eyes were absent. This must be more serious than she had suspected. Kono had always been very good to her, a tender lover, and a good friend. Well, she thought, I will do what is required of me for Kono's sake. Then I will find out what is going on!

"Why not!" she declared, mustering a brilliant smile from the depths of her broken heart.

Kono gave a big smile and wrapped his muscular arms around her in an exuberant embrace. When he finally released her, he stepped back, and reaching within the folds of his knee length half-toga, he brought forth a string of large pearls and handed them to Clarissa.

She gasped and turned them over and over in her hands. They were large pearls of different colors, white, pink, brown, gray, and black.

"Oh, Kono!" she said. "These are magnificent. Truly magnificent. Should I wear these when I meet Pualopua?"

"They are yours to wear always, whenever you like. They are a gift from me," he answered her softly. "To remember me."

There was something in his demeanor that made Clarissa look up. He was smiling, but there was something, a sort of pathos, swimming in his eyes. This was all very mysterious, but she would play along. Whatever was making people act in so bizarre a manner would reveal itself eventually, she was sure of that.

"Follow me," said Kono and abruptly walked out of the hut. Clarissa fell in behind him, her curiosity piqued. Kono entered the long meeting house at the end of the village cluster. Clarissa followed him in, blinking as her eyes adjusted to the dim light.

"Greetings, my friend." Clarissa heard a deep voice speaking in the native language as they entered.

"Greetings, Pualopua," replied Kono. "I have brought you the beautiful one you requested." Kono turned to Clarissa. "Step forward."

Clarissa stepped forward as directed. Now she could see the other man quite clearly. As Eleanor had said, he was very good-looking. He stood taller than Kono. He wore a similar half-toga to Kono's, but in his hair, he wore a feathered headdress that cascaded down his back. In his ear he wore an ornament made from a shell and around his neck was a lei of fragrant flowers. He smiled when he saw Clarissa.

"I am here to join you in celebration." Clarissa gave the tradition greeting in the native tongue. She had always had a flair for language.

"I am impressed," said Pualopua. "You speak as beautifully as you appear."

"Examine her, if you will," said Kono. "You will only find that she is all you want."

Clarissa was not in a very good mood. She was trying to enjoy the experience of being with two strapping, handsome, half-naked men, but her heart pained her and visions of Adam MacLaren with his laughing blue eyes flashed in her mind. Also, she was put off by Kono's odd behavior. He was not as jolly as she would have liked to see. She made an effort to get into the spirit of the free tribal customs again as Pualopua circled her.

"She is quite small," said Pualopua.

"She has much energy," answered Kono.

"She is not fat."

"If Pualopua prefers a fat woman —" began Kono, but Pualopua laughed.

"I prefer this woman. She is different from all the rest!" He grabbed Clarissa by the wrist, quite roughly, she thought, and pulled her forward. He reached a hand up under her sarong, groping between her legs.

Like dynamite, Clarissa's temper, already short, went off. She swung her open hand up with all her might and smacked Pualopua on the side of his head, cuffing his ear in the process. Clarissa always knew she was stronger than most girls her age. After all, she was very athletic. She could ride, her tennis game was legendary, and she had led her girls' basketball team to Private School Championship her senior year. However, she was unprepared for what happened when her hand came into contact with Pualopua's unprotected ear. Pualopua's eyes bugged out, his mouth opened, and he collapsed to his knees. Apparently, the force with which her open palm hit his ear produced a very painful concussion. Pualopua rocked back and forth on his knees, both hands clasped to his ear.

Clarissa and Kono stood still, stunned. Clarissa was the first to recover. Horrified at what she had done, she knelt beside the groaning man.

"Oh, dear! Oh, dear! I am so very, very sorry! Are you hurt? Tell me!"

Finally, Pualopua looked up. Clarissa drew back, expecting some sort of retaliation. Instead, Pualopua grinned at her from ear to ear. "I will have her! She will be seated next to me tonight," he said to Kono. "She is very brave and has her own ideas in her head!" He began to laugh. Then he said, "Go, go! Prepare for the feast. We will celebrate this woman you have shown me, as well as the friendship of our two nations. I will tame her to my ways!"

Kono said to Clarissa, "Come with me now. I will take you to my wives. They will ready you for the feast."

He turned and exited the longhouse, leading Clarissa by the hand.

The celebration site was empty and quiet as Clarissa followed Kono across the beach. The women would be getting ready, donning their best sarongs, dressing their children in festive loincloths and shell necklaces, braiding each other's hair.

It was dusk and Clarissa looked out across the ocean. The yellow, pinks, and mauves of the sunset reflected in the softly undulating blue-green waters. Away on the horizon, the tramp steamer still sat. Clarissa could see the lights on the deck.

"Kono," said Clarissa pensively, as they made their way past the huge fire pit. "What is going on? Has Pualopua threatened you? Something very mysterious is afoot. Please tell me what it is."

Kono stopped in his tracks. His face was somber as he turned to face her. He said, "Pualopua is a powerful chieftain. Every so often, he must flex his muscles, show his strength to the other nations of these islands."

"You are also a powerful chieftain," said Clarissa, looking up at him.

Kono snorted. "My responsibility is to my people. When Pualopua comes, I give him what he wants. Big party, much flattery, his choice of women. The women are eager to serve him. They know it can only help our people. When Pualopua has what he wants, he goes away. We will not see him for several more years."

"You should stand up to him, Kono! The men here do not go around putting their hands up the women's skirts! Your people should not fear a bully like Pualopua."

"I do not wish to bring the wrath of Pualopua down upon our village. We are a peaceful people."

"The people of this island are brave and strong. You have nothing to fear from Pualopua."

Kono sighed. "I do not like to talk about this," he said softly. "My father was killed by Pualopua's father. He was speared in the back as he left a feast on Pualopua's island. As he died, he made me say I would not fight, that I would not risk the lives of my people. I am doing what was bidden."

"Oh, Kono," said Clarissa, shocked by the story, "I am so very sorry, but there has got to be a way to come out from under the power of Pualopua. He is a bully and a fake."

"Let us go to the feast. We will talk of this later."

Clarissa squeezed his hand in sympathy and followed him to the longhouse.

Inside the longhouse, the women were scurrying here and there. They were bedecked in all their finery, and they descended upon Clarissa as she entered.

Margaret took her arm. "Clarissa, dear, come with us. We will primp you for the celebration. You will be sitting next to Pualopua."

"You must be turned out in the finest couture we can manage," put in Eleanora.

Pi appeared in her usual silent manner, holding a beautiful sarong of pure silk. It was blue, like the sea, and shimmered in the fading light.

Kono had disappeared. The wives took possession of Clarissa. They bathed her, combed out her blond hair, which had grown quite long, falling onto her shoulders in golden waves. Maya plaited fine braids into her hair, bejeweled with white shells. Clarissa wore the pearls around her neck, so the wives adorned her with cuffs of flowers around her wrists and ankles.

Finally, they were all of them ready. They clustered around Clarissa in an unusual formation and made a procession to the center of village.

The torches were lit. The coals in the fire pit were glowing. Drums beat softly in the background, and all the men and women sat cross-legged on colorful mats laid upon the sand. Kono and Pualopua sat side by side in large cane chairs, facing the fire pit. Facing them, on the opposite side of the fire pit, was another large cane chair, but this one was hooded and long fronds hung down in front of it, so that the seated person was hidden from view. It was to this chair that the wives of Kono guided Clarissa.

"You are guest of honor," said Pi, holding the fronds open. "Please be seated."

Clarissa felt this was getting a bit ridiculous, but she obliged and seated herself within the chair. Drums began to beat. Six women appeared and began to dance to the rhythm of the drums. Clarissa could just see them from between the palm fronds. Suddenly, she heard a voice, whispering at her.

"Psst! Psst!"

Clarissa turned in her seat. "Who is it?" she whispered back. "Where are you?"

"It's me, Eleanora. I am hiding behind the chair."

"Eleanora!"

"Shhh. Do not make a sound. Just listen to me. I feel I have the responsibility to inform you of the reason for this celebration."

"I know," Clarissa hissed. "Kono told me about tribute to Pualopua."

"He did not tell you the entire truth. Did he tell you that you were to be the tribute?"

"What!"

"Shhhh. You are to be married to Pualopua. Tonight."

Clarissa was greatly affronted and said so. "I am greatly affronted! I will not marry Pualopua! No! I will not. The man is a boor and a bully!"

"Clarissa, please! I warn you. For the good of the people here, do it. He will take you to his village. It is a wealthy village. I have been there. And he is most comely!"

"Oh, really, Eleanora! The man is odious! I am not going anywhere. These people must banish Pualopua once and for all!"

Eleanora whispered desperately, "Clarissa! What do you mean to do?"

Clarissa did not answer. She burst from chair and, ignoring the drummers and dancers, marched around the fire pit and stood, hands on her hips, directly in front of Kono and Pualopua.

She looked back over her shoulder and shouted, "Stop that infernal drumming!" The drums were at once silent. Clarissa stamped her foot in the sand.

"Now you listen to me," she expounded, pointing a threatening finger at Pualopua. "I do not intend to marry you. I do not intend to leave this village until I am good and ready. You are just a big bully. Go home to your own village! Go find your own wives! We will not tolerate this!"

Pualopua watched Clarissa carefully, his eyes narrowing. When she had finished, he was quiet, staring at her. Then he erupted in loud, raucous laughter. "Marry me or no. I will take you to my village now." He stood up and grabbed Clarissa in both of his arms, throwing her roughly across his shoulders. He shouted something in the native tongue, and his handful of henchman fell in behind him. They began to march toward their beached outriggers.

Clarissa yelled, "Kono! Help me! Do not let him have his way!" She pounded on Pualopua with her fists and squirmed to free herself.

In her fury, she saw Kono stand and motion to the men of the village. Just as he took a tentative step forward, she heard a loud male voice shout, in English, "Drop that girl now!"

The voice pierced through Clarissa's very soul. She looked back over her shoulder and saw a small dinghy beaching itself on the sand. Several men were climbing out and running up the beach. Even in the deepening dusk, she could recognize Adam MacLaren in the lead.

Suddenly, Clarissa was filled with surge of energy. Her heart soared. She twisted her body in Pualopua's grip.

"You heard him! Drop me right now!" And so saying, she clapped both her palms over Pualopua's ears as hard as she could. The results were predictable.

Pualopua roared in pain and collapsed in the sand, holding both ears. Clarissa sprang lithely away just as Adam reached them. Adam grabbed both her hands. Clarissa gazed into his eyes, forgetting everything around her. The only real thing was the warmth of Adam's hands holding her own.

"Back to the boat!" he shouted to his men. "My darling, follow me!"

Clarissa would have followed him over broken glass. They ran toward the boat. Out of the corner of her eye, she saw Pualopua and his men rally and begin to start after them.

And then a curious and marvelous thing happened. Kono, followed by the young men in the village, rushed between them, surrounding Pualopua, knocking him and his men to the ground.

"Good-bye, my dear!" Clarissa heard Eleanora yell.

Margaret echoed her, calling out, "Come back as soon as you can!"

Two minutes later, she was seated in the small wooden dinghy next to Adam while the other two men rowed out across the darkening sea.

Clarissa's heart was beating as if it were trying to escape her chest. Adam had both arms around her and was holding her close to him. She could feel him breathing, hard and sharp. She drew back, seeking his face with her hands and her eyes. The moon was rising and she could make out the features of his strong countenance.

"Adam," she breathed the name, as if uttering it would wake her from a dream.

"I'm here, my darling. I have you now. I have you now."

"How did you get here? How did you know where to find me?" Her fingers traced the outlines of his face, his eyebrows, his cheekbones, his lips.

"Did you think I would not seek you to the ends of the earth? I was wild with panic. Finally, Chauncey and Bruce found the letter from Eleanora in your room and showed it to me. It gave me something to work from. We have been sick with worry!"

Clarissa listened to him and hung her head. She murmured, "I am quite a selfish girl. I was only thinking of my own heartbreak. I thought you were marrying that awful woman at Christmastime. It was more than I could bear." She looked up into his face again, her eyes shining with tears of remorse. He could have been killed on her account. "You came for me!" she said softly. "You came to bring me home."

"I am an investigative reporter, after all." Adam smirked. "And yes, I have come to bring you home."

Suddenly, Clarissa was aware of a huge wall that seemed to have heaved up out of the ocean.

"All hands down there?" It was a voice from the deck, far above the waves.

"It is the tramp steamer!" said Clarissa, suddenly putting two and two together. "I saw it on the horizon, before the fiasco began. It was you! I would have swum out to you, had I only known."

"No need," quipped Adam. "Your chariot came for you!" Then he cupped his hand and called up, "Aye aye, Captain. And one more."

"Stand by for the ladder."

Out of the darkness, a rope ladder fell, dangling just above the gently rocking dinghy.

Adam stood up, swaying slightly to keep his balance. "Lady coming on board," he called. Then he turned to Clarissa. "You first, my lady."

Clarissa smiled and stood up. She took Adam's outstretched hand and allowed herself to be guided to the ladder. "Hold tight, darling," said Adam. "Hold tight as you climb. The crew is waiting to help you aboard."

Clarissa gripped the ladder and climbed easily to the deck above. Several pairs of hands reached out for her and lifted her gently onto the steamer. The two men who had accompanied Adam came next. Adam came up last, heaving a great sigh when he at last stood with both feet on the ship. Clarissa ran to him, wrapping her arms around his rugged form.

A moment later, a tall, thin man with thin blond hair and a white goatee stood before them.

"Allow me to introduce Captain Arvid Anders of the tramp steamer Rover," said Adam.

Captain Anders smiled broadly and reached out a hand to clasp hers in a warm handshake. "Welcome aboard, young lady," he said, in a thick Scandinavian accent that Clarissa found charming. "Follow me to your accommodations."

Clarissa followed the captain, Adam bringing up the rear. Captain Anders led them down a narrow stairwell below deck, then down a long, narrow hallway with small doors off it every few feet. Near the end of the hallway, he stopped and opened a door.

"Your accommodations, miss," he said gallantly. "I know you must be used to First Class, but this, I'm afraid, is First Class aboard the Rover!"

"I am sure it will do just fine, Captain," said Clarissa. "Thank you so very much. You are most kind."

"Well, I shall run along and get Cook to rustle you up something to eat. Please refresh yourself and feel free to ask for anything you might want. If it's aboard the ship, you may have it."

Clarissa thanked him again. He bowed and left them standing in the doorway. Clarissa stepped into the cabin. It was dimly lit by a nearly imperceptibly flickering industrial sconce on the wall. There was a bed in the room. It was a real double bed, and not a cot. There was also a locker of sorts to hang clothing, and a sink with a mirror above it.

"All the comforts of home," chuckled Adam, stepping in behind her and closing the door. He had her in his arms. Clarissa lifted her face to his, and their mouths crashed together in a most passionate kiss that lasted until they both found themselves breathless.

"I thought I should never taste those lips again," she whispered into his chest as he held her close.

"I thought I might never lay eyes on the woman I love again," he said, resting his chin in her hair. "I was prepared to die trying, though."

"And you could have! And it would have been my fault! Oh, Adam!" Her eyes filled with tears again at the thought of her own selfishness.

"Why didn't you give me a chance? Why did you leave?"

Clarissa heaved a big sigh. "I was so sure you were marrying that woman. I…I couldn't bear to be in the same town. London society would have been buzzing about it for months."

"You have a vivid imagination," he said, somewhat dryly. "Well, no matter. We are together now. Clarissa, believe me when I say that I love you more than I have ever loved anybody. And I'm a selfish cock, too!"

She allowed herself a soft giggle. She kissed him lightly this time, drawing back, saying, "Adam MacLaren, I will never doubt you again. Never, even in a million years!"

"I am glad to hear it," said the man, finally loosening his grip on her. "We are headed for New York on this bucket of bolts. How do you think the fashion doyens will fancy a sarong?"

"New York!" exclaimed Clarissa. "Why, Adam, I don't even have a pair of shoes! And what time of year is it, anyway? I have completely lost the season!"

"It will be coming spring by the time we arrive. The daffodils might even be out in Central Park. Not to worry, we can buy shoes when we get there."

"With what? There were no newspaper editors to offer me a paying job on that island! I will have to telegraph my father and explain matters to him."

"My dear, you are traveling with the editor-in-chief of the *Tribune*! My credit is good all over the world. Besides, I have family in New York. They must meet you as soon as we dock. Fortunately, this state-of-the-art vessel does at least have a telegraph system."

Clarissa was happy. She stepped back and looked at the love of her life, actually there in the flesh, warm and breathing, and looking better than he did in any of her dreams.

"By the way," he said, "you look lovely. The sarong is silk, isn't it? They are usually bark cloth or cotton. Is it a special sarong?"

Clarissa laughed. "It's a wedding sarong! I'm dressed up for my wedding! I was supposed to be married to Pualopua! Imagine! Just to keep him placated. Well, I hope we taught him a lesson he'll never forget! I hope they all learned a lesson!"

Adam smiled and opened the door.

"Where are you going?" asked Clarissa.

"To get the captain," he replied. "It would be a shame to waste that sarong!"

And that is how Miss Clarissa Hardy became Mrs. Clarissa MacLaren and spent her honeymoon aboard a tramp steamer bound for New York.

EPILOGUE
Present Day

I looked up from my reading. The mismatched bits and pieces of the manuscript lay scattered around me on the sofa, on the floor, on my lap. The story had mesmerized me. I had been so absorbed, I hadn't noticed that most of the day had passed. I hadn't noticed that the rain had stopped and a misty late afternoon sun was shining in through the window.

The dogs whined when they saw me look up. Automatically, I got up to let them outside. Soon, the house would bustle again with children, a husband returning home from work, telephones ringing, televisions blaring. And everybody would be expecting dinner. I looked around. The only thing I had done all day was read that manuscript. And it had captivated me!

I galvanized myself and raced around, pulling a Bolognese sauce out of the freezer and putting a pot of water on to boil for some linguine. All the while, I couldn't get Clarissa's story out of my head. Who had written it? Was it biographical? Autobiographical? Purely fiction? It appeared to have been written over a period of time, weeks, even years, but definitely by the same person. I had to find out more. Where should I start? Could the person responsible for this amazing little gem be part of my own family? After all, one family member or another had occupied this house for the last two hundred years. I decided to call my mother. She would at least know more or less who lived in the house during specific time periods.

"Hi, Mom," I said, pushing the ear plug into my ear so that I could talk while I set the table. "I was housebound today. Yes. Cleaning the attic, stuff like that. Anyway, do you know who lived here, say, like, the late twenties?"

The silence that followed my question was my mother thinking. Finally she said, "Hm. Let's see. After World War I, during the twenties and into the early thirties, it was a summer place. A lot of the family used it. You know, people evacuated the cities during the summer. Afraid of polio! Yes. Anybody who could afford it had a place in the country."

"Who would have used it, then?" I persisted. My mother had a way of drifting off topic.

"Well, most of the family, I guess. I know my grandfather did a lot of work on the place. He rebuilt that fireplace. My mother, your grandmother, spent almost all of her childhood summers there. It was a busy place. My mother had two brothers and a lot of cousins. You remember her stories."

"Yes, I do. So my great-grandmother and great-grandfather were the primary occupants?"

"Probably," mused my mother, as if she were still searching her memory.

"And their names were?"

"Caroline and Andrew Adams."

"What was Great-Grandmother's maiden name?"

"Hamilton."

"Caroline Hamilton. Did she have a brother or sister?"

"No, she was an only child. Why this sudden interest in the family tree?"

"Oh, I ran across some interesting things up in the attic," I remarked nonchalantly.

"I'm not surprised. No telling what's up there!"

"Was anybody in the family called Clarissa?"

"Why, yes! That was your great-grandmother's middle name. I always remembered it because I liked it so much. I almost named you Clarissa!"

"Wow!" I exclaimed, "Really! Caroline Clarissa Hamilton Adams."

"Yes. She was quite the character, as I recall the family stories. She left home as a young woman and traveled the world. She met her husband, my grandfather, overseas somewhere. Worked for a newspaper. A modern girl. And then there was some kind of story about her being married on a boat on the way home from the South Seas! Really shook her family up. Apparently, they made them get married again, when she arrived home, in the church, just for good measure."

"I don't believe it!" I spoke more to myself than to my mother.

"What did you say?" she asked. "Oh, it's true. Or at least partially true. She and Andrew arrived in New York on some tramp steamboat and scandalized both families! They were a colorful pair. Did you find something of theirs?"

"I think I might have found some...ah...letters about them. Only they were called Clarissa and Adam. Sort of a...um...diary, I guess you'd say."

"How interesting! I would like to see those. She always said she wished her name had been Clarissa Caroline instead of the other way around. And of course Adams was their surname, so it very likely is about them."

"The story of the boat is here."

"Really! Well, I would say you've found Great-grandmother's personal diary!"

Personal. I guess so! "Well, I've got to go, Mom. Everybody will be streaming in here in half an hour and I haven't done anything all day!"

"Okay. I want to come over and read it soon. Let's make plans. I'm sure it's fascinating."

"Absolutely. It's quite fascinating. Bye, Mom. Talk soon."

"Bye-bye, dear."

Later that evening, after the dinner had been eaten, homework had been done, and the kids were in bed, I was still thinking about Clarissa's story. I readied the kitchen for morning and went into the living room. My husband was breathing softly, asleep in front of the television. I opened the drawer to the writing desk that stood in the corner and took out the manuscript. Clutching the random pieces of paper in my hand, I gently squeezed my husband's shoulder.

"Humpf!" He started out of his sleep. "Oh, sorry," he said, "I drifted off."

"No problem," I said, "Let's go to bed early tonight."

"Sure," he said, standing up and stretching. "What's that in your hand?"

I curled my arm through his and guided him to the stairs. "It's a bedtime story I want to read to you," I whispered in his ear.

ACKNOWLEDGMENTS

Thank you to my parents who brought me up with a healthy, accepting view of the sexual self. Thank you also to the person who left both *Fanny Hill* and *The Story of O* lying around for curious young women to read. And thank you to my Omnific team, all of whom seem to honestly enjoy my story, which, after all, is the point.

ABOUT THE AUTHOR

Chloe Gillis is fascinated with history and the history of human sexuality. After spending years writing about this subject clinically in grants and research papers, Chloe has begun writing historical fiction, applying her knowledge of human sexuality to create fun, romantic erotica.

check out these titles from
OMNIFIC PUBLISHING

⟵—⟶Contemporary Romance⟵—⟶

Keeping the Peace by Linda Cunningham

Stitches and Scars by Elizabeth A. Vincent

Pieces of Us by Hannah Downing

The Way That You Play It by BJ Thornton

The Poughkeepsie Brotherhood series: *Poughkeepsie, Return to Poughkeepsie* &
Saving Poughkeepsie by Debra Anastasia

Recaptured Dreams and *All-American Girl* and *Until Next Time* by Justine Dell

Once Upon a Second Chance by Marian Vere

The Englishman by Nina Lewis

16 Marsden Place by Rachel Brimble

Sleepers, Awake by Eden Barber

The Runaway series: *The Runaway Year* & *The Runaway Ex* by Shani Struthers

The Hydraulic series: *Hydraulic Level Five* & *Skygods* by Sarah Latchaw

Fix You and *The Jeweler* by Beck Anderson

Just Once & *Going the Distance* by Julianna Keyes

The WORDS series: *The Weight of Words, Better Deeds Than Words, The Truest of Words* &
The Record of My Heart by Georgina Guthrie

The Brit Out of Water series: *Theatricks* & *Jazz Hands* by Eleanor Gwyn-Jones

The Sacrificial Lamb & *Let's Get Physical* by Elle Fiore

The Plan by Qwen Salsbury

The Kiss Me series: *Kiss Me Goodnight* & *Kiss Me By Moonlight* by Michele Zurlo

Saint Kate of the Cupcake: The Dangers of Lust and Baking by LC Fenton

Exposure by Morgan & Jennifer Locklear

Playing All the Angles by Nicole Lane

Redemption by Kathryn Barrett

The Playboy's Princess by Joy Fulcher

The Forever series: *Forever Autumn* (book 1) by Christopher Scott Wagner

⟵—⟶Young Adult Romance⟵—⟶

The Ember series: *Ember* & *Iridescent* by Carol Oates

Breaking Point by Jess Bowen

Life, Liberty, and Pursuit by Susan Kaye Quinn

The Embrace series: *Embrace, Hold Tight* & *Entwined* by Cherie Colyer

Destiny's Fire by Trisha Wolfe

The Reaper series: *Reaping Me Softly* & *UnReap My Heart* by Kate Evangelista

The Legendary Saga: *Legendary* & *Claiming Excalibur* by LH Nicole

The Fatal series: *Fatal* & *Brutal* (novella 1.5) by T.A. Brock

The Prometheus Order series: *Byronic* by Sandi Beth Jones

One Smart Cookie by Kym Brunner

Variables of Love by MK Schiller

New Adult Romance

Three Daves by Nicki Elson
Streamline by Jennifer Lane
The Shades series: *Shades of Atlantis* & *Shades of Avalon* by Carol Oates
The Heart series: *Beside Your Heart, Disclosure of the Heart* & *Forever Your Heart*
by Mary Whitney
Romancing the Bookworm by Kate Evangelista
Flirting with Chaos by Kenya Wright
The Vice, Virtue & Video series: *Revealed, Captured, Desired* & *Devoted*
by Bianca Giovanni
Granton University series: *Loving Lies* by Linda Kage
Missing Pieces by Meredith Tate

Paranormal & Fantasy Romance

The Light series: *Seers of Light, Whisper of Light* & *Circle of Light* by Jennifer DeLucy
The Hanaford Park series: *Eve of Samhain* & *Pleasures Untold* by Lisa Sanchez
Immortal Awakening by KC Randall
The Seraphim series: *Crushed Seraphim* & *Bittersweet Seraphim* by Debra Anastasia
The Guardian's Wild Child by Feather Stone
Grave Refrain by Sarah M. Glover
The Divinity series: *Divinity* & *Entity* by Patricia Leever
The Blood Vine series: *Blood Vine, Blood Entangled* & *Blood Reunited* by Amber Belldene
Divine Temptation by Nicki Elson
The Dead Rapture series: *Love in the Time of the Dead, Love at the End of Days* &
Love Starts with Z by Tera Shanley
The Hidden Races series: *Incandescent* (book 1) by M.V. Freeman
Something Wicked by Carol Oates
Chronicles of Midvalen: *Command the Tides* (book 1) by Wren Handman

Romantic Suspense

Whirlwind by Robin DeJarnett
The CONduct series: *With Good Behavior, Bad Behavior* & *On Best Behavior*
by Jennifer Lane
Indivisible by Jessica McQuinn
Between the Lies by Alison Oburia
Blind Man's Bargain by Tracy Winegar

Historical Romance

Cat O' Nine Tails by Patricia Leever
Burning Embers by Hannah Fielding
Seven for a Secret by Rumer Haven
The Counterfeit by Tracy Winegar

Erotic Romance

The Keyhole series: *Becoming sage* (book 1) by Kasi Alexander
The Keyhole series: *Saving sunni* (book 2) by Kasi & Reggie Alexander
The Winemaker's Dinner: *Appetizers & Entrée* by Dr. Ivan Rusilko & Everly Drummond
The Winemaker's Dinner: *Dessert* by Dr. Ivan Rusilko
Client N° 5 by Joy Fulcher
The Enclave series: *Closer and Closer* (book 1) by Jenna Barton
The Adventures of Clarissa Hardy by Chloe Gillis

Anthologies

A Valentine Anthology including short stories by
Alice Clayton ("With a Double Oven"),
Jennifer DeLucy ("Magnus of Pfelt, Conquering Viking Lord"),
Nicki Elson ("I Don't Do Valentine's Day"),
Jessica McQuinn ("Better Than One Dead Rose and a Monkey Card"),
Victoria Michaels ("Home to Jackson"), and
Alison Oburia ("The Bridge")

Taking Liberties including an introduction by Tiffany Reisz and short stories by
Mina Vaughn ("John Hancock-Blocked"),
Linda Cunningham ("A Boston Marriage"),
Joy Fulcher ("Tea for Two"),
KC Holly ("The British Are Coming!"),
Kimberly Jensen & Scott Stark ("E. Pluribus Threesome"), and
Vivian Rider ("M'Lady's Secret Service")

Sets

The Heart Series Box Set (*Beside Your Heart, Disclosure of the Heart &
Forever Your Heart*) by Mary Whitney
The CONduct Series Box Set (*With Good Behavior, Bad Behavior &
On Best Behavior*) by Jennifer Lane
The Light Series Box Set (*Seers of Light, Whisper of Light, Circle of Light &
Glimpse of Light*) by Jennifer DeLucy
The Blood Vine Series Box Set (*Blood Vine, Blood Entangled, Blood Reunited &
Blood Eternal*) by Amber Belldene

Singles, Novellas & Special Editions

It's Only Kinky the First Time (A Keyhole series single) by Kasi Alexander
Learning the Ropes (A Keyhole series single) by Kasi & Reggie Alexander
The Winemaker's Dinner: RSVP by Dr. Ivan Rusilko
The Winemaker's Dinner: No Reservations by Everly Drummond

Big Guns by Jessica McQuinn
Concessions by Robin DeJarnett
Starstruck by Lisa Sanchez
New Flame by BJ Thornton
Shackled by Debra Anastasia
Swim Recruit by Jennifer Lane
Sway by Nicki Elson
Full Speed Ahead by Susan Kaye Quinn
The Second Sunrise by Hannah Downing
The Summer Prince by Carol Oates
Whatever it Takes by Sarah M. Glover
Clarity (A *Divinity* prequel single) by Patricia Leever
A Christmas Wish (A *Cocktails & Dreams* single) by Autumn Markus
Late Night with Andres by Debra Anastasia
Poughkeepsie (enhanced iPad app collector's edition) by Debra Anastasia
Poughkeepsie (audio book edition) by Debra Anastasia
Blood Eternal (A Blood Vine series single, epilogue to series) by Amber Belldene
Carnaval de Amor (*The Winemaker's Dinner*, Spanish edition)
by Dr. Ivan Rusilko & Everly Drummond

coming soon from
OMNIFIC PUBLISHING

The Hidden Races series: *Illumination* (book 2) by M.V. Freeman
The Ground Rules by Roya Carmen
Trouble Me by Beck Anderson
The Forever series: *Forever Winter* (book 2) by Christopher Scott Wagner